Prism Literary Series 4

A VOICE OF THEIR OWN

Short Stories
by
Egyptian Women

Edited and Introduced
by
Angele Botros Samaan

MINISTRY OF CULTURE, EGYPT
FOREIGN CULTURAL RELATIONS

Prism Literary Series 4
Published by
Foreign Cultural Information Dept.

Prism Publications Offices
44, Messaha St., Guizeh, Egypt

Cover by : Mohamed Nadi
Layout by : M. El Kady

First English Edition 1994
Second Print 1998

© *Prism*
All rights reserved for the publisher

Dar Al-Kuttub Registration No. 16753 / 1998
ISBN 977 - 235 - 166 - 8.

Contents

FOREWORD

When the Foreign Cultural Relations Central Department planned the publishing of a selection of short stories by Egyptian women writers as a much needed addition to its series of literary publications, it was decided to ask the assistance of an expert to make the choice of both the writers and the stories. It had to be someone who can, in addition, undertake the editing of such an ambitious book. The most obvious choice was Dr. Angele Botros Samaan who has been working for many years with great insight in the domain of Egyptian literature and in particular women's contributions in this respect. And we are proud to say that we have made the right choice.

Angele Botros Samaan, B.A. (Honours) and M.A. (Cairo University), Ph. D. (London University) is professor of English Literature, Faculty of Arts, Cairo University. She has published critical articles in Egypt and abroad in the areas of the English novel, particulary the modern novel, the Arabic and African novel in addition to Utopian writings, translation and women studies.

Among the books she has written are the following titles :

In Arabic : The Novel and the Novelist, 1972; The English Novel, 1977; Studies in the English Novel, 1981;Studies in the Arabic Novel, 1987.

In English : Views on the Art of the Novel, ed., with an Introduction 1965; Critical introductions to : Joseph Conrad, Heart of Darkness, 1970; James Joyce, A Portrait of the Artist as A Young Man, 1977, 1987; D.H. Lawrence, Sons and Lovers, 1990; Arabic Literature in Egypt in

English Translation : A Bibliography, Compiled by Angele Botros Samaan; **Women in Society : Egypt,** Singapore Times Publishing, 1993.

Translations : Into Arabic : Chinua Achebe, **Things Fall Apart,** 1971; Thomas More, **Utopia,** 1974, 1987.

Into English : Nehad Gad, **Adila** and **The Bus Stop : Two One-Act Plays,** 1987; Naguib Mahfouz, **Al-Sukkaria (Sugar Street),** 1992.

She is ex-Member of the Shoura Assembly (Second House of Parliment), 1983-9, ad is currently member of the Translation Committee of the Supreme Council for Culture, the International Association of Thomas More's Friends (Amici Thomae Mori), the Board of the University Women Association, Cairo, the Egyptian Women Writers Association, as well as member and Egypt correspondent of the International Association of University Professors of English (IAUPE).

INTRODUCTION

This collection of short stories by Egyptian women aims at representing in English translation a cross-section of stories written by two generations of women : Egyptian women who began writing in th late fifties and early sixties and are still writing represent the first generation after the pioneers. They are followed by a generation of younger women who started publishing short stories either in the seventies but largely in the eighties or in the eighties and early nineties. It is in the eighties and nineties, however, that the crop of short stories by women writers have increased dramatically. With one exception,[1] all the stories in this volume have been published in these two decades.

The stories are rather loosely arranged according to the date of birth of the authors or the beginning of their writing careers. The aim of this collection is to offer as many short stories as would be possible in a handy book, taking into account the need to represent as much variety of both issues and modes of writing and to stress innovation and development.

Considering the large number of Egyptian women contributing to short-story writing, it was inevitable that during the process of selection, we had to draw the line somewhere. Fifteen writers have been chosen, each to be represented by two stories. Eliminated owing to lack of space is the generation of the pioneers, including Saheir al-Qalamawi, Aisha Abdel-Rahman and Amina al-Said, as well as most of the writers immediately following them, such as Sophy Abdallah, Naguiba al-Assal and Gazibieh

Sidky, some of whose stories having been already translated. Also eliminated are two well-known writers who have been widely translated : Nawal al-Saadawi and Alifa Rifaat.

Several of the women included in this volume have already had some of their stories translated into English in various short-story collections. Some have been published individually or in collections in French, German, Dutch, Russian and Hungarian. However, it has been felt for some time that there is a need for a representative collection of more than one generation of short-story women writers in English translation. Translation being one of the most effective means of cultural encounters, these short stories are addressed to both lovers of this literary genre and readers who take an interest in the culture of the other.

Forerunners

In the field of story-telling, a tradition of women participation in Arab culture goes very far in time[2]. An early antecedent is Shaherezad's **Arabian Nights (Alf Laila Wa Laila)**. Shaherezad is a pioneer, universally acknowledged. Not only did she succeed in keeping her despotic husband fascinated night after night but in saving her own neck and the necks of countless young women. By weilding the tool of arousing her listener's curiosity and keeping him in suspense, she set a standard of story-telling and left the world an enormous wealth of ever-living stories.

Our grandmothers, unknown preservers of a long tradition of oral story-telling, kept generations of children, entertained, out of mischief, fascinated by their magical tales, as Etidal Osman has potently illustrated in her short story, "The Sultana", included in this collection. She has conveyed the magical skill with which a marvellous uneducated woman could tell a story of multi-layered meanings.

A tradition of women short-story writing also goes quite far. In the late nineteenth century, Aisha al-Taymouria, member of a talented family and sister of Mahmoud Taymour and Mohamed Taymour, widely regarded as the founders of the Egyptian short story, wrote and distributed tales.

In the first half of the twentieth century, a time of experimentation and innovation, Saheir al-Qalamawi, a pioneering short-story writer, who came to be the first woman professor of Arabic literature, has paid tribute to her grandmother— and indirectly to all our story-telling grandmothers, by giving her collection of short stories the title, **My Grandmother's Tales**[3] (1935). Qalamawi is a forerunner of a line of Egyptian women short- story writers who increased in number along the years.[4]

The short story became the most popular form of writing during the fifties and sixties.[5] This is exactly when a group of young women, mostly new university graduates in either literature or journalism, started writing short stories, and soon made a name for themselves. In the sixties and seventies the short story flourished. It is on record that when it became a popular form of writing, "women were not far behind men."[6] The eighties and nineties witnessed a greater flourishing of short-story writing, recalling that of the sixties, when a group of young men and women brought new life and vitality into Arabic literature in Egypt. These decades saw not only the establishment of women as short-story writers but also the appearance of notable talents.

The increasing volume and improving intellectual and aesthetic quality of women's literary writings in general is a reflection of improving conditions of women's lives, socially, economically and culturally. Reform in the fields of education, and work for women opened the gates for them to participate more actively in public life and to express themselves more freely in writing.

Several of these women are still preoccupied with woman's place in society, woman's worries and the discrimination she has suffered from for so long. Most of these women, however, are not feminists in the strict sense. According to a useful definition :

> Feminism involves more than one sense : an awareness by women that as women they are systematically placed in disadvantaged position; some form of rejection of enforced behaviours and thought; and the attempts to interpret their own experiences and then improve their position or lives as women. [7]

It seems to me that Egyptian women express, in different degrees, feminism in the first two senses, but it is the third sense which is truthfully involved in their literary writings : the attempt to interpret their own experiences. With few exceptions, they are not militants but would naturally hope to improve the position or lives of women through their writings. It is specifically by interpreting their lives as women and human beings that they would achieve such an objective. Preoccupied with woman's issues as they are, women writers are no less concerned with the human predicament as a whole. What is interesting is that they interpret it from their own perspective and through their own voice.

A Voice of Their Own

The claim that women writers have a voice of their own is supported by both male and female critics. According to Salwa Bakr, novelist, short-story writer and critic :

> A woman's eye is different from that of a man in looking at life and things. Their worlds differ. The world of one is different from that of the other. It is thus

inconceivable that a woman's experience in writing literature would be the same as that of a man. A woman has to create a way of writing to express herself first and foremost, taking into account that this is not as easy or as simple as it seems since the male literary tradition is the most common and the most influential.[8]

Commenting on Ibtihal Salem's short-story collection, **The Seagull,** Edward al-Kharrat, eminent creative writer and critic, writes :

> She draws without hesitation, with the hand of a craftsman .... Moreover, she is a woman, who always sees things, persons and scenes, and feels them with the perspectives and feelings of a woman.[9]

However, as much as one needs to stress woman's distinct voice, one needs to insist that literature is literature whether written by a man or a woman.

Abdel Qader al-Qot, distinguished Arabic literature specialist and critic stresses this point :

> Literature with regard to its artistic qualities cannot differ when written by a man or a woman. It is the concerns of each of the sexes that differ as a result of the experiences of each sex and their impressions of life and society... Thus we should not look in women's writings for a special kind of literature with distinctive qualities. Nevertheless we must admit that woman has her own interests which are the outcome of her psychological and social circumstances.[10]

Issues and Modes of Writing

A chronological listing of the short-story titles in this collection would reveal increasing variety and diversity. The choice of issues and techniques reveals development and enrichment in Egyptian women's output, attained through innovative modes of writing together with greater boldness and outspokenness. Their short stories no longer focus on women's experiences but reflect social, economic, political and cultural issues of life in Egypt. At their best, they investigate aspects of the human condition. The more traditional approaches are gradually superseded by more positive attitudes and more original modes of writing.

Etidal Osman, short-story writer and critic, commenting on women's concerns, rightly states :

> In a number of texts there appears to be a serious endeavour on the part of women writers towards a more profound discovery of the self and a revelation of the specifity of the feminist consciousness with its points of strength and weakness in addition to the influence of social transitions and economic crises on the status of women and their consciousness. [11]

War, economic policies, such as the market economy, privatization and increasing individual investment are not simply part of the socio-economic and political background but decisive factors that have their impact on individual lives and changing values. In these short stories, they are viewed in terms of personal lives and attitudes. Foremost among the ravages of wars is the premature loss of dear ones as in the short stories of Fawzia Mahran, Sekina Fouad and Ibtihal Salem. The widening gap between the wealthy and the poor, the rising cost of living and the financial hardships of hard-working people are vividly dramatized in Latifa al-Zayyat's "The Narrow Path" and Ibtihal Salem's "The Bet" for example.

Other stories depict cases of loneliness, failure to communicate and lack of human compassion as in Sanaa el-Beesy's "The Old Man and the Night", Wafiya Khairy's "A Mood of Optimism" and Salem's "The Bet".

Modes of presentation vary according to the quality of the situation or moment depicted and to the author's attitude and outlook. Realism is dominant in some early texts, especially those portraying the external world, a blending of realism and impressionism in later short stories, specifically when the inner self or individual consciousness is being rendered. The narrative voice is mostly a woman's voice, often using the first-person method of narration or some form of the interior monologue as in Zayyat's "By Cadlelight." Time, place and character play different roles in different stories. Despite the predominance of female characters, male characters are often objectively and convincingly portrayed. Atmosphere painting and local colour are essential technical devices in a number of stories. Style and language are ingeniously experimented with in Osman's and Radwa Ashour's stories. Classical Arabic blends with the colloquial variety at times, producing a sense of immediacy and liveliness especially in dialogue.

More innovative writers experiment with the use of myth, legend and ritual as in Osman's "The Sun Tattoo." She also makes good use of intertextuality and traditional ways of telling stories to children.

The first two stories in this collection can be said to set a pattern regarding treatment of personal and public issues. Zayyat's "By Candlelight" focuses on the consciousness of a woman character involved in a painful personal relationship. She competently renders the agony of an unhappy marriage which starts with attraction and ends with disillusionment and estrangement. Her portayal of the intelligent, educated and politically-active heroine, her suffering, hesitation and final resolution to act are beautifully dramatized. No less wonderful is the presentation of the character of the husband and the forced intimacy of the relationship. In contrast to the husband, she introduces the wife's group of congenial friends. The journey to a village in the heart of Egypt symbolizes a quest for a solution. The beauty of nature in the village functions as a metaphor of a better and healing way of life, the room at the top of the land-keeper's house as an image of phoney values.

"The Narrow Path" reflects several facets of external reality through the experience of a working woman who is a wife and mother of two daughters growing before their time. Also basic to the structure of the short story is the presence of a mad man and his imaginary train. Zayyat resorts to symbolism, contrast, life-like dialogue to depict the external and inner reality as well as reality and the dream.

The same pattern with slight variations may be easily detected in Mahran's "So Near.. So Far," which presents an evocation of the past in the middle of the present. Mahran focuses on a woman character, recalling a chess match betwen her late husband, a combat plane pilot, injured in action, and his best friend. Reminescences of the past and awareness of the present are woven not only together but with the ravages of the war and the son's determination to follow in his father's footsteps, use his technique and win the chess game with his father's friend. Love, friendship, loyalty, patriotism blend in a poetic text. The symbolism of the chess game and the time-shifts are structurally functional.

In "Music at the Bottom of a Mug," once more through the consciousness of a woman character, Mahran exposes the consequences of economic policies in physical and emotional terms. The declaration of the beautiful town, Port- Said, a free zone changes both the place and people's attitudes and values. Profiteering and the rush for foreign consumer goods become the norm. Contrast serves to highlight the change : the daughter rejecting the beautiful present from Port-Said and the mother cherishing it. are symbolic of the change.

In other short stories such as Ihsan Kamal's "An Uncommitted Crime" and "The Game is Over," the author is mainly concerned with public issues, specifically injustice and the mishandling of the law and their impact on human beings both men and women. Despite the obvious reformist aim, human suffering and the human predicament are Kamal's basic concern. Although a more traditional narrative technique and a realistic mode of depicting character and action are employed, humour and fantasy function as effective tools of social satire.

Wafiya Khairy in both "A Mood of Optimism" and "A Man and a Woman" focuses on woman's place in society and the family-still a burning issue in large sectors of society, despite the many gains attained by women. As a script writer of film and television serials, she tells a good story, occasionally marked by a romantic strain, but generally faithful to many aspects of Egyptian life.

Iqbal Baraka and Zeinab Sadek concentrate on more personal issues, and attempt innovative techniques. In "A Cup of Nescafe," Baraka depicts a man-woman relationship from an original angle. Two young people who belong to two totally different backgrounds are placed in an unusual situation, but both the situation and the characters' behaviour are credibly rendered. In "Abortion," she chooses a theme which is no less original. She presents a situation that can easily deteriorate into sentimentality and culminate in a cheap ending. However, she successfully evades these pitfalls. Seen against popular cultural attitudes towards childless wives, the contrast between the first two husbands and the third one reinforces the realism of the situation.

11

Representing women writers who focus on the different facets of the perennial theme of love, Sadek contributes two interesting portayals of women in love to this volume. "Warm Memories" unmistakably carries "A voice of her own." She renders not only the tender emotions of a woman in love, but also her self-assertion. Her use of the dialogue form throughout the short story is a rare technical achievement. In "Sparrows," birds are not simply part of atmosphere painting. They function as symbols of innate wisdom, capacity for love and loyalty, that can initiate the heroine into true love. Both Baraka's and Sadek's stories are marked by optimism and faith in human nature and in woman.

Sekina Fouad chooses young girls as protagonists in both her stories. In "She Will Come," the central character first appears as a child who grows in the shadow of grave national happenings. The impact of the 1967 Israeli-Egyptian War upon the inhabitants of the sea war-front, Port-Said, is faithfully conveyed through the viewpoint of the young girl who experiences the loss of her parents and witnesses the extensive damage of the war. The story blends elements of the political short story with the personal details of the girl's striving to achieve success. War, love, hero-worship and personal achievement are skilfully woven in an exciting story. "The Pasha's Beard" which literally stands for a tree and symbolically for the grand father's love, both represent a haven for a little girl in difficult times.

Sanaa el-Beesy's "The Old Man and the Night" is an investigation of the experience of a lonely bed-ridden old man who accidentally overhears a telephone call involving a clandestine love affair. Torn between the excitement of listening to the lovers and his awareness of what they are immorally plotting, he makes a habit of eavsedropping. "Let's Go Skiing" satirizes some present-day social phenomena: immigration for the sake of financial gain, easy divorce, showy lavishness in obituaries and funerals, as reflected through a long interior monologue of a male character, who is not an image of perfection.

With Osman, we are in the company of a younger generation of Egyptian women writers, who combine a bolder attitude towards life and woman's predicament, and a capability for experimening with the form and language of the short story. Osman is an original writer, passionately in love with the Arabic language, which plays a central role in her writings. It has taken an equally original and devoted fellow writer, Radwa Ashour, to translate her stories, and preserve the rich quality of the language as much as is feasibly possible. In both "The Sultana" and "The Sun Tattoo," the present moment blends with historical traditions: reality, myth and legend working together in a well-wrought structure.

Ashour writes short stories of compelling emotoinal and intellectual compact. They reveal a depth of vision and brilliant craftsmanship. She selects moments of life involving both women and men, mostly seen through a woman's perspective. "The Man Seated in the Garden Waiting," besides capturing glimpses of childhood and old age joyfulness and gloom, symbolically conveys to the child's mother some mysterious fear lurking in the human heart: of doom, perhaps death, both aspects of the human condition. The mother's sudden determination to continue the ball game with her son may reflect faith in life and survival. The story certainly lends itself to other interpretations. Ashour's very short stories, of which only a few are included in this volume, are concise, concentrated, poetically rendered moments of a man-woman relationship. The intimacy and vitality of the experience are vividly conveyed through her individual style and original use of language.

Bakr is a committed artist, deeply concerned with woman's predicament. She focuses on poorer women who suffer most as a result of unsuitable living conditions, economic changes and traditional attitudes. In this collection, however, she is represented by two stories exemplifying the poetic trend in her works. Using the poetic device of pathetic fallacy, she paints a vivid picture of the life-story of a lonely flower in a murky swamp. Bestowing the human quality of contemplation on the flower, Bakr succeeds in sensitively depicting the consciousness of the flower, through a series of significant moments. In "The Camel," she employs a dramatic technique depending on situation and dialogue. A small boy wants a real living camel and after a frustrating dialogue with his weary working mother is given only a substitute. In both short stories, the symbolic undertones are unmistakable.

Aisha Aboul-Nour's heroines are determined, strong-willed young women, rebellious females, seeking independence and self-assertion and often resorting to violence. In "The Rebel," the protagonist, an elegant, sophisticated young woman, symbolically finding herself locked up in a room is determined to free herself. Rather ironically, she resorts to her feminine make-up implements for the purpose. In "Meeting at the Time of Lost Love", the conflict between the man and the woman, a common theme in her stories, is only resolved by resorting to violence, and rather romantically, the woman wins.

Salem, unlike Aboul-Nour, has her feet firmly rooted to reality. In both her stories, "The Seagull" and "The Bet," she uses telling details and evocative symbols to create the right atmosphere for her significant moments. In compact structures, she pin-points major changes at a particular time and place. In Port-Said – once more the scene of action – the seagulls, the beautiful sea birds, are decreasing in number. Some of them are dead on the shore, others are escaping from the war-devastated port. Khaki is the dominant colour at the present moment. The past is symbolically evoked through stolen moments reminiscent of a tender past love relationship. In "The Bet", Salem focuses on another aspect of reality, changes resulting from the mad pursuit of money after the declaration of Port-Said as a free zone, at the expense of true values and human contact. This is forcefully reflected in a car-drive on which the heroine is taken by an old friend, poor then, lavishly rich now.

Mona Ragab introduces her women characters in action, whether individually or in a group. 'When Women Revolt" is a satirical portrayal of a women's meeting, to which some men are also invited, to work out a plan for combating terrorist events. The women participating in the meeting are a representative sample of so-called militant women. The irony of the situation resides in the excuses they give for leaving the meeting. "The Fervent Heart", is an impressive dramatization of an ambitious woman's predicament. The protagonist is torn between her academic ambition and love for her young daughter.

Neamat el-Biheiri's two stories may be regarded as variations on the theme of love. "The Sand Dream" is a tender rendering of young love – a dream that a girl and her cousin drew on the sand. The natural background reflecting the innocence and beauty of the relationship stands in deep contrast with the "sinister" represented in the boy's mother's response to the dream. "The Infatuated" paints a vivid scene from every-day reality. Biheiri excels in capturing the mood of a group of young army trainees, when a pretty young woman boards the bus taking them to a night out in the city. Unusual as the situation is, both character and incident are convincingly rendered, through a woman's perspective and a woman's voice.

Varied as the voices of Egyptian women short-story writers are: angry, tender, rebelling or optimistic, they represent "a voice of their own".

Reception

To answer Mary Eagleton's question, "How has criticism responded to women's work? an attempt will be made to assess the reception of the short stories in this volume, as an example of Egyptian women's writings. Owing to lack of space, only a few representative reviews, introductions and critical assessment will be examined. Also illuminating, as a sign of recognition, is the volume of short stories by women writers in translation.

To begin with, it would be fair to claim that critics' reactions are not always as "dismissive" as they are sometimes thought[11]. Judging by the number and quality of the reviews of several women short stories, criticism has been responding favourably, even warmly to some of them. It is on record, for example, that Kamal had nine reviews bewteen 1968 and 1970, and Baraka no less than ten assessments between 1964 and 1975. With the eighties and nineties, there have been greater signs of recognition.

One of the earliest short story collections of the second half of the twentieth century, Mahran's "The Women Students' Hostel" (1961), was reviewed in Al-Magalla (The Journal),[12] the most important literary periodical at the time. It was also treated in Experiments in Literary Criticism 1967, in both cases by serious academic critics: Fatma Moussa and Shukry Ayyad.

As for introductions to short-story collections in

general, there have been several along the years. A memorable early precedent is Taha Hussain's introduction to Qalamawi's **My Grandmother's Tales** (1935). Introductions to Kamal's **A Prison of My Own** (1965), Saadawi's **The Thread and the Wall** (1972), Salem's **The Seagull** (1987) were all written by eminent literary specialists and critics: Abdel Qader al-Qot, Ali al-Ra'i and Edward al-Kharrat. More recently, Ragab's **When Women Revolt** carries an introduction by Youssef Idris, our eminent writer.

In addition, the seventies witnessed the birth of the first selection of short stories by Egyptian women. Youssef al-Sharouni edited **Al-Layla al- Thaniya Ba'd al-Alf (The 1002 Night)** (1976), a source of information of reviews and assessments of women's short stories, among other useful information.

A quick investigation of a few representative reviews will reveal that discerning critics have been quick to discover talent and to attempt objective assessments of women's works. Traditional prejudices against women writers have not completely disappeared, but they are less frequently voiced than before except by chauvenist critics. Such accusations as involvement with the self, women's problems and marginal issues are repeatedly refuted not only by the short-story writers themselves but also by objective critics and reviewers.

Reviewing Zayyat's "By Candlelight," Farouq Abdel Qader writes :

> I would like initially to state a fact that I regard as necessary and important : we are at a rare moment of our Arabic literature in general and the literature produced by our women writers in particular. We are confronted with a high

standard of objectivity and self-analysis, satisfied only with stripping off all masks of deception, one after the other and reaching down to the deepest depths where the self, the subject of analysis appears to the examining self, shining in perfect nakedness.[13]

Another critic adds that Zayyat's pure soul "views life and the universe from an extraordinary human stance."[14] Her technical ability and profound analysis of the human soul are noted and commended. Zayyat is also praised for having "beautifully blended her own autobiography with the biography of her characters and with significant selected details of the social reality," - another refutation of the autobiographical stigma.

Of the other women whose writings have been widely reviewed: Mahran, Kamal, Khairy, Baraka, Sadek and Bakr, among others, only some can be cited here. Mahran is praised for her inspired style, her use of the interior monologue and her writings being "always related to the life of the country and the people." Most reviews follow the same pattern pointing issues treated and characteristic technical devices employed. Kamal's resorting to symbolism in "The Game is Over," is regarded as a means of denouncing political coercion and as part of the human condition. Khairy's portrayal of man-woman relationship, whether negative or positive, is favourably received as part of Egyptian life. Sadek's most important concern is rightly viewed as an attempt to register woman's attempt to achieve progress and freedom. Her portrayal of men and women characters in every-day life, according to one critic is commended for being executed through an isnpired angle of vision and truthful rendering.

It is good to note that reviewers are often quick to

perceive development and innovation in modes of writing. They favourably receive experimentation as a contribution to the development of the short story in Egypt. This is evident in the reviews of the works of such writers as Osman, Ashour, and Bakr. In assessing Osman's achievement, reviewers focus almost completely on her technique and style. She is rightly hailed as a serious creative writer seeking solutions to problems of expression, with one foot in poetry and the other in prose. As an innovator, she is regarded as having a social sense in terms of a value system and a desire to communicate.

In an attempt to match Osman's poetic prose, one critic writes, "Osman tells one story inside another, one story after the other like the shell and the pearl... *The Sultana* is a tale embellished with many colours, adornments and ornamental flourishes."[15] According to another critic, Alaa al-Deeb the stories in **The Sun Tattoo**, reveal a balance between the author's desire for experimenting with structure and the fulfilment of the function of the social and human story: "a synthesis of language, plot and theme, to create her special world."[16] In more specific terms, Ashour commends Osman's achievement. "In **The Sun Tattoo**, Osman establishes a link between Egyptian folk heritage and mystic Arabic tradition and finds a link between the legend and reality."[17]

Osman's case illustrates how a woman who is a true artist is objectively assessed both individually and as a contributer to the national culture and literature in general. Al-Deeb adds :

> **The Sun Tattoo** collection both renews interest in the short story and emphasizes the fact that the Egyptian woman participates in creative writing with full artistic and intellectual responsibility.

Ashour's short-story collection title, **I Saw the Palms,** with its apparent symbolic evocations has produced an interesting interpretation. According to a woman critic, Zeinab Montasser, it implies lifting one's eyes from the grass to the treetops and the horizon. Ashour is regarded as observing the footsteps of a number of human beings : rising or falling, withstanding or collapsing, but ultimately triumphing, looking forward to the future and holding on to the last ray. Commenting on this hopeful vision of the human predicament, Montasser adds :

> Ashour delves in the depths of human
> beings.... She sees them in relation to
> reality and the dream: visions will shine
> and human beings will triumph. This is
> why she moves between two worlds: the
> virgin world of childhood that advances
> to the future, unhindered by fetters and
> the world of adults, with its rigorous laws
> and changing moods. By mingling of the
> two worlds, children become the nourish-
> ment that renews the parents' blood.[18]

This interpretation is particulary true of "The Man Seated in the Garden Waiting".

Salwa Bakr's reputation rests on her deep concern with woman's issues in the context of national, social and political issues. To pin-point her concept of women's writings, Al-Deeb, quotes her own words to the effect that "Women's literature plays a preaching and an enlightening role and contributes to the emancipation not only of woman but also of man." He stresses Bakr's endeavour to convey a message. "She is committed to a progressive stance towards social issues."[19] Other critics dwell on her close attachment to the Egyptian reality and her truthful and stubborn representation of life, in an attempt to expose its defects and reform it." Nehad Seleiha, commenting on one of the characteristic qualities of Bakr's social satire, writes : "Amidst her deep awareness of the ugliness and falsification she depicts, she does not drown the reader in a torrent of grief and bitterness, but resorts to a sense of humour, rare in such writinge.[20] Nor is her work lacking in optimism. "A Flower in the Swamp" is rightly regarded as a symbol of life and hope amidst a siege of sterility and infertility."[21]

Salem's attempts at experimentation are regarded by critics as a vehicle for conveying a message. Anger is rightly seen as "a dominant note in her short stories" which are strongly marked by the local with its human, social and cultural dimensions. She is also praised for depicting personal experience with determination and sincerity.

Reviews of Aboul-Nour's short stories highlight h - attempts to innovate by resorting to dramatic structures, images and symbols to convey analysis of characters. Critics point out that she particularly concerns herself with conflict between man and woman. According to Seleiha, "She uses writing as a revolutionary existentialist act."[22] Her stories are described as beginning with social rejection and ending with existentialist rebellion.

A pertinent question to pose at this point and attempt to answer briefly is, "How do these women writers respond to their reception?"

Bakr comments regarding the situation of women writers in general :

> Since the end of the past century - the era
> of Aisha al-Taymouria... the attempt of
> women to march into the world of litera-
> ture has not stopped. Yet the doors are

still kept ajar, warily receiving these attempts.[23]

However, "there has been some change lately," she adds.

Osman, too' has her reservations, but she states :

> It may be possible for anyone studying Egyptian women's writings to notice an increasing amount of interest in these writings by the critical establishment.[23]

Noteworthy also is the recent appearance of a special issue of the Egyptian magazine, **Ibda' (Creativity),** Jan. 1993, on "Woman's Creativity", including a section on womens' writings.

Translation of short stories by Egyptian women, as a sign of recognition, has been considerably on the increase since the sixties. Almost everyone of the women writers included in this volume has had specimens of her stories translated into one or more foreign language.[25] Several of them are included in short-story selections in translation, of which only those showing progress will be cited here.

Mahmoud Manzalaoui's pioneering selection of short stories by Arab writers, both men and women, in English translation, **Arab Writing To-Day : The Short Story,** is a landmark in the story of the reception of Egyptian women writings world-wide. By simply being included, and regardless of the ratio of representation, they are placed on an equal footing with men. Out of the thirty stories in this selection, twenty six are by men, twenty two of them are Egyptians. Out of the four women writers, two are Egyptian: Saheir al-Qalamawi and Ihsan Kamal. By 1987, in William Hutchins', **Egyptian Tales and Short Stories of the 1970 and 1980,**[26] the number of women is eight out of a total of thirty-two. Between 1963 and 1983, Denis Johnson-Davies published several collections of Arabic short stories, including both men and women in varying numbers. With the beginning of the nineties, Egyptian women short-story writers received the recognition of a whole volume to themselves in Marilyn Booth's excellent collection, **My Grandmother's Cactus** (1991),

In addition, three selections of short stories by individual authors have appeared so far – a more significant sign of recognition. First appeared Alifa Rifaat's **Distant View from a Minaret** (1983), translated by Denis Johnson-Davies.[27] Achieving a new record, Salwa Bakr has had two complete selections to her name: **The Wiles of Man**,[28] also translated by Denis-Johnson-Davies, and **Just a Beautiful Voice**,[29] translated by Hoda al-Sadda, both appearing in 1992.

According to a recent **Bibliography of Arabic literature in Egypt in English Translation**, (1991),[30], the ratio of women to men short- story writers is 19 / 91 – a percentage of over 20% – a far cry from the 1968 ratio of 2 / 22 – a percentage of 9%.

Egyptian women's voices certainly seem to be getting more widely heard.

Angele Botros Samaan

Cairo, 1994

Notes

1. *Ihsan Kamal's short story "The Game is Over" was published in a newspaper sometime before it appeared in a collection in 1982.*

2. *See author's introduction to Al-Hilal's edition, 1978.*

3. *See Shukry Ayyad and Nancy Witherspoon,* **Reflections and Deflections : A Study of the Contemporary Arab Mind.** *Cairo : Foreign Cultural Information Department, 1986, p. 218.*

4. *Sayed al-Nassag, "The Egyptian Story in the Seventies,"* **Prism : Quarterly of Egyptian Culture** *(10 - 1984), p. 29.*

5. *Margot Badran and Miriam Cooke, eds.,* **Opening the Gates : A Century of Arab Feminist Writing.***London : Virago Press, 1990, p. xviii-xix.*

6. *"Reflections on Feminist Writing in the Arab World," Paper delivered at the Comparative Literature Symposium, Department of English, Cairo University, Dec. 1992, and published in the Symposium Proceedings, 1993.*

7. *Critical Assessment,* **The Seagull,***(1987), p. 118.*

8. *Introduction to Kamal's* **A Prison of My Own***(1970).*

9. *Paper on "Gender Encounters," delivered at the Comparative Literature Symposium, Department of English, Cairo University, Dec. 1992.*

10. *See Marilyn Booth,* **My Grandmother's Cactus : Stories by Egyptian Women.** *London : Quartet Books, 1991, p. 12.*

11. *(Jan. 1962).*

12. **Al-Hilal,** *March 1987. Quotations throughout this part of the Introduction are translated by the editor.*

13. *Abdel Badi,* **Ibda'** *(May-June, 1990).*

14. *Farouq Abdel Qader,* **Rose al-Youssef,** *No. 3312.*

15. *Alaa al-Deeb,* **Sabah al-Kheir.**

16. **Al-Hayat** *(14 Dec. 1992)*

17. *Zeinab Montasser,* **Rose al-Youssef***(4 June 1990)*

18. *Alaa al-Deeb*

19. **Al-Ahram** *(24 Nov. 1987).*

20. *Abdel-Rahman Abou Oaf.* **Al- Ahali** *(9 Sept. 1992).*

21. **Al-Akhbar** *(3 Aug. 1988)*

22. *"Reflections on Feminist Writings in The Arab World," See above, note 7.*

23. *"Gender Encounters," See above, note 10.*

24. *See Biographical notes.*

25. *Cairo : The American University in Cairo Press, 1987.*

26. *London : Quartet Books, 1983.*

27. *London : Quartet Books, 1992.*

28. *Cairo : General Egyptian Book Organization, 1992.*

29. **Arabic Literature in Egypt in English Translation.** *Compiled with an introduction by Angele Botros Samaan. Cairo : Supreme Council of Culture, 1991.*

*LATIFA AL-ZAYYAT was born in the coastal town, Damietta in 1923. She is professor of English and Comparative Literature at the Girls' College, Ain Shams University, Cairo, novelist, short-story writer and critic. She graduated in English Literature, Cairo University, 1946, obtained a Diploma then a Ph.D. in Journalism, in 1957. Besides teaching and writing, she occupied the position of Director of the Arts Academy (1970-1972). Her novel : **The Open Door** (Al-Bab al- Maftouh), 1960. Was one of the earliest novels written by Egyptian women. She has also published **Old Age and Other Stories** (Al Shaykhoukha Wa Qissas Okhra), 1991 and **An Inspection Campaign : Personal Papers** (Hamlat Tafteesh : Awraq, Shakhsiyya), 1992.*

She has also written two important critical studies in Arabic :
Protrayals of Women in Arabic Stories and Novels *and* **Naguib Mahfouz : The Image and the Example,** *both in 1989.*

Her short stories : "By Candlelight" and "The Narrow Path" appeared in **Old Age and Other Stories.**

BY CANDLELIGHT

Latifa· Al-Zayyat

She stood behind the door of her apartment hurrying the departure. An old desire urged her release from the apartment overlooking the Nile and from the confines of a husband who as a morning habit sleeps in.

Waiting to be picked up to the Bani-Sweif bus- stop by the hostess of the country house at Sannour village with her playwright husband, she stood hurrying the departure.

At the last minute she shoved into her small suitcase the project of her second novel in the hope of... of what? For the past two years she has been deconstructing, on the left-hand side of her golden notebook, what she has been constructing on the right- hand side of it, so the project has never been accomplished. The comments of the political being– still alive in her– flowing on the left- hand side in successive dates from 1960 to 1962 refused to portray an individual's failure as the failure of mankind, conveying thus to the public a message of despair.

But is it conceivable that in two days a crisis which has lasted for two years gets resolved? Two years or ten years? In bitterness she wondered while still standing behind the closed door. Finally, in her usual manner when trodding forbidden grounds, she repressed the question deciding thus to go whole-heartedly through the new experience of living in a village.

She got onto the Bani-Sweif bus. The group was joined by a friend who is a literary critic and the friend's sister, a physician, with her husband, a professor of psychology.

29

She felt a certain belonging to the travelling group: a group less pretentious, more genuine and more honest than the groups within which she moves behind her husband. With this group one could drop one's mask and relax without being on one's guard for the next impending blow. This group is definitely not like the groups which carouse at the "Night and Day" cafeteria of the Semiramis Hotel or which go out for candlelight dinners in chic restaurants or decorate opening nights at theatres, painting exhibitions and public seminars.

She shares with this travelling group common interests even close political ones though not identical. However, due to her political past she remains the black duck of the group or, as many would say, the "red" one. But, even to her, the difference is now blurred.

* * *

The bus travels along the agricultural road of Upper Egypt, a road distinguished from most agricultural roads of the Nile delta by palm trees on both sides. The palm trees thicken into a forest and desert hills loom on the horizon. The bus radio is playing a song : "Whoever said that love is like honey; love is sweeter than honey". The tedious rhythm of the song repeats the same stifling tone while the sand hills get closer and smother the green valley. Through the radio the Arabic translator talks about Gagarin and man's first trip into space while the sand hills suffocate the valley down here.The bus reaches Bani-Sweif as Abdel Halim Hafez sings : "For the sake of your moon-like beauty I would travel up to the moon".

A taxi carries the group to the nearest spot to Sannour village which borders the eastern desert. Having crossed

30

the valley, the taxi stops as circulation in the sand becomes impossible.

Together with the group she delves into the sand dunes. She sits by the Nile bank waiting for the ferry. At last, crossing the Nile is the final leg to reaching the old country house, a house seldom used in the decade following the law of Agricultural Reform.

* * *

Waiting for the ferry she sits on the sandy edge watching the eastern bank of the river. Here, the Nile curbs into a semi-circle blocking the view on both sides. Here, life begins and ends with this turquoise green bracelet of tall palm trees and with this bank of soft fine golden sand glittering in the sun as a field of amber. Here, the turquoise is laced up by the amber in infinite tranquility.

If only existence were to begin here and end with infinite tranquility! She notices the sand hills in the horizon enveloping the Nile, the bank, the palm trees and her. She leafs through her golden notebook looking for the paragraph in the prospective novel which describes the options available for her heroine. And what formidable options they are :

One of two paths is open to her who became impaired beyond hope of recovery : either give in and live the rest of her life in bitterness or accept reality with courage.

But, there are no two paths, there is one and only path : in between one death and another death there is death and the reality she is to accept "with courage" is also death. Startled, she jumps up to her feet hastily picking her belongings while the ferry is boarding.

* * *

The ferry gets crowded with peasants in festive clothes returning from the unavoidable trip to the city and peasants employed in the city returning after a long absence for a short visit to their families. There is also the group of Cairene intellectuals, two donkeys and one sheep. The ferry is filled with a warm and festive atmosphere as the peasants are exchanging greetings, asking after family members and sending regards to the loved ones dispersed across the banks of the Nile looking for a living.

She sits listening to the exchange between the villagers and the ferryman who connects the isolated village with the outside world. The ferryman relates the prediction reported in Cairene newspapers about the closeness of doomsday. The white donkey gives a prolonged bray. The peasant woman who is bringing back her sheep from the veterinary hospital laughs and says :

"For God's sake captain, when death comes round don't ferry him, then he won't cross over to our side."

The problem of survival remains the one reality beside which other realities dwindle as long as there are in this world people struggling to survive. "Being and Non-Being" do not worry the peasant woman as it had worried Kierkegaard. Neither Sartre's "Nausé" nor Camus' "absurd" worry her. Unlike intellectuals, the peasant woman treats death - or the supreme reality as an Egyptian writer calls it- with great simplicity and surprising light-heartedness. She transforms death into a living being with whom she co-exists acknowledging his presence but transcending it in her struggle for survival.

The wind gets stronger and the ferry leans over to one side, its surface touching the water. At the possibility of drowning in the Nile, she exchanges anxious looks and affected stoic grins with the group. The ferry continues to lean over while the villagers and the ferryman continue their conversation in a warm and festive mood as though the interval between life and death has been cancelled and the opposites have been reconciled in a warm and festive moment.

The ferry reaches the bank and she becomes over-whelmed by the joy of living. The ferryman requests the "carpet"[1] She looks at some men approaching the ferry carrying a wooden object. Instead of the "carpet" she identifies the coffin of a young child. Life and death clash at this intense moment. Her eyes meet those of the friendly peasant woman who reports the situation in an objective manner devoid of emotion :

"You see, we don't have cemetries here... so we bury our dead on the other bank."

She observes the peasant woman pulling away her skinny sheep and walking down the "carpet" to the sandy bank in firm steps. She feels embarassed because in her long seclusion from people she has slipped into reflections about the absurdity of life and the doomed failure of the human quest.

Everything has to follow the schedule planned by the hostess for the short weekend : as she sets it the afternoon is given to a free tour around the house and the surrounding fields. The morning of the following day is also free except for the evening which has, for a special event, the singer of the village singing the local songs unique to

---

(1) Used figuratively to refer to the wooden ramp for going on or off a boat.

the area. Sometime in between the afternoon and the evening of that day the hostess and her husband will have to visit the keeper who collects the rent of what remains of the family's land. The visit is optional and those wanting to rest can stay in the house. However, it would be appropriate for the physician to join in the visit to the keeper's house especially that the keeper's wife is sick and there are no physicians in the whole area. At any rate, the choice is totally up to her.

Soon after the hostess has finished setting up the schedule the physician asked :

"Where's the village?"

Nothing appears from the window except a stretch of green bounded by sand. The hostess assured her that the village is not far away and that those who opt for the visit to the keeper's house in the afternoon of the following day would have to pass through it.

As soon as the hostess had finished talking, a peasant from the village came in holding her dying baby for the guest physician to examine.

* * *

She started with the garden which due to ten years of negligence had turned into a weedy growth of plants, even the weeds had dried up. As she strolled about, it occured to her that since a long time she had ceased rambling and meditating. She pictured the tears flowing noiselessly down the veined cheeks of the peasant mother. She wondered whether her misery had reached the extent of being afraid of the process of thinking freely. She would plan her thoughts for a lecture, a seminar, an article, a broadcast or a televized interview. Otherwise, she would read anything and everything in order not to think freely. If short for reading material, a medical brochure would come to her rescue. Has she become like a train which loses its balance and gets destroyed if it goes off the track?

"What is important is the journey itself not its consequence, the continuation of man's quest and not its results. There is no oasis somewhere or some time to be reached by man. Man sees the oasis and lives it during the quest. The journey is the green oasis."

So said she summing up the central theme of her prospective novel at a time when she still had hoped to write it. Her friend, the professor of psychology, commented :

"The project of this novel turns failure into a philosophy and makes general what cannot be generalized. Certainly, the human quest is not doomed to failure."

He kept silent for a while then added :

"Are you trying to justify a situation you cannot bear?"

For the first time ever she contemplated the truth of his comment. She realized that she had overlooked the comment as well as other gossip in order for the train not to lose its equilibrium and get overturned. A colleague of her husband whose political stance is totally opposed to his, told her :

"People are amazed that you have written such an excellent novel despite of everything."

On that day she had treated as nonsense the colleague's comment. What is the source of amazement when, despite of her marriage, she is the same being? Her old belief has not altered, neither has her will for change. As a young woman she strove for social change through action and now, as a woman, she strives for it through writing.

Amidst the thrill of success of her first novel she had forgotten a promise she had made to herself : if only I can complete this novel, I would be able to free myself from my husband, from this house and from this style of living. She had completed the novel but forgot the pledge which she now remembers.

She followed the garden paths covered with jagged pebbles and wondered: have the pebbles become flat over the years or have her senses become so dull that she no longer feels their prick thrusting at her every now and then? Is she really the same being after ten long years of marriage?... She had escaped from the baby with scrawny legs and swollen stomach leaving him behind dying inside the house and going out for a free tour... Probably at night on her cushion, she would choke a little with tears for the baby but then her breath would return to normal as soon as the process of purification takes place. If she would choke again at any pressing form of misery or deprivation, here and there, novels, plays and films would be accessible to all. She would go on crying in the darkness of the theatre, the cinema or the bed instead of participating as much as she could in changing social conditions. She would continue to play the game of crying to make herself believe that she is not dead but still living. Is this flow of tears one of expiation or one of purgation? She mumbled as she felt the prick of the pebbles :

"Something is wrong with my constitution !"

Then asking the help of people who no longer have a real daily presence in her life she added :

"For God's sake show me wherein lies the ailment. People say that you dream on paper, struggle on paper, achieve on paper what you can't achieve in actual life."

So told her an actress whom she respects as a comment on her first novel while at the cafeteria of the broadcasting house. This time she felt the thurst, but instead of admitting the truth she retorted sharply and proudly :

"Let anyone who can, dream up a novel equally good."

As soon as the hot comment and the sharp reply had ended both went on doing their roles to the best of their abilities. The actress playing one of many roles which change everyday, while she.. which role does she play? The role of a writer who suddenly emerges from the unknown to the known and who possesses the keys of the writing game, the role of an artist who can bestow the keys of the game upon anyone who wants to play.

But worst of all is the fact that it is not a game at all. By the end of her first novel she had become similar to Goha[1] who had lost his box but retained its keys. All the keys to the writing craft in themselves cannot create the utterly devoted passion for life which is the subject matter of art and without which art turns into a leisurely or ornamentative game. Now, where does she stand vis a vis this utterly devoted passion for life ?

"I wanted to seize my vision of reality as a young woman before it slipped away for ever from me."

She was struck by the sentence given in reply to the correspondent of a foreign broadcasting company asking :

"Why this particular novel and at this particular time, the year 1960?"

On that day she was surprised to hear herself admit a truth she had long suppressed and no doubt repressed anew, for here again, while walking in a dried up garden,

_____
(1) A comic folkloric charater.

37

the same truth hit her again as both old and new, known and forgotten. She had to admit that the vision in her first novel was not that of a life really lived but rather that of a bygone life which had slipped away from the person playing the game of crying.

She climbed up, then down the abraded steps which divided the garden into heights and depressions... These definitely meant much at a time when the flowers used to be opened to the sun, the air, the tall trees with their roots deep into the soil and their branches upward into the sky. Now, they mean nothing anymore... Equated are the ascent and descent now that the garden had withered.

When her first novel admitted her to the hearts of people, achievement meant both a great deal and nothing. It was as though another person had got there, as though she had masqueraded the passion for life of another creature and not hers. She saw in the eyes of girls and in the grateful handshake of a bashful young man the glitter of recognition.. One night she dreamt that she had been invited to a reception. She stood with other guests on one step of the stairs leading to the party hall. People preceded her and others followed and she recognized among them some famous Egyptian writers. While queuing up she felt electrified into a state of consciousness; have the other guests experienced the pang or is she the only one who feels it?

On that day she felt that in order to reach the hearts of people she had cheated a little and as a consequence she caught the pang. From that day on the sense of failure followed her while moving in the circle of stars who cross the halls of the television and broadcasting house with confident steps and artificial smiles posing and saying: "Really..." and there is no reality in what they say.

38

She collapsed on a seat of rocks as she found herself in a dilapidated kiosk. She admitted that the kiosk had changed from a green to a sandy colour. The comment on the left-hand side of her golden notebook which destroys the project of the unfinished novel on the right-hand side, came back to her. She found herself unconsciously repeating its words :

To escape confrontation does not represent a solution. It amounts rather to an attempt of suicide as an alternative to waiting for the completion of the act of killing.

She had to admit that the rope of self-deception is long and eventually surrounds the neck of the human being. This admission frightened her, so she ran away to an open field near by.

She tried to identify the plants in the field. It was imperative for her to do so. She stretched out a trembling hand to one of the leaves, plucked it, brought it to her nose and focussed all her senses on smelling it. But she could not identify the plant. She cut the leaf in two, tasted it, chewed it, sucked it, savoured it but could not identify it. She spat the extract and went on rolling in the field.

She recollected that in her youth she had eaten a raw marrow straight from the field and had liked it. The passion for life naturally bestows upon every small or large object a special and unique flavour. In her youth, she had dreamt of running with her beloved barefooted in a field of green beans, of lying down with her beloved embraced by the greenery and the scent of the fertile soil, of eating with her beloved beans and cottage cheese. She ended up having dinner with her husband by candlelight as lovers would do, while no love remained between them. Whenever he would drag her to one or other glittering circle she wanted to cry

39

out: a lie are those candles, a lie is our marriage, a lie is every circle we move into. But instead of crying out to shatter the lie, she lived it. She wondered: has she herself turned into a lie,– into the inseparable part of an institution addicted to analgesics, avoiding the clashes and taming the words in order for the living, far-sounding conflicts not to erupt?

Instead of crying out she read to her hsuband one morning a poem by Salah Abdel Sabour[1] published in the Friday *Al-Ahram* [2] which deals with the pretentious intellectuals who carouse at the "Night and Day" cafeteria. All she can recall now of the poem is the meaning of one line not its wording. A woman tells the man who is staying late with her in the cafeteria :

"Let's go darling before the morning rises and my varnish vanishes."

She recalls, however, that while reading the poem her eyes had been filled with tears and that she had experienced catharsis. So, she resumed living the lie. She also recalls that despite the intensity of emotions she had not forgotten to read the poem as a good poem ought to be read by an appreciative reader. And between the intensity of emotions and the necessity of tact, she lived the lie.

In the elegant restaurant she sits face to face with her husband. The candles separate them, but also do the half-truths, the bitterness of reality, the cruelty of deception, the mutual rejection of each other's identity, the fear of clashing, the preservation of a social image, the pretended success of a project long bankrupt, the words tamed by love and later by social cowardice or the so-called civility of intellectuals: words, obscure and mercurial

---

(1) *Eminent Egyptian poet.*
(2) *The Friday issue of Al-Ahram includes a literary section.*

beating about the bush and its cowardly alleys, wanting to exclaim but never do. And why should words be proclaimed when the session of candles is but another ritual in a series of rituals which shapes their lives and their movements together and with others. It is simply another of the many rituals which destroy her and yet which she keeps on contributing to perpetuate.

Their nightly conversation is another one of their rituals. A conversation, if it can still be termed so, for it used to be but is not any more. Over the days she had been transformed into an ear listening with a mind burdened by an ever- increasing accumulation of lies and half-truths which would multiply day after day without ever stopping. He would keep on weaving more lies and more half-truths while her mind kept on being bewildered day after day with the increasing bewilderment passing unnoticed by her.

Under the impact of accumulated lies her mind is often distracted now while speaking, as people do, in a gathering. A sudden look of surprise from one of her listeners would hit her, causing her to realize that she was losing control over her mind. Yet, instead of crying out "enough" she would become silent and tongue-tied.

The ritual of all rituals is at night when she becomes the listener. If she were sleeping he would wake her up, for the day is not complete unless the nightly ritual takes place. He brings her dinner on a tray, sits on the side of her bed and relates to her his endless conquests of the day. When he reaches the emotional conquests half-truths creep into the story : "Would you believe it people are saying I am having an affair with so-and- so?" Once upon a time it was difficult for her to imagine an affair with so-and-so because so-and-so would have been like a daughter to him. But, if and when the story reaches her, he would retort : "Haven't I told you so?" and would emerge innocent, his innocence being that of a wolf from the blood of a lamb, as the saying goes. Two years ago she cried out at him :

"Stop telling lies, please. Your constant lies are despicable to you and to me. It is an unwarranted insult to both of us. I have never asked you for an explanation and I shall never do so."

But he never stopped. He could not live without a nightly listener to his daily conquests which never ended or to his daily bitterness at the ingratitude of people or of life which also never ended. And over the days, she had been transformed into an ear which listened and into a mouth which was tongue-tied. She would want to get some sleep to be fit to get up early and do her work. But in case she would argue he would keep her up throughout the night until she got convinced or worse still until she pretended to be so in order to sleep. For years she had stayed up late to discuss matters in the hope of an intellectual encounter, but then she turned into a listening ear and a tongue-tied mouth when she had realized that there was no meeting ground between them. Even their meeting in bed had become unbearable and had been transformed into a destructive ritual.

Many years back he had shouted at her in bed but then shouted no more. He would not utter a word while performing his "marital duty" and sleeping right after. But once, when their marital encounter had not been yet a ritual he had shouted at her :

"You despise me."

She looked at him then with wonder and surprise and he added :

42

"Your body rejects me, scorns me."

She did not know then that at times the body could be more intelligent and more expressive than the intellect. She did not know that self-deception was permissible by the intellect but not permissible by the body. Nothing would delude the body from its sensations. She knew but had not become any wiser. She had expected that he would stop the sexual act but he did not. She intentionally deferred it but it did not stop. Intercourse became a destructive ritual. He had transformed her into an object for his own satisfaction. Yet, instead of crying out "enough", she carried on with swollen eyes, permanent nausea and frustration.

"But your personality is not that of a fighter."

So had remarked a colleague a few days ago when all efforts needed to be recruited in a nasty and open fight against corruption with the administration. She had replied then perhaps as a justification or as an apology :

"Let's try. I usually buy my peace of mind with a lot of small concessions. But when it is a matter of principles you will find me as stubborn as a mule."

She admitted while lying amidst the unidentified greenery that the foot of a mountain was indeed its bottom and that there was no end to making concessions. Usually a small concession would lead to a bigger one and so on. Unprincipled concessions would get confounded with principled ones over time. Then, one day one would wake up to find oneself falling into a bottomless abyss.

She admitted that she had never exclaimed at her husband because she had been transformed into a lie playing the same game and abiding by the same rules. She also acknowledged that her husband was much better than her because he did not pretend to be other than what he was.

She admitted that anger was no longer her right since it was only the right of a person capable of disconneceting and reconnecting what had been severed.

On the eve of their travel back to Cairo, the singer sang to the group who got back tense and gloomy from their visit to the village and to the keeper's house. The singer related the story of a village suffocated by rocky and sandy hills and of a people who lived in the village turning, over the years, the rocks into green. The miseries and joys of people over the years diffused the tension and gloom of the group. Tearless, she sat listening to the stories of sowing and reaping, of hope and hunger, of passion and death realizing that the game of crying had become of no use.

She had not participated in the tension and gloom which followed the visit to the village and to the keeper's house. She had gone beyond the stage of feeling guilty as well as the stage of attempting to get rid of guilt by blaming others or blaming unknown forces. She felt separated from the group by a new consciousness that her world up in a flat overlooking the Nile in Cairo had ended.

Something had happened between the sunset and the evening of this day which ended her world for ever. She was not certain when exactly it had happened. Was her world over when she was going through the mudddy paths of the village resisting a spell of fainting and succeeding? Or was it at the keeper's house when suffocating she had cried out "Get me out of here"? Irrespective of when, she was certain it had ended. Neither brooding over her misery by candlelight nor dreaming on paper was possible any longer.

The feeling of the inevitable end obligated her to face the necessity of taking action. Separated from the group she was wondering: "Am I able to do it?.. Has anything remained from the young woman I was which would help me to amputate the existing condition and reconnect what had been severed?"

It was not difficult to surmise what had occured at the house after the visit of the group to the village and to the keeper's house. She had lived similar moments several times though none were as severe as these ones experienced on this day. The members of the group sat facing each other as though they were strangers. Each was avoiding the other's gaze for fear of disclosing their hidden complacencies. As she had expected, soon the gloom turned into tension. Each was attempting release from responsibility by throwing the blame either on unseen forces or on others.

To admit responsibility amounts to the collapse of the beautifully glittering shell that each one had built for oneself back in Cairo in order to shelter oneself and live. The question "What have I done to change conditions?" is an issue conveniently avoided because much is at stake.

As she had expected, tension replaced gloom. Each accused the other of treating the event as a tourist would by simply visiting the village to look at the misery of its inhabitants. The accusation narrowed down and was directed at the physician who did not simply watch like the rest of them. Rather, the physician had made contact with the peasants by talking to them, treating their children who were either in a critical stage or dying, sending for the purchase of medicine from Bani-Sweif and recommending long-term treatment beyond her stay. The physician had been distressed when she realized that none of the patients' families owned enough money to secure long-term treatment. She had appealed to everyone even to the stones of the earth complaining about the total absence of medical care from the village and from the whole region.

It was said that like tourists the physician had asked questions which should not have been addressed to the villagers.

At sunset, the village appeared in the twilight as having one dominant and fixed colour, that of mud. She felt dizzy as mud houses were losing their dimensions in the dimness. People of mud were sitting by the doorsteps of houses with swollen stomachs and parched lips. Muddy coloured blood was streaking out of the mouths of children in extremity. People were vanishing in the alleys of the village as though they were mud puppets. Similar to children's toys were animals with skinny, stiff and restless necks. Nothing shattered the silence except a bloody cough and a woman wailing her baby with an almost inaudible lament.

In agony she faltered like a drunk. She realized that there was a thin margin separating her from losing consciousness and that her survival depended entirely on going beyond that margin to stay conscious. Instead of running away this time too, she slowed down while still reeling over. Instead of closing her eyes as not to be stabbed by the suffering, she kept them wide open to see. She stared, she heard, she assimilated, she stopped and ruminated upon every bit of detail committing each to her memory and to her whole being so as not to forget but as to get furious.

No, this time she did not escape from the village or

46

from its mud people. To them she returned after a long absence.

From the Keeper's house, she escaped.

There is something sham and artificial about the Keeper's house. The man had wanted to extricate himself from a house of mud to one of red bricks. It seems though that he could not afford to, so he remained trapped with no real house similar to the one who dances half-way on the stairs.[1] Neither did he belong to the peasants nor to those who owned red brick houses. The house of the Keeper is not a house at all, but a room on a second floor suspended in the air by a flight of steps that has no railing. The ground or first floor has nothing at all, no rooms for the children of different ages, no pen for animals, no oven to make bread or cook meals. The house is just a room hanging up in the air on stairs with no casing similar to the decor of a play about to be dismantled.

Climbing up to the suspended room was not difficult due to the twilight at sunset but getting out of the room in the absence of any light represented the real difficulty. Yet, exit was imperative however deep the darkness and difficult the attempt. The only alternative to the exit was death by suffocation.

While listening to the village singer relating the stories of sowing and reaping, of hope and starvation, of passion and death she wondered : had they forced the sick woman up there or had she contributed willingly to the show which was staged for the sake of the Cairene guests?

She opted out for the latter possibility as nobody could

---

[1] *A saying implying failure to achieve an objective, like a dancer who dances half-way on the stairs and is seen by neither those upstairs nor those downstairs.*

force anyone to do anything against one's will.

How alien and uprooted did the sick woman look spread on a black metal bed in a room suspended in the air with some plaster still on its floor. How alien and uprooted did she look sleeping on a bed probably for the first time ever and in a position unusual for her. Would the sick woman be able to return to where she belonged now that the game was over?

She did not know exactly what had happened to the woman when the black metal bed had fallen apart... At the doorstep stood the men guests and the hosts. Inside the suspended room stood the women guests stuck to the wall to make room for the physician. After the exchange of courtesies and greetings started the medical examination.

The physician stripped off the woman. No sooner had the physician leant over to put the stethoscope onto the heart than the bed collapsed with the naked woman on it. As for herself, she went out of the room suffocating in her own shame, and whispering to the friend, the professor of psychology :

"Get me out of here."

In the open air outside the Keeper's house she stood trembling with shame, touching her body, feeling the depth of the wounds she experienced when the bed had collapsed with **her** on it naked.

She wondered after the departure of the singer and as the owner of the house was putting the tapes of the recorded songs in her suitcase in preparation for their return to Cairo. Does the woman have the strength to amputate the existing condition and to connect what has been severed? She nursed her anger as would a pregnant woman her foetus, being aware that crying out for help was no longer useful. Now, that the game is over, the woman has to stand up on her own feet and to return back to her people, herself, her own and her home after an absence of ten years.

Translated by Amal Kary

THE NARROW PATH

In the afternoon, the mother waited impatiently for her two daughters' return from school. She bent out of the window, hoping to catch a glimpse of Siham and Mona in the distance. She soon straightened up, realizing she never learned from experience. Nobody could see anything in the distance from that window. An old grey house, two houses away, blocked the street, leaving only a narrow path. Thus the way looked as if it was blocked. Siham and Mona would not be visible except after passing the narrow path, with Siham leaning her head back and her lips tightly closed, while Mona would breathlessly follow her running in order to catch up with her quicker and firmer step, running and holding on to Siham's arm, as if afraid that she would slip out of her grasp and she would be lost.

The mother retreated from the window, wiping with the back of her hand the drops of perspiration falling from her forehead onto her eyes. Something different marked Siham's walk during the last year, something painful to the heart. The girl walked as if getting ready to defend herself in a battle waiting for her at the next step, a battle that she would miraculously bypass with every step.

The sun was setting but it was still very hot, as if the street tiles had stored the heat in the ditches, sending it out like a strong wind, carrying the smell of roasted chopped onions, old urine and rotten rubbish heaped in the corners.

51

A cat joined Om[1] Mohamad's children in what seemed like a process of sorting out the rubbish. The cat got out of a heap of garbage, yawned in the shade of a wall and stretched wiping her back with her tongue, satisfied and traquil.

A train whistle was heard shattering the midday calm of the street and the cat crept on her belly terrified. The mad man living on the roof of the house opposite came out riding his make-believe train as usual. He gave the starting whistle, breathing in and out like a train, his legs and arms acting as the train wheels. The train sped up slowly and gradually, ending with a mad rush, as if there was a wall to the roof to stop the rush. The madman escaped from reality to the world of make-believe. There was no narrow path in the world of madness, nor was anything impossible. Everything was possible in that world and so was nothing. The madman bumped against the wall and gave the starting whistle once more, ending where he began and his blood kept flowing.

The madman's blood accumulated on the wall day after day and he did not stop bumping his head against the wall. "God alone is the all giver and all powerful," said Amm[2] Gom'ah, the grocer who had in the last few years become the owner of a boutique, as she listened to the starting whistle. On the recorder belonging to Sayed, the mechanic's boy, who now owned a kiosk dealing in imported cigarettes, sweets, toys, narcotics and women's good name, Soad Hosni, the popular singer, was heard singing her new song for the thousandth time.

_____

(1) The Arabic word for mother. A woman is often called by the name of her first- born male child in some sectors of the society.
(2) Amm : uncle, often applied to an elderly man not necessarily a relative.

The mechanic's boy looked stealthily at a house on the opposite side of the path, together with two men, strangers to the neighbourhood. Almost immediately, the strangers disappeared along the narrow path, and soon after, the door of one of the houses which at one time had a blameless record opened, revealing a woman. Who could the woman be this time? Whose daughter was she?

She knew that the right path had become the hard path, that the current was overpowering and that nothing was incredible any longer. She was stunned and frightened every time the door revealed this or that woman with a friendly face or a girl she had carried as a baby, while Soad Hosni went on with her song "rejecting the sweet potato"[1] and repeating the rest of the song saying, "Go get me chocolates, laddie, or forget all about me." Meanwile, flies covered Om Mohamad's bare breast as she fed her new-born baby, while her other children, both boys and girls, the eldest not quite eight years old, carried to the hut built of palm tree branches in the middle of nowhere, the sorted out garbage as soon as it arrived: rags, glass, food remains, to appease their hunger. And the madman's blood did not cease to accumulate on the wall. What was really strange was that he who was sane did not go mad.

In the kitchen, the mother was pealing egg- plants, and getting the slices ready for frying, while the rice was still cooking as a result of her having been delayed that day on her way back from the school because of bad traffic. Mona would scream the moment she would discover that lunch was not ready yet. And Siham! But Siham's is quite another story. The girl of eleven had prematurely grown up.

At Siham's age, she herself was as ignorant as a blind cat, as the saying goes, knowing nothing about life. She

_____
(1) A cheap kind of sweet compared to chocolates.

53

used to hang her feast dress on the foot of her mother's brass bed and go round jubilantly contemplating it all day, and when she went to bed she would dream of the moment when she would wear it the following day. She did not know anything about the latest fashions or the best fabrics to go with those fashions, nor did the other children in the neighbourhood or at school know anything of the kind. The dress to be worn on the day of the feast was to be new and that would be enough to make it beautiful in her eyes and in the eyes of the other children. When she happened to fall ill on one of the feast days, the dress remained on the front of the bed which she shared with her mother three days of the week, and she feverishly contemplated it. Otherwise it carried her joyously to the street, alive with colours, children's laughs and cries while friendships grew suddenly and those who quarrelled soon made up as if nothing had happened, enjoying a sense of belonging and make-believe games, in which every child had a part to play with all seriousness, whether he belonged to the policemen or the thieves. The children's world was a magic world, closed to the grown-ups. It had its language, its jargon and its values, according to which all were equal and all alike.

The mother cut her finger on the knife blade and suddenly realized that having to face her daughter, Siham, had come to frighten her sometimes. She washed her finger, watching the water getting coloured with blood then clearing up as she resumed what she had started. The wound hurt as she dipped the egg-plant slices in salted water. She decided the world had changed and children were no longer children, and wealth, poverty, black and white existed side by side in children's schools, even in the alleys.

The barrier between the world of children and that of

adults had collapsed, and a great power and a hard life, had transformed the white into black bestowing on what was black the glitter of wild, fierce gold and authority. Everyone saw and knew this and aged with the knowledge.

The mother placed the pan with some oil on the stove and thanked God that Siham was not a good mixer. She did not pay visits to friends and declined invitations to birthday parties. Her mother wondered, as she watched the smoke rising from the oil turn dark grey, whether Siham really hated appearing in front of her school mates wearing dresses that her younger sister, Mona inherited when the hem could no longer be let down.

Two days before, Siham had asked her a question which still bewildered her. The girl had asked how much a Rollsroyce cost and whether it was 80,000 pounds. The mother could not believe this for more than one reason .. so she asked her daughter to repeat the question. The girl did and the mother asked sharply what Siham had to do with that sort of thing.

She later realized that she had deliberately been sharp with her, in order to gain time to understand the meaning of the question first, and then the significance of the girl's asking such a strange question. She guessed that the Rols-royce was a more expensive car than the Mercedes, a thing which she had not known until that moment, nor could she distinguish one car from another even then. She wondered at the fact that there existed a car which cost 80,000 pounds no less than at the fact that at her daughters' school there were parents who could afford such a car. She was appalled that Siham showed an interest in a matter so totally and incredibly out of context in the framework of her family and her environment. The more she realized the significance of the question, the sharper her tone became as she told the girl that it was no concern of hers and that she should concentrate on her studies.

The girl went on asking if when she grew up, she would be able to buy a car, even a low-priced Nasr if she did well all through school, saved every possible piastre of her pocket money and of her salary when she finished school. The mother was puzzled by Siham's questions and took refuge in repeating the proverb, "If there is a will there is a way." She could hardly believe herself as she parrot-like repeated a proverb which applied in the good old days, but no longer did. Nonetheless she thought one may hold on to a proverb as a drowning person holds on to a rescue line, in order not to go astray or go mad.

The mother moved backward as the egg-plant slices settled in the pan to avoid the spatter of the boiling oil reaching her. She recalled Siham's look examining her mother's clothes as she proceeded on her way to work.

"This style is no longer fashionable, no one wears it any more," said Siham.

"Maybe if this dress is shortened, it would look better," she said as she examined her with a strange look as if she were one of her pupils and not her own daughter. How painful was that look for Siham herself as well as for her. How distressing it was to be viewed through others' eyes and for our loved ones to see us with the eyes of strangers. At such moments we become naked, and both we and they suffer alienation, she felt.

The mother turned over the egg-plant slices in the boiling oil and once more she felt guilty, as if she had done wrong. Siham would notice the absence of a meat dish at lunch time for the sixth time running, she thought. If she were in a good mood, she would refer to this saying.

"Has the cat eaten the meat, mother?"

She might go along with Siham's irony or be content with a smile. The atmosphere tinged with irony, but free from bitterness and replete with small exchanged confessions, would carry the family merrily along to the end of the meal. Neither irony nor clowning really mattered. Things would not be so bad if Siham did not resort to silence and did not comment. She no longer knew how to treat the girl and this made her task as a mother more difficult.

The fried egg-plant slices made a hissing sound as they were being put in a glass dish containing a vinegar and garlic sauce and the mother wondered how often she was on the point of disclosing the truth of the financial situation of the family to Siham. The father's monthly salary from his regular job in addition to his earnings from moonshining, together with her salary as a teacher plus her income from private tuition could hardly cover the two daughters' school fees, necessary clothing and food under the condition of the mad rise in prices. All the necessities of life were gradually turning into luxuries. Years before, she had classified meat as a luxury, except for one day or two per week, and after meat came fruit and now it is almost time for vegetables. She was no longer able to provide a salad daily, despite the importance of vitamins for the two girls. If the flat rent had not been what it used to be and had not gone up, even the bare necessities would have been impossible.

How often had she been tempted to get Siham to share in shouldering the responsibility, but ended by taking pity on her. How often was she provoked by the knowing angry face to start explaining the situation, to complete the knowledge in order to remove the anger? How often did she change her mind as a stab suddenly went through her and she realized once more that the knowing face was a little face, the face of a child made mature before her time by a need that had crossed no one's mind, the child of parents who held university degrees and occupied highly-respected government posts for more than twelve years, whereas Sayed, the procurer, owned a whole block of flats, a grocery had been converted into a boutique and a civil servant, supposedly earning an income equal to that of other civil-servant, parents of school girls, owned a car which cost 80,000 pounds.

She would not add to Siham's worries. She had already learnt more than enough before her time. The future would teach her still more.

* * *

Mona was seen in the distance, but unlike what usually happened, unaccompanied by Siham, hurrying, bouncing like a ball, the place still very hot after the midday heat, and the mad man still bumping his head against the rock. Mona stopped under the window making ambiguous gestures out of which her mother could make nothing. She put her school bag on the ground in the street and started jumping higher and higher every time.

The mother almost screamed in terror as a boy on a bicycle just missed her daughter. Siham picked Mona's bag and dragged her home against her will.

The mother opened the door for the girls, wondering what made Mona behave in that strange way, as she headed towards the kitchen to warm up a pot of vegetables, all that remained of the week's rations. She heard Mona rushing into the hall, and turned to see to the frozen vegetables she had taken out of the fridge.

She almost fell over the stove and the pot as Mona put her arms round her legs in a mad rush. She tapped Mona's shoulder in an attempt to make her let go of her legs and turned her face towards her. Mona raised a pair of eyes shining with a thousand and one gleams to her. The mother walking away from the stove with Mona, pushing her towards the middle of the kitchen, asked:

"What is the matter Mona? What is it, darling?"

Standing at the kitchen door cross-armed Siham answered scornfully:

"She's going mad, mother. She's going to take part in a play for the school party."

Mona added with a self-confidence quite new to her :

"I'm going to play the part of a silk merchant in a play about the Khalif Haroun al-Rashid."

She laughed in her way which resembled the cock's crowing and started going round in a circle which became larger and larger, while her ringing laugh got mixed with the madman's whistle and the circle continued to become larger until the mother cried in terror :

"Mind the fire, Mona. Mind the fire."

Mona stopped for a moment speechless, facing the fire and the frying egg-plant, then turned round, her face all black. She then heard the madman's train whistle, laughed in her crowing way and rushed towards the hall, inhaling and exhaling the air, like a train whose wheels are her legs and arms.

The mother caught Siham's eye, as she handed her the bread plate to take to the table. Once more she felt the bewilderment that recurred whenever she tried to read her elder daughter's thoughts. Words stumbled on the tip of her tongue and when she could finally utter them, they carried the tone one uses to address children, mixed with that one uses to address grown-ups :

"What about you, Darling? What role are you taking in the play: The Queen's?"

Siham's hand stopped half way to the bread plate for a moment and before she turned her eyes down, the mother noticed the knowing look that shone in her daughter's eyes, a look which seemed to say :

"Are you laughing at me mother, or at yourself? I already know my place in life and no illusions will make me forget it."

The mother extended a trembling hand to hold the child's hand that rested on the bread plate. Siham blushed and withdrew her hand in a violent movement which nearly toppled the bread. Standing at the kitchen door, she said, possibly by way of an apology or, perhaps, in an attempt to escape a moment of intense emotional contact :

"I'm hungry, mother. I'd like something to eat."

Responding to her daughter, the mother, trying in turn to lessen the intense pressure of the moment, said :

"Straightaway, darling. Just keep Mona busy for a moment, else she would start grumbling."

Mona, however, no longer needed anyone to keep her busy. During lunch, she showed that she could do without all of them, showing an indepedence which exasperated Siham whom she was in the habit of following like her shadow. The father was not present to witness the new development of the relationship between the two girls, and had he been present, he would not have noticed it, as he was always occupied with matters of earning a living out-of-doors or in-doors.

Mona did not touch the food. She continued making a noise on her plate with the knife and fork, moving her hand from one side of the plate to the other, slowly and elegantly, listening to the rhythmical sound rising from the plate and setting it right whenever it was out of tune. Siham tried more than once to stop that noise, but Mona only once claimed that she was playing the xylophone, then she did not listen any more to Siham's don'ts. Her tunes mingled with the madman's starting whistle as he took off.

When the meal was over, Siham tried to restore the situation between her and her sister to what it had been before. She headed towards their room without helping to clear the table or wash up, deliberately made a noise with her chair as she left the table, moving away slowly to give Mona a chance to get up and catch up with her as usual. But Mona did not leave the table, nor did she notice that Siham did. Siham slammed the door behind her, once more to draw Mona's attention but Mona noticed the door shutting, without taking any notice. The tunes rising from her plate, if anything, became louder.

Rehearsals for the school party continued for two weeks, during which Mona left home in the morning with Siham, and returned from school alone at 5.00 o'clock in the afternoon. Siham boycotted the party on the pretext that it was mere play-acting and child's play and persisted in refusing to wait for her sister to finish rehearsals, despite her mother's repeated pleading that she accompanies her sister home.

The fist time Mona returned home alone, she said that she knew the way, and in a newly-acquired pride insisted that she was no longer a baby and, counting on her fingers, said she had only three months to go before she would be nine.

After that long speech, Mona was silent, keeping to herself in a persistent and continuous attempt to stay alone. Siham predicted that Mona would soon go mad, whenever she passed her as she sat rolled up in an isolated or dark corner. The house no longer echoed the cock-crowing sound that Mona made, nor Siham's ironical remarks that aroused laughter.

Throughout the week of rehearsals, the mother attempted in vain to get Mona out of her isolation, and to convince Siham that Mona's isolation was not madness but simply physical exhaustion resulting from the rehearsals. As it happened that she was so busy marking exercise books and running the household, she did not notice the strange symptoms that Mona began to show. Siham, however, was not too preoccupied to observe how her sister had completely dissociated herself from the circle of her influence. She closely observed those symptoms day after day, though she did not comment on them until it was too late.

A few days before the school party, the mother was busy making a new dress for Siham, who had chosen the fabric herself and obtained the pattern from one of her school friends. The mother was sitting in the hall stitching the hem of the new dress and had just finished it when Siham tip-toed from the girls room, beckoning her mother to follow her.

Once inside the room the mother found Mona sitting on the bed gazig at nothing, now and then screwing her eyes which shone with a dazzling glow as if she saw a vision of extreme beauty.

"She will go mad. I told you she would," said Siham.

Mona regained consciousness as from a dream, and looked at Siham then at her mother, wiping the drops of perspiration that had gathered on her forehead as she recognized them and was silent for a moment. She looked around the room, stopping to stare at the bare tiles, at a sofa with the stuffing spilling out and at a crack in the

62

opposite wall getting deeper and deeper every day. She looked like a rat caught in a trap.

Mona signalled her mother and sister to leave the room then lay down in bed, pretending she wanted to go to sleep.

Convinced that her daughter was feverish, the mother left the room and went to look for a thermometer. She could not remember where she had put it, and Siham would not let her concentrate, insisting that Mona had not been eating at all, while the mother continued to put things upside down on every shelf of the wardrobe during her search for the thermometer. How often had she decided to rearrange her things, but no time was ever left for that in the whirlpool that one lived those days, no time to arrange things and take one's breath. And there was Siham saying triumphantly :

"Look, she has even forgotten all about the sandwitches that she gives to the children every day."

The mother was still looking feverishly for the thermo-meter, while Siham insisted that Mona had not been sleeping and that she spent the night lying on her back with her eyes wide open. But she was really cunning, the moment she caught sight of someone putting the light on, she closed her eyes and pretended she was asleep.

Having found the thermometer at last, the mother turned round reproachfully saying to Siham:

"Mona is sick, Siham."

She pushed the thermometer in Mona's mouth once and twice but the temperature did not even register 37 degrees centigrade, and Mona protested saying:

"I am not sick."

Nonetheless, the mother uncovered her, turned her over, felt her body all over, clinging to the idea of there being some physical ailment to justify her strange behaviour, while Mona's body stiffened under the mother's hand, reminding her of the futility of her attempt to help her, in fact rejecting her, discarding her and banishing her.

The mother turned off the light, defeated, and Mona pulled the cover over the whole of her body up to her head.

* * *

The lights were put on in the hall and the curtain raised for the parents to greet the children, then it was lowered. While the curtain was raised, the children on the stage and the parents in the dress circle, the higher circle and the boxes exchanged smiles and greetings and the place shook with words like "Well done", "Bravo" repeated again and again accompanied by intermittent clapping after the parents were exhausted with continuous applause.

The mother tried in vain to catch Mona's eye more than once. Mona stood on the stage, there and not there. Much as she seemed happy throughout the play, much as she seemed miserable when it ended. All through the show, Mona seemed happy and absorbed in her part and in the beautiful imaginary world of which she seemed to be an indivisible part. She moved with steady steps and spoke with unusual eloquence and unlimited freedom. She was whole-heartedly given to the world of singing, dancing, music and the warm silken colours, the diamond jewellery and golden crowns, and that world was entirely hers. She was not out of this magic world for one moment, nor was she aware of anything else. Thus she excelled in playing her part as none of the other boys and girls participating in the play did. Why then, was she so despondent now that the play had come to an end? Why did she have that look of a trapped rat as she stood amidst those who looked resplendent as they were greeted?

The mother waited for Mona for some time in the lobby. If she had not allowed Siham to go home with their neighbour, she would have sent her to look for Mona. She watched parents leaving with their children, one group after another. As a pattern emerged, she could distinguish those parents who did not own a car, those who had one, driven by the father or the eldest son, and those whose car was driven by a chauffeur dressed in a unifiorm like those in television plays.

The parents who did not have a car, walked along the theatre wall and disappeared in the darkness even before they came down the last steps of the front stairs. In the case of the parents who owned cars driven by the father or the eldest son, whoever drove made an unnecessary and conspicuous show of the car keys, maybe because the sight of the luxury cars which sped by, shining and stopped blocking the theatre entrance surprised him as much as they surprised her. The owners loitered about in front of their luxury cars, conversing while the uniformed chauffeurs opened the car doors one after the other and the ladies gathering their long dresses entered first, either dressed in evening gowns, embroidered with sequins and beads, or veiled. But what veils, by God! What an amount of genuine pearls tied the head-cover like a crown and circled the soft relaxed neck like a bracelet.

The mother caught the eye of another mother waiting for her son or daughter, and they exchanged a smile which broke the feeling of isolation in this hostile and provoking, atmosphere. Each of them indentified the other as a working woman, perhaps a teacher, each wearing that stern classic suit, ready for such occasions, a suit that lasted for ever was altered as days went by, by means of a new scarf or a new blouse and maybe an artificial flower. Suddenly

the mother felt anxious when her working woman companion bade her goodbye and disappeared in the darkness.

The last bunch of parents had left and yet Mona did
not show up. The place was almost deserted and the theatre
lights were gradually put out. She wondered what took
Mona so long. She entered the lobby, noticed a side door,
went up the stairs leading to it, walked up a long corridor
partly lit by the dim light showing on the doorstep of a
closed door and called out Mona's name, but there was no
answer. She pushed the door open, went in and found
herself in a dimly-lit long room like a corridor, containing
heaps of costumes, taken off hurriedly by the children. She
called out Mona's name once more, but there was no
answer. At the far end of the room, she found Mona, still in
her costume, sunk to the ground in one of the corners. She
shook her, saying:

"What is wrong, Mona? Aren't we going home yet,
dear?"

Mona bent her head down, bit her lips and with a dark
face, submitted to her mother who helped her take off her
costume. However, she wanted to put on her own clothes
herself, then calmly followed her mother.

At the door of the costume room, Mona stopped to
cast a look at the place. A bad smell came out of decaying
silken clothes, the remains of food, empty soft drinks tins,
bottles, whose remaining contents melted the silver and
golden crowns that were thrown on the floor in disorder,
artificial flowers that had been trodden on, as the children
went out, and Haroun al-Rashid's golden chain, made of
brass, surrounding a paper lantern, that gave no light.
Mona opened her mouth and looked as if on the point of
crying, then slowly shut the door as she went out.

Mona's tears fell down her cheek noiselessly as she

walked along the narrow path on the way home. She snatched her hand from her mother's grasp, the moment she caught sight of the children, gathered as they usually did every evening to chase the madman. She covered the distance from the path to the house in a run, protecting herself against the pebbles that erupted from the ground and fell from the sky.

Mona's sobbing increased in the stair-well, while the children dispersed, followed by the madman's curses, then gathered once more to chase him with pebbles, laughs, and a song was heard repeated for the thousandth time about "chocolates, not sweet potatoes."

* * *

Siham opened the flat door, and stood for a moment watching the tears in her younger sister's eyes. Mona stood in the middle of the hall wiping her tears with the back of her hand. The mother standing behind her, put her arms around her, patting her on the shoulder and kissing her hair. Mona freed herself from her mother's embrace, ignored Siham's extended hand and walked heavily to their room, holding her head back and pressing her lips stightly together.

The mother realized that Mona too has grown up. She felt dizzy as she perceived the quick rhythm of life. She leaned on the edge of the table to avoid falling under the pressure of the whirlpool. Siham grew up when she was ten and Mona was not yet nine.

There were tears in the mother's eyes as she stood upright. She remembered that her father wept when she menstruated at the age of twelve. He wept out of fear for her in the days when righteousness was the rule, not the exception, on all levels. She felt the magnitude of her new responsibility as a mother and regretted the good old days.

The mother prayed God, as she took off her special occasions suit, to help the two girls go through the narrow path in peace.

Translated by Angele Botros Samaan

FAWZIYA MAHRAN was born in Alexandria in 1931. As a result of being brought up in a coastal city, the sea plays a significant role in her writings. She graduated in English Literature, in Cairo University, 1956. She had such a passion for writing that she started her writing career a few months before graduating. She participated in launching **Sabah al-Kheir,** *an important weekly magazine, then began writing for* **Rose- al-Youssef,** *a prestigious political and cultural weekly magazine, established, 1925 by the pioneering woman journalist whose name it carries. Mahran has published short stories, novels and plays. In 1961 she issued one of the earliest short story collections by women writers,* **The Women's Hostel** *(Beit al- Talibat), inspired by her stay at Cairo University Hostel for women students. Her war trilogy* **The Sea Horses** *(Guiado al Bahr), 1980;* **The Break-water** *(Hagiz al-Amwag), 1984 and* **The Ship** *(al-Safinah), forthcoming, representing: Defeat, War and Victory is a praiseworthy achievement. Also noteworthy is her play* **Caputchi,** *1978.*

Her short stories : "So Near... So Far" and "Music" were published respectively in **Al-Hilal,** *1988 and* **Hawaa,** *1992.*

SO NEAR... SO FAR

Fawziya Mahran

The chessmen move like ballet dancers.

They meet.. separate.. escape from the opponent's rook or stand firm for confrontation.

(I listen to their internal rhythm with longing and anxiety).

They advance.. retreat on selected squares : rise and grapple, take to flight or lie in waiting for manoeuver. It is a game of intelligence and struggle – as if drawing a plan for the future, and contemplating a move for advancing, making of the struggle a supreme pleasure.

(My heart beats faster.. something like delicious numbness flows in my blood. I have got used to patience and the gift of waiting and watching. My thoughts fly, compelled. They fly over large areas, roam over horizons of memories and visions.. soon to descend on the magical chessboard).

Neither my ears nor my eyes stray from them. Despite the book in my hand, I was fully conscious of the two of them. From time to time I am aware of a hesitant sigh.. a weak whisper.. a faint gasp.. disconnected words.. a chess move or a gambit.

The two opponents occupy crucial squares in the heart of the arena : a moment of combing and memory. From time to time, I raise my head from the book, I try to hide my anxiety and worry. I make an exhausting mental effort.

(I do not know what the lines or the words mean.. I am overwhelmed by longing and anxiety).

The sitting has become disquieting : the whole universe depending on moving a small piece from its place.
The end begins with one move.

The game itself does not interest me.. Nor is the result
of the race what I desire or watch for. The pleasure
depends on the way the game is played.

The basic law of the fight stipulates, "Devise whatever
solution you wish, provided you preserve your strength and
not let go of any chance to win. Sieze such a chance nobly
and honourably).

I wish for something really difficult– an image of what
mostly used to happen.

The achievement of justice always means comfort,
satisfaction and the hard option.

(Two specialists in High Mathematics are involved in a
complex problem.. As much as they enjoy the competition,
they are dazzled by the original solution – two generals at
war, each of them has the initiative, knows what the other
is thinking and appreciates it.

The rhythm is slow. Advancing is replete with danger.
The spirit of adventure is fettered by deliberation, confidence and the need not to overestimate one's ability. The
straight line here is not the shortest way. You cannot
proceed in a straight line, exposing your horse to a sudden
blow dealt by a ruthless soldier.

Suddenly the match warms up.. breathing becomes
difficult.. the arena of the battle extends (I can almost hear
the neighing of the horses, the rattle of the swords, the
shaking of the forts and the rumbling of the conflict. But
can the arena accomodate three?)

"The threee of you are dearest to me in life."

That was what he said when his dark face was

surrounded with bandages, his body covered with dressings and his eyes shining and full of fire.

"The three of you.. are my most beloved on earth."

His friend tried to lessen the tension:

"You still prefer the aeroplane to us."

He looked around sorrowfully.. He surely remembered what happened. All he said was that a brilliant light suddenly flooded the pilot's cabin, turning everything into a dazzling glow. He could hardly see anything. When he regained consciousness, he found himself in hospital and we anxiously looking at him.

(What we saw was appalling : people bleeding, wounded persons and doctors, restless movement, cries for help, painful groans – a scene that will remain engraved in the mind).

"We are fighting for our land, Victory is dear."

(Victory is dear indeed. Many beloved ones are gone. Among them I lost my martyr).

The boy cried :

"I am getting close to the target."

The book fell from my hand.. I raised my head inquisitively. I woke up from a peaceful nap.

The two of them are all that is left to me : my son and my husband's friend, together with the memories of our shared love.

Would the chessboard accomodate three?

I would never interfere, nor comment on how the game proceeded. I never tried to play it, nor did either of them ask me to.

"You stand between us like a referee," he said one day.

I love this exquisite game.. this comfortable.. perturbing sitting. He is resurrected with it. He gallops on the backs of horses.. I see him alive amidst us. (His enthusiasm for flying and chess is connected with his love for life and the homeland).

Winning absorbs the boy's thinking.. While concentrating on the centre of the black square, his opponent seems to be watching what I am thinking about, and following the stream of memories and images inside me.

He does not want to allow the boy a quick or an easy victory.

(He wishes to test his metal, sharpen his ability and arouse his defiance and firmness, in order to enable him to know his capacities and to draw him into the circle of anguish, of always seeking solutions).

I was getting weary with concentrating and watching.. with analysing the situation and the progress of the game. I retreated to the joyful visions of the past.

(At first I never thought I would ever be a pilot's wife. Women around me were surprised: a violent pilot who loves flying, is enamoured with the aeroplane and deserts you most of the time).

"Flying an aeroplane," he said, "surpasses all the pleasures of life."

"What if you don't return!" was my comment.

"I cannot promise you anything," he said.

"Without you, how can I stand it," I retorted.

(I wished I had never uttered those words).

I was destined to remain suspended in the sky in this way.. to say "goodbye", and "See you," watch him in outer space, and freeze with terror if the plane tilted.

(We lived together moments that were equal to a whole life).

"We are all destined to die," he said merrily and acquiescently.

74

"Whether inside the belly of a whale or high up in the clouds, one knows not what is hidden for one."

"Be reassured," he added, "I have made a pact with the aeroplane. I would rather die than 'expose it to destruction."

"I fear flying," I said.

"Everyone of us fears something," he said. "There are those who dread water or shudder at the thought of living on high floors. Personally, I cannot stand walking slowly. I suffocate in a crowd. I wish to die flying."

He died the way he wished. He carried out the mission and saved the aeroplane. He landed it safely. He was kind to us. Embracing us with his eyes, he said:

"The three of you together."

The boy made a sudden move. He moved a chessman from its place and put it in the next square. The friend's eyes followed the move with interest.

"The risk is too great," he said.

"Are you up to it?" asked the friend.

"The main thing is to beat you," came the answer.

Concentration and eagerness were written all over his face. He had to choose one of two options of equal significance. His thought process did not proceed only on the level of consciousness, but extended to the area of inspired creativity. He adopted a style which was both offensive and tender – my husband's identical style and mode.

I told him once: "The plane stands between us."

"We both take an interest in it, and this common interest binds us together," he said. "A pilot's wife has to be patient. The spirit of a fighter becomes you," he added.

The two opponents were absolutely silent. He pushed back the window pane.. a cool breeze rushed in.

"Fresh air helps one to think," he said.

I remember their games together – difficult and enjoyable. They were equals in every respect: in mode, style and occupation, friends since their childhood, in the village alleys, in the classrooms and around the chessboard.

Before the last flight, he promised his friend to return and continue the game with him. ·

I said, "You almost forget me during the game. I no longer exist, perhaps."

"Rather the room is vibrant with your presence," he said playfully "and don't forget the victory is always for you."

Once the game lasted all night.. Many rounds ended with a draw.. That night, he did not like the draw.

He stretched out his arms, as if to embrace life itself. "Let us take a rest and leave the situation as it is. The position itself is a triumph for us," he said.

In the calm of the night, he whispered in a voice marked by neutrality and innocence,

"I see that he is determined to win for you."

(Not to answer was the right thing to do, so I resorted to silence).

"The boy is an image of his father; he has the same spirit, the same merriment."

The friend urges him to excel, trains him for violent resistance (out of loyalty to the martyr – to his unspoken promise to look after his family – and for my sake, perhaps).

"Pilots are a special breed."

(Being bound by a mission, the aeroplane and common training is a tie stronger than the ties of blood, says his twin).

"Flying creates love and intimacy."

"Had we been in the far ends of the world.. separated by continents and oceans, flying in foreign skies.. we would have carried out a mission in the same way without a predetermined agreement. We carry our lives in our hands. We sacrifice ourselves for the homeland."

(What do you think soaring up in the sky demands? it demands sacred love and identification. In the pilot's cabin, I am always flooded with light).

Those were his last words before he left, and in the hospital he did not exactly know what happened, except that a thrilling light broke through to him. Seeing with one's eyes became impossible. Everything was transformed into a glow.

In the abyss of grief, his friend wept saying :

"I wish it had been me.. He has a son who needs him."

His words shook me... I heard them before he uttered them..

I became aware of the boy's anxiety,

"Why does he distance himself from us? Will he, too, leave us? Shall we lose him?"

From time to time he comes, and resumes a conversation that had been interrupted. He enquires about how we are getting on.

He comes as a flash of warmth. We continue reminiscing. He sees the loved one's phantom amongst us).

The last time he came, he measured the boy against his own chest and said:

"You've become a man already."

He looked at me, and addressed the boy :

"Look after her and get ready for the next round."

He stayed longer than usual that time. The chess game restored warmth and cheerfulness to the sitting.

Absorbed in the game, he said:

'He has his father's style of playing."

"That's why I must beat you," said the boy.

"Think before you make a move," the friend said.

"One more move and I win," retorted the boy.

"Remember," his opponent said, "Victory is so near so far."

He said that and looked at me. (He has eyes that watch what I think.. follow memories and images. In one moment we realized the intensity of our feelings).

The chess game mostly ended with a draw. The situation remained as it was.

(I felt that he was so near.. so far).

Translated by Angele Botros Samaan

MUSIC AT THE
BOTTOM OF A MUG

This bowl-shaped ceramic mug brought back music to our home. Pardon me but whenever the tune starts I have to listen. I become connected to the source of the music and swim in the ripples of its beautiful notes.

His image is reflected to me on the water as he is holding the young girl and teaching her to swim. The image embodies life. The drops of joy glitter. My own particles get liberated and start racing. His voice comes to me : "Let her know how to enjoy life." The music gets louder with joy while his words are all over me :

A twin to life is one's country. If you open your arms like this you can hold a piece of your country. Your embrace has room for the trees, the plants and the sea. You are then embracing life and the prettiest things in it, the things for which you may sacrifice you life.

Music brought back joy to me and freed me from my worries.

But how did this friendship between me and this living tune start? It all started while I was shopping for a present to my daughter from the historic sea town which had witnessed events, memories and the times.

The town is despised now and treated as a market for imported goods. My daughter had requested a list of these goods while I was attending a conference there.

I found it, the gift of a mug. When it tilts forward the

music starts. It gets louder with joy but also suffers with me about the martyred town whose key I have lost and whose doors have been closed to me.

My colleague said : "The sea was filled with the bodies of martyrs." He too had been wounded and martyred. He had been posted here but they broke his camera as well as his bones. Under the blast he kept trying until he found a woman looking for her son. He pointed to the film hidden inside his shirt. In a flash the woman understood everything. She took the film and hid it in her bosom. Few days later the pictures were all over the newspapers of the world shaking the human conscience. The port city by the beach and in one's heart is a free zone now. Could I dare buy something other than a musical mug?

My daughter was not pleased with the modest gift. Perhaps out of politeness she accepted it and pretended to be happy. It seems that she has treated it roughly or lightly similar to the way my city had been treated. Consequently, its musical bottom fell off.

My heart pounded. I carefully carried the bottom and safely placed the mug up the highest shelf of books.

The gift was returned to us. I felt as if it were a part of me, of my homeland: a fresh wave, a foetus from the womb of that woman who repelled all the miseries of war from Egypt by enveloping the work of martyrs in her bosom.

The music inside the mug records the hardship and the sorrow. It makes grief noble and beautiful. The music at the bottom of the mug has become my friend.

The tune plays whenever I open my library. The music resonates brightly and colourfully according to my mood. To him, its greeting is like a morning salute. I do not know how it managed to evolve itself to play its tune whenever I pass by the library. It follows my movement. I put on the lights, I open the window and it plays its music all the same.

Sometimes I would be rushing about, but I stop when it starts and remain silent until it finishes its tune. Its power of music grows stronger. It summons me when I am else. Where so I get up for it. It evokes in me fresh feelings and ideas. We need to write a great deal about the days of heroism and martyrdom, about the greatness of life and good living.

I feel it is a human being who accompanies me on the journey of my life, my thoughts, my ambitions, the subject of my work and the mission which awaits me.

Like me she was beseiged and suppressed.

She plays a round of wake-up call and good-bye one everytime I go in or out of the house. She materializes his image in front of me. She recalls the cheerfulness of voices, the excitement of the sea and the integrity of vision.

My friend is really a human being. She responds to the light, to the pressure of air, to the rhythm of paces, to the fluttering of the heart, to images and imagination.

She brought back music to our home. She reactivated the hope anew.

The key of the city is not lost. It lies in the bosom of the martyred woman. It lies in the hand of a child whose father teaches her how to swim and enjoy life by embracing a portion of the homeland sea.

Translated by Amal Kary

IHSAN KAMAL was born in 1935. She is a founding member of the Writer's Union and of the Story Club. Two hundred and fifty of her stories have ·been published in Egyptian newspapers and magazines, some in Arab magazines. She has published eight short-story collections between 1960 and 1988. Kamal is largely concerned with man-woman relationships, as exemplified in the following titles of two of her novels : **Love Never Dies** *(Al- Hob la Yamouto Abadan), 1981;* **The Strongest Love** *(Aqua Hob), 1982 and* **Wives Are Not Admitted** *(Mammnu' Dokhoul al-Zawgat), 1988. Love plays a great role in her novels, but she is also deeply concerned with social and moral reform. Kamal won three short-story awards. A number of her stories have been adapted for the cinema and television. Some have been translated into English, French, Russian, Swedish, Dutch and Chinese. She is a full-time writer – a rare thing among our women writers.*

Her short stories in this volume appear in **The Strongest Love** *and* **Wives Are Not Admitted.**

AN UNCOMMITTED CRIME

Ihsan Kamal

I woke up trembling. What a terrible dream!

I was standing on the edge of an abyss, and my foot had almost slipped into it. I had heard a roar of laughter, the source of which I had been unable to define. Was it Satan, or was it myself, or was it something else? Was it a dream, was it a vision, or was it that desire which blazed inside me as if the fire of hell itself burned within me? I am in fact standing on the edge of an abyss. In my dream I was doing my utmost not to fall into it. While in fact I longed to fall into it. To fall or not to fall... Two conflicting powers are pulling at me until between them I am almost torn into two, or perhaps I had already been torn apart a long time ago. The problem is which of these two parts is really me, and which part of me is thinking now?

Why do people hate other people so much? When somebody speaks highly of another person nobody ever repeats what is said. However, if anyone speaks badly of a person a million people would readily volunteer to repeat as quickly as a flash of lightening what they had heard. People would hear abuse and enjoy repeating it, taking the greatest pleasure in doing so. What is it that makes them so happy to hear a person abused or slandered even though there is no hostility between them and that person? My father was a kind peace-loving doctor who loved everyone and who, so I believed, was loved by everyone. But all that affection for him did not prevent them from believing that he had embezzled the large sum of money, as accused.

An inquiry was made, and my father was interrogated and our house was searched more than once, yet no

83

incriminating evidence was found. Although there was nothing more than circumstantial evidence against him my father was orderd to resign for the circumstantial evidence was thought to be considerable and accordingly he should not remain in his post, since he had been accused and had failed to prove his innocence. The case had too many loose ends. My father had been unable to prove his innocence nor could his guilt be proved by one single piece of evidence. They were consequently unable to pronounce any sentence upon him, as the head of the department in which he worked had declared. But the man lied, for a sentence had indeed been pronounced upon him, for being a suspect.

As is so often the case with any news or rumour that is heard and repeated, facts were omitted and additions were supplemented, and even with these additions and omissions, the result would more likely than not be distorted, and by the time the news reached our good neighbours, it stated that Mr. Shakir had been dismissed from his post because he had embezzled a large sum of money, and considering that every single one of these neighbours was honest, pure and virtuous, they must all avoid him, lest his handshake should infect them. The very sight of him would blur their eyesight and their wives and children would naturally boycott his wife and children. No one would play with me or with my sister Karima. One day, my best friend, Izzat, wanted to look at a toy with which I was playing. We had met on the front steps of our house, but suddenly a hand whisked him inside the half-open door of his house which was closed quickly.

What an unjust punishment I suffered! When I rang the bell in order to make sure that he was all right, the door was slammed in my face without a single word being uttered. I cried and ran to my mother, who, instead of drying my tears and comforting me, as she usually did, wept with me. I realised later that she, too, had been ostracized and that nobody would have anything to do with her any more.

Sometimes I wonder what our neighbours used to talk about before they learnt about my father's trouble. I doubt if they opened their mouths in those days, even to yawn. After that, whenever two people met, no other subject was discussed. They chewed up the gossip about my poor father as if it were a piece of chewing gum, not caring in the slightest about the pain their remarks caused him. On the contrary their delight increased every time they heard the sound of the crunching of his reputation under their jaws. Ever since then it was as if we had made an alliance with suffering. The experience he had undergone was intolerable and it hurt my father to the core, leaving its mark upon him, both physically and emotionally. His face became as wrinkled as a piece of waste paper that had been crumpled by the hand of a nervous person.

My father did not die of bronchitis as the physicians assured us. He was in fact murdered, and everybody participated in his murder. The head of the department in which he worked, his colleagues, his neighbours, friends and relations, not to mention the police and the council for the prosecution who had failed to arrest the real criminal, were all responsible for his murder. The poor man was unjustly accused and was stabbed by all and everyone.

My sister and myself grew up in this atmosphere of isolation until we went to college, where we began to mingle in moderation with our colleagues. One of these colleagues asked for my sister's hand in marriage and accompanied by his family paid us a visit. Nevertheless after several such visits, and after the necessary arrangements for the engagement had almost been completed, he disappeared and never returned. He withdrew after making lame excuses. A year later another suitor asked for my sister's hand in marriage, but he too, disappeared into the blue after several visits. Naturally the matter did not require a high degree of intelligence to put two and two together.

We were no longer able to endure the hate that continued to encircle us more and more ever day, after we had lost all hope that the cruelty that governed the souls of our neighbours might ever turn into sympathy. There was only one solution, to move to another district. In spite of the difficulty of finding another flat in those days, the owners of the house in which we lived were more than generous, and paid us a larger sum of money than that for which we had asked, to leave the house. We paid this sum as key money for a new flat, in a district far from our first home. However it turned out it was not sufficiently far away as we were to discover later on. Once more we were placed in the same situation, for in a few months, all our neighbours had learnt about our trouble, complete with latest additions.

At the beginning, the matter did not bother us a great deal, for we had no intention of mingling with any of the neighours. However two suitors came, one after the other to ask for Karima's hand in marriage, and they too, followed in the footsteps of the two previous suitors and disappeared. A fifth suitor proposed marriage, and as his visits continued, we asked ourselves how long it would take him to be infected by the mortal plague. However, months, passed by and he did not show any change in his intentions. My mother was very happy but Karima was of a different opinion with which I agreed. Indeed, how could we be certain that the danger no 'longer existed. Was it not possible that he too would disappear after we had spent a large sum of money on Karima's trousseau and furniture? Since it is better that a disaster befalls one than to be daily threatened by it, my sister spoke to her fiancé frankly about the matter. He answered her with a winning smile saying: "Yes, as a matter of fact I have heard all about the matter, but I did not believe a single word of it. My mother was so touched that she almost wept as she said :

"Thank God that you did not believe those lies and false accusations."

He answered : "They say that one's character lights up one's face, and how could the father of such a fine family over have been guilty?"

My mother was so overcome that she wept, as she patted his hand saying : "May God bless you."

We no longer had any doubts, and began to prepare ourselves to buy the bride's furniture and trousseau, when the bridegroom surprised us by asking us to furnish five rooms in addition to all the modern electrical appliances..

My mother objected saying that that was his responsibility.

He smiled again benevolently, as he looked in my direction saying :

"According to some marriage arrangement the husband has to provide household electrical appliances. When there is a sincere understanding between the bride and the bridegroom, it makes no difference whose responsiblity it is."

I began to feel suspicious, but I tried to hide my feelings behind a smile as I murmured :

"That is quite true but how can we possibly buy all those things? As you can see, we are a family of modest means?"

"My demands will not cost more than fifty thousand pounds," he replied. "And that is not too much to pay for Karima's hapiness, considering..."

My mother, in all innocence answered: "I swear to you my son that we do not possess more than..."

Karima, who had been looking at her fiancé, in a strange manner, interrupted her, saying :

"Considering what Fathy?"

She tried to look him in the eye and finally managed to do so, after he had endeavoured to avoid her gaze. He then began to mumble and stammer :

"I mean... I wanted to say..."

Karima said :

"Say it Fathy and don't hesitate to do so. You mean to say considering the sum of money that my father embezzled. Is that not what you meant?"

He answered : "No, no, not at all. I never meant that, but, but..."

Karima screamed at him :

"Get out of here immediately, and I don't ever want to see you again."

He said:

"Just listen to me, why did your father hide the money? Was it not in order that it can be used to meet yours and your sister's needs? And what event is more important than your marriage?"

Karima wept bitterly as she pulled the engagement ring off her finger and threw it in his face saying:

"My father was the most honest and virtuous person, you despicable man!"

In spite of Fathy's being exactly what Karima had described him to be and strange as it seemed, he became very angry, and his anger revealed him for what he really was. He randomly hurled his accusations :

"Stop screaming, as if your father were really honest and innocent. Everybody knows that he embezzled that sum of money. Do you take me for a fool? Perhaps your brother Raouf has cheated you all, and hidden the sum of money all for himself? If that is the case, you should be grateful to me for drawing your attention to the fact, so that you can wake up from your slumber and demand your share."

When Karima had calmed down after a fit of hysterics, she rested her head upon my shoulder, while my mother kept repeating, as she wrung her hands in dismay:

"The four suitors who disappeared were more decent than Fathy. Oh my God! All that time, he really believed that your father had embezzled the money, and in spite of that he still wanted to marry you!"

Karima answered her, the words scorching her lips as she said :

"Oh mother how truly innocent you are! He wanted to marry me because of that, and not in spite of it."

I have a job now, after having graduated from college, and I am in charge of hundreds of thousands of pounds. Every time I touch a large sum of money, I remember my father's fate which is engraved like a tattoo in my memory. It also reminds me of what happened to us all, to myself to my mother and especially to my sister Karima. The ordeal that she experienced had put out the gleam in her eyes, leaving them like two dull pieces of glass. We all paid the price dearly, for a crime which we did not commit. In fact we paid the price for something that we did not take. Should not a person who has paid for something in advance be entitled to take that thing for which he has already paid? Did we not pay back a debt which we did not borrow? To rectify what happened, I should commit the crime of which we had been accused so that I would not spend the rest of my life suffering the bitteness of the false accusation. Oh! How intolerably bitter it has been.

On other occasions, I come to my senses and dispel these terrible thoughts. I feel that I am on the edge of an abyss. I wonder what will become of me? Shall I advance and slip and fall into the abyss, or shall I move as far away from it as I can, and proceed upon the right path? Shall I

always remain at the edge of the abyss, torn between
advancing and retreating, between falling and deliverance?

Translated by Thoraya Mahdi Allam

THE GAME IS OVER

"All rise."

The court usher shouted in a thundering tone which resounded in the court room. Everybody stopped talking and silence cast its cloak over every one, while the council for the defence moved like a crow in his black gown, until he stood before the platform where the judges presided. He began to present his defence, after first refuting the accusations of the prosecution one after the other, until he had dealt with them all. He then presented fresh evidence that proved my innocence. Most of this evidence was completely new to me, and this was the first time that I heard of it.

My lawyer was very competent, and presented the case skilfully and invented events equally skilfully. He talked on and on and on, until I lost interest, and I felt that he could continue to talk on until Doomsday. I tore my gaze away from his lips as they moved, and began to think about other matters. Suddenly the loud voice of the usher shouted in the same thundering tone :

"All rise."

The dignified judges returned after having completed their deliberations. The senior judge[1] cleared his throat before pronouncing the sentence. I held my breath as he opened his mouth to say :

"After taking into account a number of extenuating circumstances, the court pronounces the following sentence

_____

(1) There are three judges in Egyptian courts according to the legal system.

91

upon the accused: He is forbidden to speak or express himself in any way."

I covered my mouth with my hand to prevent myself from laughing, lest the judge should consider this to be a sign of disrespect. Was I only sentenced to not speaking? My lawyer had previously warned me that I would probably be sentenced to capital punishment. He had also promised me that he would do his utmost for me but had also said :

"In spite of the superhuman effort I have made preparing your defence, and the effort I will make in presenting your case, if we are lucky, I believe that I can commute your sentence to penal servitude for life."

The sentence had surpassed my wildest hopes, for which is easier to endure, the imprisonment of one's whole body or the imprisonment of one organ of that body, especially if that part, namely the tongue, is not of paramount importance. As far as I was concerned it was not a sentence at all, for I had never been fond of talking. During all the meetings which I had ever attended, whether business meetings or social gatherings I had always listened to what other people said, and very rarely had I thought of expressing my opinion on the matters that were being discussed. I thus adhered to the belief that the person who listens to others benefits more than the person who expresses an opinion. Oh my God, how happy, I am. Thanks to heaven and thanks to you too you just judge. I shouted :

"Long live...."

Oh my God! what has happened? Somebody shut my mouth with icy steel fingers. He answered the pressing question that was conveyed through my eyes saying :

"Have you forgotten the sentence pronounced on you!. I am appointed to make sure you carry it out."

I raised my hand to ask for permission to utter one word of thanks to the judge; for what would he think of me, if I did not express my gratitude to him? However this person, who lacked the least degree of courtesy, refused to allow me to utter a single word. I wondered why he behaved in this fashion, for I did not intend to say anything that would hurt anybody's feelings and no one should object to a word of thanks. He shrugged his shoulders and I too shrugged my shoulders. All right! Let the judge think of me whatever he wants. The matter is not of paramount importance. In any case, I believe, and hope that I will not see that judge again.

I forgot all about the judge, the case and my sentence when I saw a sweet smile light up her face, and light up the whole world around her.. She was wearing a pretty dress which I had not seen her wearing before. I greeted her with a voice which rang with mirth and admiration as I said : "How lovely..."

I did not complete my sentence, for suddenly the steel fingers cut my words short. Oh no, have mercy, one must be tolerant even when carrying out a sentence. My wife had stood by me during the ordeal of the hearing of my case. She had always encouraged me with her smile, which had raised my morale during the darkest hours . Very few wives are as faithful and as patient as she has been, so I should at least be allowed to pay her a little compliment. The steel fingers would not let me utter one word. I felt very angry, for not hearing a word of affection from me would undoubtably hurt her feelings, after all she had been through on my account. Even if I do not consider her devotion and loyalty, I do love her. Am I not allowed to express my feelings even to my wife? She used to be as happy as a little girl whenever I told her how much she meant to me. During my trial, when I was behind bars, her eyes would brim over with happiness which would envelop me from head to toe. I did not know what to do, and sat beside her gloomily when suddenly I noticed something that surprised me. My young daughter noticed that her mother and I were preoccupied, so she made the most of the opportunity to open her mother's handbag stealthily and take a bar of chocolate from it. Without realising it, I cried out:

"That is naughty..."

The man's hand quickly shut my mouth. I turned upon him, looking daggers at him, but he did not seem to care in the least about my anger. Cannot this stupid person understand? My young daughter does not realise that she is stealing something. If I do not draw her attention to the fact and explain to her her mistake, she might do the same thing with her friends at school, and then no one would be able to predict what the result would be. I must correct any mistake she makes immediately. She is my daughter, and I cannot remain silent about her mistakes however slight they may seem. The judge who passed this sentence on me could not have meant to prevent me from bringing up my daughter well. Obviously this person who is appointed to carry out the sentence is both stupid and ignorant. If only he would remove his hand from my mouth, I would be able to convince him of his mistake, but he will not move an inch. I became more and more annoyed, although I tried to convince myself that my daughter would probably repeat what she had done and that her mother would then see her and draw her attention to her mistake.

My wife tried to dispel the gloomy atmosphere by saying :

"Imagine the coincidence! Our club's team is going to play against a famous foreign team today. How would you like to watch the match?"

I was not very enthusiastic about her suggestion, and she felt that the idea did not appeal to me, so she sat beside me and patted my arm and repeated her suggestion. It was as if her touch had absorbed most of my anger. So I nodded in agreement.

My wife was right. As soon as the game began, I began to forget the remaining traces of irritability. But, my God! Is that how the game should be played? So I started to shout, out aloud :

"Very bad.... "

I had forgotten all about my sentence, but the person appointed to carry it out, had not forgotten, and the excitement caused by the match did not prevent him from doing his objectionable duty. Must I remain silent even here? It was only one word uttered in the air, a word that nobody could possibly hear. It could not even be heard by the player to whom it was addressed. Nevertheless it expressed my opinion about what I was watching. How could it harm that man if I uttered it? I did not enjoy watching the match in the same way that I had previously enjoyed similar matches. However the goal that our team scored was such a fine goal that it was enough to delight anybody, however gloomy his mood may have been. Cheers filled the air, and everybody was cheering, and I was unable to control myself so I cheered shouting :

"Wonderful...."

His hand stretched out to close my mouth quickly, even more quickly than the ball crashed into the net. Not even the triumph of our team interceded on my behalf to allow me to utter one word. If I was unable to express my anger or my admiration about the game that was being played in front of me, what then was the point in remaining? I left the stadium, with a bitter taste in my mouth. Naturally the irritation that I felt did not escape my wife's attention, so she suggested that we should go and have a cold drink. The waiter came and made a low bow and said :

"At your service."

I did not bother to raise my head, which I supported with my hand, when I heard his words. What was the use? Would that person allow me to order what I wanted? My wife saved the situation by saying :

"Two glasses of lemonade please."

She looked at me and said :

"I ordered something that would cool you down."

The glass almost fell out of my hand. I had not yet quenched my thirst with a single sip when I saw him. I put down my glass immediately, for this was the moment for which I had waited so long. During the months, weeks, days minutes and seconds that had elapsed since my sentence had been pronounced, I had thought about nothing other than meeting him. Why had he hated me so much? Maybe it was his desire to present an interesting topic to the public that read his articles in spite of the fact that there were many more interesting and important subjects that would have interested his eager public. Nevertheless, he put all that aside and chose to write, at length, and in detail about my case. He did not bother to write about the shameful military defeat which was termed as "a set back", nor did he write about the petty state which was populated by displaced persons from all over the world, and yet occupied parts of a great state, the roots of which were buried in the depths of history. He did not write about the prisons which were crammed with all kinds of oppression, torture and humiliation. He ignored all these subjects and wrote about my case as if it were the only subject about which he could write. In addition to that he exaggerated and misrepresented the case. He had absolutely no right to try me upon the pages of his newspaper and then to pronounce a verdict of guilty. Every day he presented fresh "evidence" concerning my case, or crime as he put it, such "evidence" was completely unknown to me.

He should have been a novelist and not a journalist, and all the evidence with which he tried to incriminate me was proved false. Oh how I would love to spit upon him! But no, I shall not do so. Suffice it that I sneer at him and tell him that all the deductions upon which he had founded his expectation that I would be sentenced to death were completely wrong. After I had been proved innocent, would he now confess that he had made a mistake? I heard a chuckle of laughter. Oh my God! I had forgotten all about him, about the person who was to make sure that the sentence was carried out. He said to me sneeringly :

"Your innocence?"

I was not surprised that he knew what went on in my mind, even before I uttered it, but I wondered why he sneered at me. Of course I was innocent, can he not see that I am as free as the wind and am able to go wherever I like. I can leave the stadium and sit in the casino, comfortably, crossing my legs, as all fine people do. Once again I forgot him, or tried to forget him, but he refused to let me do so. If I so much as took a step forward, I would find him beside me. What does he want of me? Does he intend to carry out his duty here and now? Oh no! Not now! that would be unbearable. That journalist has wronged me greatly and has accused me falsely. I am now in a position to tell him that he was unjust in his verdict and I must tell him so. I had remained silent before this, and am willing to remain silent for the rest of my life, but I must speak out now. That journalist had made me drink cup after cup of bitterness. He had chewed up my reputation as one chews a piece of chewing gum. My very bones were crushed under his jaws, but he did not care. In fact he became more and more delighted every time he heard my groans. I had previously felt annoyed when this guard had prevented me from expressing my love for my wife, but neither he, nor any other person can prevent me from expressing my hate and anger, nor prevent me from feeling the sweetness of revenge. I looked at him, hoping that the determined look in my eye would restrain him. However he did not care, and he looked even more determined than before. I opened my mouth to speak, but he was prepared and his hand shut my mouth before I was able to utter a single syllable. I thought:

"Oh no, not now. Let me say just this once what I want, and I promise you it will be the last time. I just can't remain silent now. That is more than I can bear. I beg you, I implore you."

Tears streamed down my cheeks, and I almost kissed his hand, but it was useless. On the contrary, his fingers increased their pressure on my mouth as if they were bars of iron.

Dumb people really must be miserable, but at least

they communicate with each other by signs. I will try to do so, and maybe I will succeed. I raised my left hand and began moving it, but the attempt·failed as soon as it started. My guard raised his other hand which was not covering my mouth and held my hand. I thought of another solution, of writing down what I wanted to say. Writing was the same weapon that my adversary the journalist had used. Before I was able to write a single letter, my guard raised his foot to kick the pen out of my hand, but I held the pen firmly, then his pressure on the pen increased until he broke it. My rage against him had no bounds and I wanted to tell him that he had gone too far and had gone beyond the limits of carrying out his duty. I thanked God that he knew what I was thinking for he answered harshly saying :

"I have not gone beyond the limits of carrying out my duty, for it seems to me that you did not understand the meaning of the sentence passed upon you. You are forbidden to speak or express yourself in any way."

Exhausted, I dropped into a chair, pain racking every part of my body.

If only I could get this trouble off my chest, I would feel better. Suddenly I remembered some incidents that had taken place some time ago. Certain people had suffered and had tried to get rid of the source of their pain. They had come to me in my clinic, and after examining them I realised how much they were suffering. I consequently prescribed nasal drops for those whose noses were troubling them, and prescribed the necessary medication for those who had stomach problems and they were all cured. One person had contacted me by telephone after midnight for he had a case of suppression of urine.

His condition was critical and I operated on him as quickly as possible and he was cured of his suffering and had I not done so, he would have died. I wondered why I remembered all these people now. Their conditions did not resemble my condition in any way. Their problems were tangible, and could be touched and felt. As for me, I want to express my thoughts in words and words are not tangible. Everybody knows this, and I, too, am prepared to present a hundred scientific proofs of this.

I mean that I had been prepared to do so, until this morning, before I experienced these disturbing events. However, it seems that I was mistaken. Everybody is mistaken. or else... what is this awful thing that is stuffed in my whole mouth up to my very throat? It began to spread and branch out until it started to hinder my breathing. In spite of its loathsome taste, I tried to swallow it but it would not be swallowed. I began to feel suffocated and I had to get rid of it, so that I could eject my thoughts and speak, in order to find my peace of mind.

I began doing my utmost to try and utter the words, and I discovered that I was stronger than I had imagined. The pressure of my words was almost as strong as the pressure exerted by my guard's hand. I thought that if I exerted a little more pressure, I would be able to overcome him. I tried, and braced myself up to do so, but I failed completely.

Between pulling to and fro, the words that filled my mouth caught fire. The long tape of words that began at the tip of my tongue and ended in the recesses of my mind convolutions became a tape of fire, the flames of which were formidable. They scorched my tongue, my throat and my head. Later, the burning tapes began to continue on and on, causing unbelievable torture, more torture than could be endured by anyone. I lay down exhausted upon my bed. I had been deceived and cheated, and so had my competent lawyer. My sentence had not been commuted at all. It was in fact a very severe sentence, even more so than the death sentence itself, for a person is judged by the opinion he expresses. Indeed if he can utter it, he deserves to live, and if he were prevented from doing so, death would be preferable. What amazed me was that I had, at first, been happy with the sentence, for I had not then realised the importance of what had been taken away from me, and I only understood that after having experienced it for a few hours.

I must appeal against this severe sentence, but how can I do so? How can I contact my lawyer? Is he now in his office or is he in court talking and talking, while I am burning my words and becoming scorched by them? The telephone is near at hand, but my guard is even nearer. If only I could evade him for just one minute, or even for half a minute! My whole being became consumed with a desire to put an end to my torture by saying one word to my lawyer. I would just say to him :

"Appeal."

However, my guard is wide awake, and never closes his eyes. Should he do so, if only for a second, that would be my chance. I waited and waited and then I had this stupid idea. I had been a boxing champion during my college days, so why don't I use my strength to kill him. I punched him on his forehead, and he staggered slightly, but regained his equilibrium and returned the punch. I felt that I had been hit by a mountain, and that sparks were flying from my eyes, while my ears were filled with the sound of thunder.

I opened my mouth, but his hand, quickly closed it, and once more I felt the heat of the flames of the tape scorching my head. This tape was even longer and hotter than the previous tapes. I wondered why he treated me thus, for I had not intended to give him a lecture, or make a speech, or even abuse him. All I had wanted to do was to say :

"Ouch."

Once again I looked in the direction of the telephone, but this time, I neither saw it, nor saw anything else on the desk. All I could see was the letter-opener. It looked lovely and alluring. I took it, and after a second stabbed him in the heart . My wife came running and screamed :

"What have you done?"

I did not answer her, so she repeated her question :

"What have you done?"

What did I do!? Why do I not answer her? Have I forgotten how to speak, or is it because I cannot believe that I can speak?

I took my wife in my arms and uttered one sentence :

"I love you."

She sighed deeply and then asked again in a low voice :

"How could you do this?"

I replied :

"I did it, so I could say to you : 'I love you'."

She said :

"You didn't have to say it. I could see it in your eyes."

I replied :

"That is because you are sensitive but there are other people who are thick- skinned, just like that journalist and his editor. I wanted to tell them something, but since they had no finer feelings, they were unable to understand what I wanted to say from the expression in my eyes, whereas you had been able to understand me. I had to tell them that I refused their injustice."

My wife said :

"But they will hang you. Are these few words worth your life?"

I replied :

"Sometimes words are worth more than life itself."

She murmured, as if she were talking to herself :

"What a high price to pay!"

I replied :

"Oh no, it is a low price to pay."

She said :

"What about me! Didn't you think about how I would suffer if I were to lose you?"

I replied :

"Please forgive me, my dear, I know that I will cause you a great deal of pain, but it cannot be compared to the suffering I have endured because of that unjust sentence. I feel now that I have defeated them, and that I can laugh and say : 'The game is over'."

I rubbed my eyes. How strange!

I saw before me the same court room, the same people, the same order of things, the same red and green ribbons on the same broad chests, the same platform and the same background. How similar to the last time I was here. However there was one difference. The short lawyer in his black gown who looked like a crow was absent. A slight difference, but it proved that this was not a recorded video tape of my first hearing. This was my second and hopefully my last hearing in court. The absence of my lawyer drew the attention of the judge who said irritably :

"We do not want any delay. Where is your lawyer?"

I replied:

" I do not want a lawyer. What use is a lawyer? I can

defend myself. I will not impose on you, for I have very little to say. As you know I do not like to talk, and when I killed that person, I did not do so because I hated him for preventing me from speaking, for he was only the tool, by which the sentence was carried out. Likewise I did not catch him stealing my money, and I was not under the influence of any narcotic, nor was I possessed by any sudden fit of insanity. I did not find him in bed with my wife, nor did he try to attack me. Any of these pretexts would have given me a legitimate right to self-defence. In fact there is no pretext or excuse that can prevent you from sentencing me to death! The game is over."

Translated by Thoraya Mahdi Allam

WAFIYA KHAIRY *was born in 1931. She graduated in English Literature, Cairo University, 1953, then proceeded to obtain a Translation Diploma in the same department, 1979 and another in Dramatic Writing from the American University in Cairo, 1982. She has occupied the post of translator in Foreign Affairs Departments in government agencies: finally attaining the position of Under-Secretary for Research. She is an established author of plays, television serials and short stories. She has written twenty short plays since 1965 and about fifteen television serials, her last being :* **The Last Return** *(Al awda al-Akhira), 1993. She won awards for film scenarios and short stories.*

Her short stories "A Mood of Optimism" and "A Man and A Woman" appear in her two short-story collections : **More Than One Thing** *(Akthar Min Shay'), 1983 and* **A Woman Inside Me** *(Imra'a Bi Dakhili), 1989, respectively.*

A MAN AND A WOMAN

Wafiya Khairy

He stood in front of the open window, with his bulky figure and his pyjamas jacket off. Such has been his habit every morning ever since he became a permanent guest at home. He started making acrobatic movements which were incompatible with his huge body, crying with a squeal of joy that he felt twenty years younger and affirming what he repeatedly claimed that he had once been a distinguished athlete but that problems at work had hindered him from practising his favourite sport. For exclusively this reason, his figure had become flabby and out of shape, just like any other athlete once he stops practising. Now that he had retired a few days before, he has the opportunity to practise his hobby once more.

Meanwhile Nageyya was energetically moving about in their flat, with her skinny frail figure. Ever since she woke up in the morning she has been washing the children's clothes. Inspite of the fact that they have become young men and women she still considers them youngsters, and will continue to do so till each one of them gets married, moves out of the house and has his or her own separate home.

No sooner does she finish the washing, which she does simultaneously with cooking, than she rushes to the bedrooms to tidy them up after the children leave for their colleges. She can no longer clean the rooms as well as she used to do in her first years of marriage, because of the weakness and feebleness which got the better of her after spending twenty years serving the whole household.

During these long years her husband was promoted from a third-degree researcher at the Ministry of Public Works to the head of a department, though the post of director general remained a long-cherished dream which he could never attain.

The outcome of those twenty years is two young daughters and two young sons – all studying for their university degrees.

Nageyya finished her housework early in the day. She then remembered that that day was the fixed day to get the family food rations: oil, sugar, soap, rice... She knew too well that if she did not go that day to take the food ration at the grocer's, he would postpone it until the end of the month. He was such an exact and meticulous man at work that he allotted a specific day for each ration-coupon holder to pick up his rations. He would not allow any alterations in his schedule, whatever the reasons or justifications might be.

Nageyya grabbed her handbag together with her shopping bag, made of a cheap, coarse material which she had made herself so as to carry heavy shopping materials especially the monthly food rations. She then hurried out. While walking, Nageyya was totally unmindful of her surroundings, until she reached the main street. This was her first time to pass by this street, as some road repairs made it impossible for her to take short cuts through the narrow streets which she was in the habit of taking to avoid going through the main street.

The drivers' hooting, pedlars' shouting, the hubbub of the crowds in the main street pierced Nageyya's ears. What on earth has happened to this world! Why has it become so crowded and noisy? Where do these people come from? What are they doing and where are they heading?

Nageyya continued wondering, though these questions did not apply to her for she knows her goal, and where she is heading too well. For twenty years, ever since she was a young girl of sixteen, when she married her husband Mounir, he has always treated her as though aiming a whip at her every single moment of her life. She has since become involuntarily involved in never- ending responsibilities and duties, for he has always been there ready with his sharp tongue sometimes more stinging than a whip. His screams could wake up the whole neighbourhood if she failed to carry out her duties or if she showed any signs of being lazy or any tendency for negligence.

In the main street, Nageyya pushed her way through masses of human bodies absolutely unconscious of anything around her. Suddenly the hubbub, the din and the roughness of the street disappeared. A soothing breeze penetrated her, caressing her on all sides, tenderly and affectionately. This sudden transformation happened when she saw in front of her a huge picture of a man and woman embracing. Smiling, Nageyya gazed at the advertisement outside a newly–built cinema. She was mesmerized and bewildered. How beautiful the woman was and how handsome the man. Both figures were slender and gracefully-built. She noticed the long loose hair of the woman. Nageyya touched her hair which she had tied in a bun at the back of her head, hiding it under a large scarf tied in a knot right under her chin. It was a trick which she resorted to of late to cover her hair to save herself the trouble of washing, brushing and combing it. Her tedious housework, besides her meagre income did not give her a chance for such a luxury.

How handsome this man looks with his symmetrically-built muscles, stretching his arm with its fine, slender fingers to caress the woman's shoulder, his eyes full of love, tenderness and affection for her.

Nageyya suddenly realized that she was standing in the queue, and stretching her hand with the three pounds to give to the box-office attendant to book her a ticket for that film. The girl at the box office told her, smiling that many ladies came accompanied by their husbands to watch the film, for its title is, after all "A Man and a Woman". She added that the film was made twenty years after the internationally famous film director had produced his film a "Man and a Woman".

Listening to this torrent of information, Nageyya was dumbfounded. Why did the girl shake off her dreams! What did she care about the film or its producer, or even its implications? She only wanted to see that look which that man directed to the woman – a look which penetrated her whole being, her soul and awakened something dormant inside her.

She quickly took the ticket from the girl, not even bothering to wait for her change. She found herself groping her way to settle at last in her seat among the rest of the audience.

Nageyya kept gazing at the pictures quickly moving infront of her, breathless and stunned by what she saw.

Two young men seated behind her were talking in a fairly audible voice about the cinema festival and the parties held on this occasion, expressing their dissatisfaction concerning many things which she failed to understand.

Throughout their conversation which reached her ears, against her will, thus dispersing the sweet feelings that she saw on the screen, she wished she could shout at them to stop them talking. She wondered why these two young men took the trouble to come to the cinema, pay for the tickets then sit there talking, dissatisfied, in this way.

Nageyya was about to turn to ask them to be quiet, when she noticed that they had already stopped talking. The effect of the film on them was stronger than their feeling of frustration or resentment. Thus they remained silent till the end of the film which gave her the opportunity to follow the events whole–heartedly.

When Nageyya was late returning home, her husband Mounir was very worried. It had never been her habit to be so late when she went shopping, especially when she went to get the food rations for she had a fixed date to do so.

Mounir thought of going out himself to the grocer's to inquire about her but he changed his mind for his huge figure did not make it a simple matter for him to move or walk easily. Moreover by such behaviour he could become a target of ridicule if people saw him asking the grocer about his wife, they would probably think that he had become over anxious and infatuated with his young wife, eaten up with jealousy after his retirement and his sudden discovery of the difference in age between them.

Hours passed quickly, one hour after another until it was almost one o'clock – it was lunch time. Nageyya could never forget lunch time for the children. His heart throbbed. He was panting for breath. What could have happened?

At that moment, Nageyya was coming out of the cinema, and like Mounir, her heart was throbbing. Like him too, she was panting for breath but for completely different reasons. A sweet vague feeling penetrated her. She wished she could fly. If only she could walk bare-footed, on tiptoe like a ballerina, if she could only sing and laugh, if she could only caress all those she saw around her.

A sweeping feeling of joy and happiness overwhelmed her – a feeling of love for everyone, foremost among whom came her children, her husband, even her neighbours and the passersby. Suddenly, Nageyya remembered the empty coarse-material bag dangling in her hand. She has not bought the food rations and now that she had spent the three pounds allotted to buying them, she could not do so.

She felt terrified and frightened. She envisaged her

111

husband's face, huge and frightening, yelling at her until his facial muscles contracted, while he denounced her despicable deed in the presence of her neighbours. How was it that his wife, this honourable lady, with whom he had lived for twenty years, during which time she had been the prodigy of honour and righteousness, had committed such a despicable deed by squandering the household budget to buy a single cinema-ticket? Yes! by God and to watch a film alone!

A strange shiver went through her. She would be terribly disgraced and her good name will be destroyed together with her future life as a wife and mother. How can she ever face her husband and her childern when they come back from college! With these tumultous thoughts and feelings raging inside her, Nageyya suddenly heard the shrieking of brakes and something heavily falling on the ground. She found herself lying infront of a car, she had been knocked down by a speeding car and the passersby were crowded round her.

She felt all her body, but there was nothing that hurt her. She heard loud voices of the passersby in unfinished utterances. "The woman is finished". "Will somebody call an ambulance." "Feel her pulse."

To the amazement of the passersby Nageyya stood up tidying her clothes and putting her scarf back round her head. She grabbed her handbag, collected its contents which had been scattered on the ground of the main street and hurried towards her home, while the crowd shouted after her:

"Thank God." "It's all right." "God has been merciful to you."

"True! God has been merciful," muttered Nageyya to herself on getting home. For when her husband met her with a worried, concerned look on his face, she told him, in simple terms what had happened to her in the main street without making the slightest reference to the details of the accident or when it happened, so as to give his imagination a chance to rearrange it in the fashion that could appeal to him. Thus, she would save herself the trouble of making up excuses for her delay, her failing to get the house provisions or for the loss of the three pounds she had.

The strange thing about this matter is that while her husband Mounir expressed his anxiety and worry over what had happened to her, Nageyya seemed to notice the same tender look in his eyes that she had previously seen in the actor's eyes for the actress in that huge advertisement which was the main cause for the way she had behaved that morning for the first time and probably for the last time in her life.

Translated by Amal Mazhar

A MOOD OF OPTIMISM

It happens sometimes that you get up one morning feeling optimistic and cheerful, but quite unable to find a reason for it. Such a mood, in many cases, makes you feel that you are capable of performing extraordinary feats. Since you have been overwhelmed by this cheerful mood you undoubtedly start reconsidering your life to assess your achievements. Undoubtedly, also, and since you are going through this unusual state of mind, you must have found that you have achieved a great deal, made gigantic steps ahead, and that you are capable, against all odds, of fighting the battle to its very end and attaining self-fulfilment as a working woman, a housewife, a member of society and even in the entire world.

This is precisely what happened to me yesterday. In that cheerful mood, I spent my day at the office working so diligently, and actively that I attracted everyone's attention. With a meaningful look that tried to fathom me, even Mohga, commented :

"You must have spent a wonderful evening. Where did you and Medhat go?"

"I don't remember what I did yesterday. But today I'm overwhelmed by this strange feeling which makes me see everything in a rosy hue – I don't know why!".

"Does that include Mr. Fathallah, the general manager?" she asked.

"I feel that even his nuisances are justifiable. Don't forget that he's in charge of a large family. Besides, his wife is ill and..."

I point out that this optimistic mood is also generally accompanied by a feeling of love for everybody, an immense tendency for forgiveness and the ability to justify the nuisances of others.

115

Despite the fact that Mohga kept looking at me doubtfully and suspiciously, at midday I noticed that her frowning, moroseness and endless complaints about everything had completely vanished. She started laughing heartily. When she noticed my questioning looks, she commented on my mood in the cheerful, naughty tone which had first attracted me to her and made us friends. With time, that tone had almost vanished under heaps of petty, daily annonyances which destroyed her innate, natural cheerfulness. This has made her wear a mask - a mixture of frowning rigidity and continuous complaining, saying, "You know! You're right! Why be pessimistic? Let's take things as they come. Let's even try to love our enemies, maybe life will be less bitter."

It seems that the effect of optimism is stronger than that of any other feeling. Thus, by the end of the day, everyone in the office caught the infection. Even the general manager amazed us by calling us to his office to bury the hatchet concerning a misunderstanding and turn a new leaf marked by co-operation and love.

That day while I was having lunch with my husband, I caught myself telling him in the tone of a person who had reached the peak of maturity and wisdom after a great deal of experience and suffering:

"You know, Medhat, we ourselves cause our own miseries. Life is much more beautiful and wonderful than we imagine. All we have to do is to take off this pessimistic mask, smile to the world and inevitably all causes of misery will definitely vanish."

With this cheerful mood I started to help my children to study their lessons, tidy up the house and get ready to go to the university in the afternoon.

In the wide road, the autumn breeze caressed my face, penetrating every particle of my being, invigorating it. I started reconsidering my life. Undoubtedly, this optimistic feeling is justifiable. I have achieved a great deal – a respectable post in a company and despite this, have managed to strike a balance between my job and my family life, I'm a happily married wife, and a mother of two children who are doing very well at school. Moreover, I'm studying for my M.A. degree. Isn't all this enough to make me feel optimistic! Had it not been for the daily, petty nuisances which we all have, I'd have definitely never parted with this optimistic feeling.

"Taxi ! Taxi!"

Why doesn't this taxi stop when I call it! There are no passengers in it and what is more, it is heading in the same direction as mine and inspite of that the taxi - driver has not even bothered to answer me, being quite indifferent to my calling. But no matter – I'll find another one soon. I continued walking looking left and right, looking for any means of transport to take me to the university. Suddenly, I felt water splashing on my clothes and face. I looked around and I saw a butcher's apprentice throwing dirty water from a bucket infront of his shop. He screamed at me impertinently:

"Why don't you watch out!"

I almost lost my temper, but I resorted to the wisdom, which I had acquired earlier that morning.

I smiled at him, suppressing my fury and said:

"Sorry".

I continued walking, calling out for a taxi. Both occupied and unoccupied taxis dash past me, and still I get no answer.

Looking at my watch, I find it is almost seven o'clock and I have to be at the university at seven sharp. I feel at a loss. How am I to solve this problem of overcrowded means of transport!

The voices of two children fighting and calling each other names pierce my ears, "son of a bitch." I felt shocked. Why drag mothers into insults! How horrible! But then it makes sense, for no one has taught these children good manners. No one explained to them the sacredness and holiness of motherhood. I continue walking, calling out "Taxi". To my pleasant surprise, at last a taxi stops for me. I jump into it, thanking its young driver:

117

"You've come to my rescue."

He looks at me sideways and asks:

"Where to?"

"Cairo University."

Scrutinizing me thoroughly through the mirror fixed infront of him, he asks:

"Student or teacher?"

"A student, studying for my M.A. in business management."

He does not comment, but gets out a piece of paper from his pocket, asking me:

" Can you read this prescription for me?"

I take the prescription and read the names of different medicines and a prescribed diet. I explain everything to him in the simplest terms then ask him:

"Is this for you?"

"No, it's for my mother-in-law."

"May God grant her health."

The driver takes back the prescription, folds it and puts it in his pocket. I take a glimpse at the hard, look on his face and feel sorry for him. A young taxi driver of his age working in a big city like Cairo and in spite of this is illiterate, unable to read or write. With the same optimistic, affectionate feeling for everyone, I feel the extent of my responsibility as an educated person in this country to help those miserable people and to alleviate the darkness of their ignorance. How can we possibly live happily in a society harbouring so many illiterate people?

Suddenly, silence prevails for a while, but he interrupts it by asking:

"Are you married?"

For a while I feel that he has no right to talk so informally to me. But I cannot help answering him proudly:

"And, I am also a mother of two children."

The hard look on his face returns, while he stares at my reflection in the car mirror.

118

"Can you cope with both your studies and your home?"

"Rather my home, work and studies."

"So, you're a working woman?!"

My self-esteem inflates within me now that this mood has been kindled since the morning.

"I'm a department manager in a big firm, I'm in charge of ten or more clerks."

I catch a glimpse of the contractions of his facial muscles in the mirror. His hoarse voice interrupts my indulgence in proud self-esteem,

"Pleased to meet you."

I instantly feel that my words have insulted him and hurt his masculine ego. But with the same optimistic feeling, affection and thoughtfulness for others which have filled me since the morning, I add to ease off the effect of my words on him:

"However, I never neglect my duty as a wife and mother. I consider my first duty is to have a happy family and to look after my husband and children."

He does not answer but he, suddenly stops infront of the university gate and says:

"Here we are."

I look at him tenderly and feel that I have actually, though unwittingly, humiliated him.

Suddenly, an idea occurs to me. Why don't I suggest that I teach him to read and write? I am capable of doing it. He can come to my place for one hour daily and learn how to read and write. In that way he would not have any grudge when dealing with an educated person such as he had when he talked to me.

I am about to discuss with him my idea as I give him the fare. But suddenly I find him rigidly fixing his gaze on me. He coldly asks me, as I, for the first time, glimpse a very faint smile in his eyes:

"And does your husband approve of this?"

I am stunned and a shiver goes through me utterly shaking me.

"Approve of what?" I ask him.

"Going out day and night!"

I scream at him:

"What!"

"I was married to a woman like you - she worked in a factory but I divorced her. I don't approve of my wife working. I'm a conservative man."

Translated by Amal Mazhar

ZEINAB SADEK graduated in journalism in Cairo University and is on the staff of **Sabah-al-Kheir** *magazine, where she has been contributing a weekly article entitled* **Ana Wa al-Hayat (Life and I)** *since 1973.*

She is a dedicated and prolific writer. Her work includes two novels: **Day After Day** *(Yawm Ba'd Yawm), 1969 and* **Don't Steal My Dreams** (La Tasreq Ahlamy), 1978, in addtion to six short-story collections.

She is mostly concerned with personal relationships, especially love and marriage, as exemplified in the following titles: **When Love Draws Near,** *(Indama Yaqtarib al-Hob), 1975;* **You Are the Sun of My Life** *(Anta Shamso Hayati), 1987.*

The same thing is true of her studies : **Stories About Love** *(Qissas 'an al-Hob), 1971 and* **Love and Marriage** *(Al-Hob wa al- Zawag), 1985. Nonetheless, Sadek's output is varied. A number of her stories have been translated into Bulgarian, Italian and German and her first novel was adapted for the cinema.*

"Warm Memories" and"Sparrows" appeared in **Nisf al-Dunya,** *magazine, 1991 and 1993.*

122

WARM MEMORIES

Zeinab Sadek

It was her in particular, of all the women in the world whom he knew, or befriended or had fun with or even disappointed - he didn't ask to see anyone of them at this critical moment of his life. She was the only one whom he asked to see, without the slightest feeling of weakness or humiliation. She was the only one whose hand he wanted to kiss in an attempt to seek forgiveness, after more than a quarter of a century had elapsed since he caused her that pain of their aborted love story.

His voice reached her weak, like the sound of voices in old dreams. She thought he was calling her from a distant continent. He told her he was in Cairo and pleaded that she go to him at the hospital.

When she entered his room, he was sitting in bed. She laid her hand out to greet him – he touched it with his lips. She sat next to him on a seat. A moment of silence elapsed. He looked at his weak body and said regretfully: "In the prime of my youth and manhood I loved you." She said: "And in the prime of my youth and womanhood I loved you."

He held his head low. She looked at him and smiled.

She said: "We came to know each other at a time when songs were sentimental, when music was romantic and when the future was full of hopes and the State's motto was "Raise your head brother..."

He raised his head, smiling. He said: "Cairo was then flourishing with Afro-Asian political conferences."

She said: "and I used to work as an interpreter in these conferences."

He said : "and I used to work in an Egyptian news agency. I met you at one of these conferences. I was feeling bored so I plugged into my ears the translation earphones. I switched it on to English and then French. I heard your voice. I liked your voice and your fluency in translation. After the session I went to the translators' lounge and introduced myself to you and told you how much I liked your fluency and invited you to coffee. We started to meet outside the conference hall when a mutual liking developed – do you remember?"

She said : "We used to go to the cinema when it was a pleasure to go there and watch the beautiful international films. We went to night clubs when dancing was romantic, and to theatres when plays were the high-class refined comedies..."

His body started to feel alive again with the warmth of memories. He said : "Cairo at that time was flourishing with big hopes, with boosting the morale to overcome the enemies, with the ever- repeated motto, "Let there be no louder sound than the sound of the battle."

She said laughing : "But my voice became louder on some of the lovely evenings we spent together when I asked for your commitment in marriage..."

He said sadly : "and my voice was even louder than yours when I protested that I couldn't. I had all my attention for my future career, and I didn't have enough money for marriage. I was a fool..."

She said, teasing him, "and you once told me, in your arrogant manhood, that whenever you meet with a beautiful female, you are not able to resist her, and you asked if I would put up with that if we were married."

124

He shook his head saying : "But that was ages ago!"

She said : "and I told you that the eye may fall for many but the heart can only have one, that your admission means no more than just being mean... and you laughed at my words.."

He said : "and I cried a lot afterwards."

His eyes flooded with tears. She pretended not to see them and said merrily : "In spite of your playful words, you never stayed away from me, and my feminine pride then refused to believe that you would ever leave me for another woman. You were so attached to me, calling me every evening to invite me out, calling me every morning because you said that hearing my voice then would bring you luck... you were everywhere in my days, my heart and my dreams and even my future which I never planned with you..."

He sat upright as if he regained more vigour and said : "These were the loveliest days,in work,in life, in love, until..." He didn't finish his sentence – he remained silent.

She said : "until there was the big shock for all the big dreams.At that time Cairo lived the humiliation of defeat in war, and I lived the humiliation of defeat in love when I found that you were attracted to an exciting beautiful female, the daughter of the then famous politician,and you were then no longer reluctant about marriage, as you had always been.... The shock was great, not only for my love, but also for my whole life."

He said : "I'll tell you now the story of my sudden marriage, which I couldn't explain to you before. I came to know her when I went to meet her father at the club to get news from him. Our relation was no more than an exchange of greetings and talk about sports and hobbies. It is true that I admired her beauty, but just like any man admiring any beautiful female. Believe me, I never thought

125

of taking her out, until that day.... I went to Alexandria to cover an important political meeting. They put off the press conference until the following day– that was in May, before our defeat in the war. So I had to stay the night there. I went to a restarurant in a small night club and I saw her with a group of her friends– boys and girls. She greeted me at a distance and I answered her back, but she surprised me by coming to my table and saying that she was bored with her group and asking me to dance with her. She was determined to stay in my company even after her group had left. At the end of the evening I took her home to her father's house there. That was all, I swear, that had happened that night. But when I got back to Cairo, her father surprised me by saying that her friends had told him that she spent the night with me, and that it had become a scandal at the club. He had to tell his colleagues – who were just waiting for anything to get at him, politically or socially – that I was her fiancé. He begged me to fulfill what he said. I found myself in an embarrassing situation and tried to explain what had actually happened that night but he said that, even if he believed me, rumours were stronger than the truth... and thus we got married."

She said : "Why didn't you explain to me these circumstances at the time? I would have found an excuse for you, instead of beginning to lose confidence in my femininity and feeling hurt in my pride."

He said : "Would I have told you that I married her because I was afraid of her father's influence? I preferred to let you think I was mean rather than a helpless coward."

She said : "They advised me to fall in love again or get married, that there was no cure for a broken heart like a new love or a rational marriage. But I was afraid – I didn't

126

want to go through another experience of love and I couldn't marry any of those who proposed to me at the time.... I found the cure in my work, in hard training and competition with colleagues until I became the first to be selected for translation in overseas conferences. My fame reached the Arab countries and they asked for me to work in their conferences. I even excelled in English translation too, and I began to find happiness in travel, and pleasure in culture and politics and wealth..."

He said : "Do you remember the first time we met in Europe after 3 years of my marriage?"

She said : "Our encounters remain memorable dates in my life."

He said : "For me, it was like the first time we met. I heard your voice through the earphones, I liked your voice and went searching for you in the translators' lounge. I invited you to have coffee and I was afraid to see a look of hatred in your eyes."

She said : "I never hated you, never rejoiced at your misfortune when you told me that you were unhappy and that you kept the family together simply for the sake of the twins."

He said : "And I told you that day about my work in the foreign agency, which I got through my father in-law. I told you that I spent most of the year abroad, hoping that you would agree to get together again away from home. But you made me understand that you didn't want to renew our relation."

She said : "I didn't want my old dreams with you to stir up again, I didn't want to start living through another desperate illusion."

He said : "You avoided meeting me aferwards, whenever we were together at a conference."

She said : "I used to watch you at a distance in the company of many women, in Cairo and abroad, and remember your old arrogant words that you were attracted to every beautiful female. I used to wonder whether your wife knew all about this. I heard many exciting stories about you in the conference translation rooms. One day I saw a beautiful female quarrelling with you and once I saw another one doting on you.."

He shook his head sadly and said : "I felt lonely and my unhappy marriage led me into these affairs."

She said : "And I remember the last time we met seven years ago, when you told me about your divorce."

He said laughingly: "That day you told me the reason for my wife's asking for divorce was my affairs with other women and that her attraction for another man was due to my neglecting her. I didn't defend myself because I knew that you didn't know the story of my marriage. That day I was delighted that you accepted my dinner invitation in that charming European city."

She said laughingly : "That day I waited for you to propose and I was wondering how to answer you, but you spared me the worry – you didn't ask me anything."

He said : "I couldn't propose to you when I was so emotionally upset after the divorce, especially that my twin boys had decided to stay with me. I was also afraid you might refuse – it was obvious that you didn't want to renew our relation. I decided to give up everything relating to my previous life. I resigned from the press agency and took the two boys and went to America to work there."

She said : "And I started to miss your presence at conferences – my eyes wandered in search for you behind the glass walls at the translation rooms. I waited for you to knock at the door and say that you had heard my voice."

He said : "Be sure that I never loved any woman except you. I wanted to tell you this before I...." His eyes filled with tears.

She said : "You will recover with the help of God. Before coming to you I went to the senior doctor who did your operation – I know him. I asked him about you. He told me what the American doctors had told you, which made you despair. He assured me that many had your operation before and survived."

He said : "Last year I came to know that great doctor in America. He was on a professional visit there and I met him at some friends' and admired him much. When I fell ill and the American doctors said I had little hope I decided to come home to die here in my country. I have been back for a month. I went straight to him and he revived my hope. With the help of God he will make me live in my country. I sent for the two boys because I decided to settle down here."

He was silent for a moment and then he said : "If I am to survive, would you accept me now? Would you forgive me and accept me as a husband?"

She said : "I have forgiven you for many years now..."

He said : "Say you haven't married because you have been waiting for me,"

She smiled and got up. He held her hand and kissed it. She left the hospital, and as she was driving her car she finished what she was saying to herself. "Yes, I have forgiven him for years and he has been in my heart all the time. I didn't marry because I like to travel and I was afraid of a husband who would hate my job or with whom I would live only with my body.. But is it possible for us to actually revive our memories in reality as we have done so in conversation?"

She shook her head and speeded up the car when she found the road empty.

Translated by Afaf Al-Menoufy

SPARROWS

She woke up at the sound of the first sparrow - she realized that the first ray of daylight has begun to appear in the horizon. She was certain that she had not slept well that night: for when she does not sleep well, she wakes up at the sound of the first sparrow and then becomes wide awake and does not feel the need to go back to sleep again. But today is her weekly day off, why should she leave her bed early? Thére is no work today. Other sparrows began to sing back at the sound of the first sparrow – it was like an alarm clock for them. She wondered which alarm clock does wake up the sparrow? Is it a male or a female sparrow?

She smiled at the thoughts. She put a pillow over her head to go back to sleep. She had dreams of sparrows in her room when it was flooded in daylight. She opened the door of her balcony and looked at the close-by tree : it was full of sparrows. She smiled as she greeted them with good morning. They do not run away in fear – they wait for the bread crumbs which she puts out for them on the balcony-sill after she finishes her breakfast. She has always seen them and has always heard them: their voices do not change and they stay on the tree even when it loses most of its leaves in winter. She has always puzzled over a question: are these the same sparrows which she had seen ever since she lived in this house as a child? Although her father had answered this question for her as a child, yet it still puzzled her. She had asked her father years ago. "Don't sparrows die?" He had answered that they died like all other creatures. Then she had asked him her puzzling question: the sparrows have not changed since she saw them as a child on the tree close-by her room. Did that mean that they were the same sparrows?" Her father had replied, "They do change but they all look similar."

She had asked her father again one day after she had seen a fight among the sparrows on the tree, "Why should sparrows fight?" He had answered her that every flock of sparrows dwelled in an area of trees and if another flock from another area invaded their area they had to fight until the issue was resolved. Her elder brother had said that day that sparrows were like beggars: each group occupy an area which becomes their territory and if a beggar came from another area they would beat him. She was angry with her brother that day and said that sparrows were not like beggars because sparrows are beautiful creatures.

Sparrows are part of her life. She complains to them about her sorrows, tells them about her joys, celebrates with them the coming of spring and always wonders about the strange things with which they build their nests. They just use whatever is available to build their nests – nothing hinders them. Why doesn't she act like sparrows? Anything available is good enough for building their nests. Why is she for ever looking for things which are not easily available?

She looked at the sparrows and smiled – they are the same sparrows which she has been seeing for years!

Through the bathroom window she heard a tune from the neighbours' radio. She didn't know why that tune reminded her of the man whom she loved and who deserted her for another woman. She wondered why she remembered him with some affection. She washed her face several times to wake up from her memories. She had decided to wipe him out of her memory after he got married, and has succeeded in doing that and is now officially engaged to someone else. Why was she thinking about him today?

She went shopping for a present for her fiancé. In a men's shop, she did not like the manner of the saleswoman. Somehow her manner annoyed her and provoked her into a bad temper – the shop owner came to scold the saleswoman and apologized and served her himself. She bought the present and left the shop. She wondered at herself: she had never before lost her temper in shops. She walked in the street. She bought a pair of shoes. While she was choosing them, she remembered the words of the man whom she loved and who deserted her. He liked her taste in shoes. Before looking at her face or dress, he would look at her shoes and express his admiration. She shook her head in an attempt to drive his memory away from her. Why did she remember him today? Many months have passed since he got married. Was it merely because of that tune she had heard and which reminded her of him? And why that tune in particular? It was not that she had heard that tune with him, for instance, which would explain why it would remind her of him. She must not, really, think of the man who deserted her.

She looked at the engagement ring on her right-hand finger. She held her hand over it with a feeling of reassurance and tenderness. She loved her fiancé. But no human beings can completely cancel out their past, or completely forget all their memories. Such things nest into one's head – they never go away completely. They may get blurred, yes, even forgotten too. But they may suddenly appear, and one should not suppress one's old feelings and memories when they come to the surface again for a moment. Suppression will hurt, so let them come out like pus coming out of a wound to purify it.

Her fiancé was completely different from the man whom she loved and who deserted her. She had read once that if one fell head over heels in love with someone and then this love was not fulfilled, one would for ever be looking for someone with the same characteristics: sometimes the same physical features, or the same temperament or the same morals. Sometimes a female would choose her second man from the same profession. But with her it was completely the opposite. She chose a man who was completely different in everything.

In the evening she met with her fiancé. She handed him the present saying tunefully : "Happy birthday my darling, and I hope next year will find you in good health and still in love with me!" He said to her in amazement that it was not his birthday. She was about to argue with him and say how forgetful he was when she suddenly stopped talking as a red signal went quickly through her mind to warn her against continuing the conversation.

Today was the birthday of the man who deserted her, not her fiancé! It was true that her fiancé's birthday was on the tenth day of the month, but it was next month! She covered her confusion with a smile.

So, her unconscious mind had been playing a role since the morning. It moved memories up to her conscious mind with that tune, so she went and bought the present. She discovered why she had lost her temper with the saleswoman: it was because she looked like the woman who became the wife of the man whom she loved and whom he actually preferred to her! She began to understand why she was always looking for things for her trousseau which were rather difficult to find: to delay her wedding. All these things went quickly through her mind as she stood silent in front of her amazed and annoyed fiancé!

She said tactfully, "Next month, on your real birthday, we shall have our wedding."

He asked, "And what about the things you cannot find for our house?"

She said that she was now convinced that she should do with what was available. "And who convinced you?" he asked her. She answered, "The sparrows!"

He laughed but was not surprised. He remembered the remark she had made one evening recently when he was visiting them. He was watching the news on television with her and her father. There was a picture of a deserted area in one of the many cities in the world where local civil wars had broken out: the houses had been hit and they were empty and silent except for the voices of sparrows. He noticed how moved she was by those voices and the sympathetic remark she made about them. She had not noticed where in the world that city was. All that she had noticed was the voices of the sparrows. He was rather surprised then and asked her, "Don't you have any sympathy for the people?" She answered, "People can act and do something, but those nice helpless creatures, what is their guilt in such wars? and how will they find their food?" Her father had remarked then, with a smile, on how much she always liked sparrows!

Her fiancé remembered all this and so he did not comment on the sparrows having convinced her to buy what was available in the market. He asked her, "What did you do this morning?"

She told him about her shopping and what happened

with the saleswoman, "Her looks provoked me before her manners did. She was fat in the face as well as in the body, and her long hair was left to flow carelessly as if she had not combed it for days, which made her look even bigger. Was it possible for a woman like that to be loved?" she asked him.

Her fiancé smiled and answered her that it was she whom he liked, and she whom he loved. She felt reassured and her heart beat with a calm loving throb which she had not felt before. She was a little embarrassed and looked down at her feet. She noticed that she was wearing the new pair of shoes. She asked him what he thought of them, and he said after looking at them, "They look nice on your feet."

Her thoughts wandered. people were not all similar like the sparrows on the tree close by her balcony. People were different – although her fiancé was completely different from the man who deserted her, she treated him in the same way, as if he was the same person. She began to understand why she got angry with him and made him angry for no reason: it was because she treated him in a manner that was appropriate for another man, and was expecting him to make the same comments as this other man.

It is strange how one can discover the truth about something in a moment, as if it was a moment of enlightenment or a bright spark passing through the mind. She should take advantage of this rare opportunity and revise her calculatins. She should start relating to her fiancé in a different way.

Her fiancé asked her, "Your thoughts are far away. Where have you been?" She answered that she considered this day to be really a happy birthday for the two of them together. He said that he found her different this evening, really nice and... thoughtful.

She promised him to be like that... always! He asked laughingly, "Have the sparrows also convicned you not to be angry with me or make me angry for no reason?"

She said that she really did learn from the sparrows

Translated by Afaf Al-Menoufy

*SANAA EL-BEESY obtained a degree in journalism in 1958. She is a journalist and a short-story writer. She is editor-in- chief of **Nisf al-Dunya** and writes regularly for numerous Arab newspapers and magazines. She has published three short-story collections : **In the Open Air** (Fi al-Hawa' al-Talq), 1973; **A Woman For All Seasons** (Imra'a Li Kol al-Osour), 1984 and **Permitted Talk** (Al-Kalam al-Mobah), 1992. Al Beesy is also a painter who has held several exhibits in Egypt, U.S.A and Canada. A number of her stories have been adapted for television, notably selections from **He and She Stories,** published in **Al-Ahram** national newspaper.*

She was awarded the Mustafa Amin (well-known journalist) Prize for writing in 1993. Her stories delve in both the external world and the inner life, exposing social ills and human weaknesses, through interesting narrative modes.

*"The Old Man and the Night" and "Let's Go Skiing" appear in **Al-Kalam al-Mobah.***

THE OLD MAN AND THE NIGHT

Sanaa El-Beesy

As heaven's face grows pale and daylight bleeds to utter dark, as the sun drops down dead with the remnants of his ember eating away on a blood–coloured battle ground, as the night – the firebrand of the wounds past and the wounds future – utters its black, decisive word, all alone he remains tethered in the middle of a mute room in an empty house, affixed to a brass bed, the high posts of which are reminiscent of pharoanic obelisks guarding an ancient tomb. The lace curtains are embroidered with pictures of winged women. His wife flew away, too. She departed this life of his long ago, only to visit his dreams occasionally with the image of her broad face stretching endlessly. Before him passes a sequence of her time-worn eyes, eyeing him with her eternal look of humility, pain and anguish like that of a dog beaten too much and fed too little.

Long hours elapse with nothing to occupy him but pulling little hairs from his brow and feeling his chest with his wrinkled fingers to check his quivering blood circulation. The very thought of the short- range future makes him shudder. Can his heart withstand it for one more year? His life is but a compulsory, sluggish creeping towards the end, a never-ending plunge in a swamp of moving sands. We grieve and rejoice, fall in love and part with those whom we love, experience jealousy and undergo suffering, only to end up as bodies dumped on an old age bed, striving in vain to work their way into memories sealed with red wax. In vain we try to remove the seals. At times, we do succeed in digging small holes through which we can peep into some disconnected events, thus reminiscing for a while over a by-gone childhood or long forgotten scenes of reckless youth, yet, for all this, the present remains lost in vast seas of oblivion.

The moon uses all her cunning to make an aperture for her circle betwixt the roofs, hoping to sneak into his bed in order to see him and with her phosphoric light, wipes out the sombre darkness created by the blanket.

If only the moon would go away! If only she would trample down the silver illusion!

To the galleries of the universe he travelled. Guided by her beams, he made his way to the hearts of the cities, the gatherings of night owls, the clusters of joys, the murmur of the beaches and whisper of the fields. Together with her light he lôst himself in the arms of a flower that grows on the edge of a mountain rock, achieved a union with the magic light, creating a bridge connecting lovers' lips. He bestowed a silver touch on the scales of a fish that was instantly overcome with joy and started to dance on the waves. He shone with the moon, exposing to view the glitter of a pearl gracing the neck of a velvety belle aboard a love boat. S.. 1.. e..e..p! Can a lonely old man sleep? He hit the pillow with his head thrice and turned on his left side then on his back. He started to feel drowsy, so he fixed himself to his place. A balky mosquito buzzing near him caught him in a vortex of distraction. He tried to shoo the intruder. It went away for a moment, only to come back quickly to produce an even more irritating buzz. Dizzi-ness.... Bells toll in his head. In the moonlight, the wardrobe and the chairs engage in a wild dance. Breath-lessness! The furniture pieces subside in their place without losing a shade of their vigour in their new standstill position as though fully prepared to go back to their wild dance.

Through the window's rectangular frame glitter stars galore. He put the pillow on the back of the bed and started to mess around with the radio indicator, oscillating between the wave lengths of two radio stations, thus resulting in a mixture of song and talk. He kicked down the moon, pulled the quilt, extended his legs, feet and neck and glued his body to the mattress. When the moon deserts him he needs to muster up all his faith and prayers to rest assured that the next building has not fallen down on his window. He imagines hearing the footsteps of the emergency men while making an aperture in the wall next to him. His prayers wax in intensity as he watches the stars leaving one after the other, only to drown in dawn's sea of light. Eventually, the call for prayer comes in shattering layers of inner darkness.

At eight o'clock sharp every day he is visited by his only daughter. Her appearance is always heralded by a sound prelude that calls to mind the beats preceding the curtain rise in the theatre : the rattle of the descending elevator's wheels, the clinking of its door when it is closed at the seventh floor. Two turns of the key in the door lock. The rustle of the morning paper when lifted from the landing. Five beats of her footsteps, with the sixth of which the wood of the floor groans.

She leans on him and presses a kiss on his face: "Good morning, papa! The traffic is just awful. I took that devil of a son to school. His father is quite a nuisance. Today you look better than yesterday. I must be quick, else I'll miss the attendance register at work. Took your pills? Slept well? How is your chest today? Your panting? Remembered the eyedrops? Now come with me to get your face washed. Have your breakfast on the balcony until I finish changing the linen." She keeps on coming and going then starts playing the old tune of the necessity of his moving to live with her, quickly responding to her suggestion by noting that there too, he will remain all by himself. She curses the present conditions, laments the scarcity of housemaids, remembers her mother and asks God to bless the soul of the dear departed. She kisses him goodbye and quits in a hurry, after promising in all good faith that – in the near future – she will take him for a little stroll, to the barber and also to the physician to have some necessary medical analyses made.

His eyes are too weak to stand the beams of light which the T.V. set emits. Naturally, his only pastime is listening to the ancient radio set placed on his right and to whose news bulletin and Koran recitations he wakes up and drowses.

That night, his quaking hand bumped into the radio set when he was trying to tune it to his favourite program "Our Exquisite Language." The radio fell on the floor as a result, also dropping with it the water jar, the eye drops and the bowl containing his set of false teeth. The cologne bottle kept the table lamp from falling down, now hanging in mid air, clutching to the wire while its light was wavering. Like a guilty child he left his bed, his foot feeling its way to the other one of his slippers. Eventually, his blind fingers managed to reach the light switch. He lifted the radio set and put it back in its place after mopping up the stickiness of the wood beneath it with his cotton skullcap. He then returned to his bed, weary and panting and still saying his prayers. Suddenly, he heard the sound of a telephone ring.

142

He was surprised because there was no telephone in the house. It then dawned on him that the sound was only coming out from the radio set, now accidentally turned on as a result of its fall. "One of those radio dramas, nothing more." his reasoning went. The sound continued for a long time, but finally came out the voice of a man whispering to a yawning female :

"Dear me! How stupid of me! Did I wake up my pretty one? I'm so sorry, honey! But anyway this is not fair at all. How can you possibly fall asleep while I'm here so love sick that I can't even get a moment's sleep. I've just got in. I wanted to hear your voice before I change. The Bey[1], your husband is on his way to you, sweetie! Should be with you in five minutes' time. We were together junketing the night away. Heaven knows how hard I tried. Don't worry, honey, I wasn't born yesterday and I know better than to blow it up—You see, I was itching to see you so I proposed that we go to your place but your pig-headed husband insisted we go to Fawzi's. Fawzi's wife, Saadeyya, is an elephant that walks and talks but to give her her due she's a cook of the first order. She certainly was trying to be friendly, but it was no good, sweetie! For me, you are the best, my love. Ring me up any time: in the morning, when in the kitchen, in the bathroom, in bed, under the sofa, on top of the drawer, hanging on the chandelier. Your phone is wireless so you shouldn't have any excuses.... My! I love you, baby! He said he's going out of town this Wednesday. I could hardly hide my glee, so I took that brat, Fawzi's daughter, and tickled her until she and I could not stop giggling. Hurrah for Wednesday! Good night, Sugar! Sleep well with all my love!" At this point, the transmission was

---

(1) An originally Turkish title used in Egypt until the 1952 Revolution-here used ironically.

cut. The old man tried to tune his radio to any other station but his attempts met with no success. When dawn set in, he had already fallen asleep, his mind inhibited by clouds of amazement at the sleazy nature of new radio dramas!

In the morning, he was about to ask his daughter to take the radio set and get its indicator fixed. Due to some inner call, however, he held back the request at the very last moment. On hearing the door shut behind her, he quickly turned on the radio and all day long, the telephone continued to ring on both sides with the same man and woman exchanging short conversations that are laden with twisted meanings.

Wednesday, at last. Her fresh, youthful voice rang out through the speaker "Bon soir, dearie. Your pal has cleared off at last. I wanted to make sure that he's somewhere out of reach so I asked him to make a long-distance call. The stupid fool thought I was worried about him. The boy has gone to bed already. I'm waiting for you. You're scared? Oh, no, not you! Buy me some shrimps while on your way. I just feel like it. The janitor has been in his room since sunset. I rang up every member of the family, all my friends and acquaintances, and told them I have a terrible headache and that I took a sleeping pill and wish to be left in peace till morning. Seven floors are no problem. You said you'd climb up the highest mountain for me. Come on, honey! Get moving.

While sitting on the balcony chair, the old man heard someone humming a song in a joyful, sensual voice. He raised his head and his eyes met those of his young neighbour with her characteristic inviting smile. She was now leaning on the washing-lines while hanging her underwear on them. She inquired about his health and life conditions, then said, "If I can ever be of any help, don't

144

hesitate to tell me, sir." He stammered out his reply and nodded his head in due solemnity. From her breast came out the buzz of a small telephone set. She instantly cuddled the machine rapturously and went inside quickly after winking to the old man, saying, "Excuse me, sir!"

He surveyed the sky, looked down at the roofs of the buildings, then extended his range of vision down to the street. He suddenly realized that he was on the seventh floor and that the woman was none but his neighbour with her wireless telephone set.. same voice!.. it was her!.

He hurried inside in order to turn on the radio set which, when dropping down that night, had tuned itself to the same frequency of the neighbour's wireless phone set. He listened with great excitement to the inflamed conversation, now that the heroine had become a real, flesh and blood person.

Like a fixed life pattern, days go by, charged with an excitement that has the old man pricking his ears for every ring of his neighbour's telephone. At times, the whisper makes him as tender as a flower's heart: at others, the reckless talk across the wires kindles in him powerful emotions that are as violent as a set of inflammable fireworks. He curses her. He curses him. He admires her intelligence. He is alarmed by his lies. He is fascinated by deceit. He envies him his virility. He condemns the libertine world of Sodom and Gomorah that continues to baffle him. The journey of eavesdropping, the love game tickles his senses. He dips the lovers in a flaming fire. He swings them on a lake of mercury. He silences them. He makes them speak. He gets addicted to their morning and evening chatter.

The daughter was happy to notice that her father no longer complained of his loneliness nor asked her to take him to the barber and the physician. He also stopped pressing her to stay a little longer in the morning and even became keener than her on her not missing signing the attendance register at work. When she came with her husband to spend the week-end with him, he started to grumble nervously. He even yelled at his grandson when the child, attempting to get him the bowl containing the false teeth, extended his small hands somewhere behind the radio set.

Turning on the radio, he heard bestial, jarring mumbles, "I love you darling. I can't take it any more. I can't live with him any longer. Time and time again I yell at him and ask him to divorce me. He only gives me a cold look then goes out. I am going mad. When shall we too be together without fear? I must get rid of him. No matter how. You can't find it in your heart to do it? Now don't give me that. Let him go to hell!" The ringing goes up again conjuring the voice of a man as elusive as a mercurial shark that inhabits a mysterious ocean and whose sharp fangs often bite off the arm or leg of an innocent person whom it decides to devour.

"Honey.. I got it, a way out for us, once and for all. It's a hell of an idea that will never leave behind a single shade of suspicion. An end for all the pain and thirst. Farewell to fear and lonely nights of long separation. Just a minute, please. Hello Mahmoud Bey. Yes.. Hello. I'm afraid it's impossible. Now, you see, I have some guests at my office for the moment. Have a good day, sir. I'll ring you up tonight. I give you my word of honour that all will be well for everybody."

All day long, silence engulfed the old man, a silence that is reminiscent of that calm which follows the sound of

146

the guillotine once the chopped head has rolled down. Like a bulk of strained nerves he remained, confined to his place in a kettle boiling on a low fire, a volcano whose crater has been blocked, the bursting of the wood of a coffin in which a living man has been put by mistake, the fight of iron-horned ibexes. In the morning he reached a decision to tell his daughter the whole story of the telephone.

The cuckold must see the light and the plot must be foiled. He will invite him to his place to listen to the talk of betrayal with his own ears. Tonight, he will know the details of the plot and will tell the poor man everything tomorrow so that he may save his skin. Hours seem as slow as tortoises. Moments feel so heavy with the window before him exhibiting stars that are like fiery pin-heads. Finally, at midnight, the ringing is heard. "Honey, can you hear me? Your pal is sleeping alone in the hall. Of course, we don't talk to each other. Of course, I love you. Now stop it. Not now. Let's get to hard facts. Hurry up and tell me your plan."

The old man pricked up his ears in order not to miss a single word. He stretched his hand to raise the volume to the maximum.

In so doing, his trembling fingers bumped the water jar which, while falling, took with it the bowl containing the false teeth, the table lamp as well as the radio set, now back to its normal transmission and broadcasting the theme tune for "Our Exquisite Language"!

Translated by Hazem Azmy

LET'S GO SKIING

At the airport, he exchanged condolences with his brother-in-law: "Take heart - her last wish was to see you before departing this life. Oh yes, I surely appreciate your occupations. May God bless her soul. She was a real lady. Your mother has always been respectable and dignified, in both life and death, and has lived long enough to see her grandchildren with her own eyes. Old age, you know. She's now in peace. Her illness and helplessness required tireless care. We spared no doctor nor medicine. Time and time again we used to bring her a specialized group of doctors at very high fees. During her last coma she used to come round for a few moments in which she used to address your late father as if he lay next to her in bed. I realized then that this was the end. She felt like some Moulid sweets,[1] so I brought her a box of Turkish delight with pistachios. Now come on, man, the dear departed was a mother to me and more. Of course, don't worry. The funeral procession started from El-Tahrir square and the funeral tent was very well attended. Relatives came from the countryside in groups and spent the night at our place after we had offered them supper. Your name was at the head of the obituary, preceded by your academic title: 'Dr.' and followed by

---

(1) The word "moulid" in Egyptian Arabic refers to the birthday of some saint (whether Christian or Muslim). In this context, it refers to the birthday of the prophet Mohammad. Egyptians celebrate the feast in various forms, prominent among which is the eating of a certain set of sweets known as the moulid sweets, one of which is Turkish delight.

your job: 'expert at the World Bank.' We mentioned that your late father was the director of the pensions department not just an inspector. There isn't a big difference between the two jobs. A minister representing the President came to offer his condolences and remained in the front seat while El-Rahman surat was being recited. I have kept all the condolences telegrams sent to you. They include telegrams from members of Parliament and the Shoura Council, the army and police top officers and chairmen of boards. We'll sit together sometime so that I may show you a statement of all the bills and receipts incurred. Your building in El-Sayyeda is now old and full of cracks and doesn't even yield any good revenue. May God see to it that it crumbles down so that we may sell the land it occupies. It would yield no less than a million pounds. Of course, I know that you came in a hurry and had no time to get us any presents. Do you believe this? The grave digger insisted on charging no less than two hundred pounds for preparing the burial ground. What a swindle! The world is going to the dogs! Even in the hospital we had to pay 1000 pounds as fees for her entering the operating theatre. Your sister, you know her sharp tongue, went to the doctor and asked him sarcastically whether that room's door was that difficult to open!"

As he entered the hall he was greeted by lumps of blackness in the form of women dressed in deep mourning and occupying the chairs. At his appearance, they started to mutter words of solace and comfort. "God has taken back what belongs to Him." Many a person was as quick to embrace him, and many a hand to stroke his back encouragingly while tear drops wetted his cheeks. At last, the tide of blackness receded in awe when he dragged his feet into the room of the deceased. He entered the room alone and closed the door behind him. The brass bed with its high posters was reminiscent of a saint's shrine. The lace curtains were embroidered with pictures of winged women. The mattresses and coverings were folded and laid aside against the wall. The sofa was covered with a spread embroidered with pictures of pale-coloured flowers. He remembered his mother in her eternal sitting on that sofa with her back leaning on the wall and her swollen legs in black stockings. He tried to remember when she first started to sit in this place. But probably that took place before the time and place he grew in. The broken mirror in her wardrobe still produced its familiar creaking, a creaking that he often heard as a child and as a young man when, in response to his pressing, she used to stoop inside the dark cave, open a hidden purse in order to supply him with some money which he grabbed and ran. Her cheap perfume greeted his nose from within the heap of clothes. He found nothing that he did not expect. Her dark dresses seemed cold and conspicuously empty. The piece of fabric he had sent her long ago was still new in its foreign wrapping. Time-worn purses containing old papers, a number of amulets, a kohl container, and.... in an old folded scarf that used to grace her head like a flag for years, was his old wedding picture. There he was, smiling with a thin moustache and standing next to him was his bride, that cousin of his whom he divorced, then emigrated. He remembered how his mother used to describe her : lady-like and very pretty. In the mirror's sharp edge, caused by the breakage, he saw his shrinking hair and the portruding veins of his gaunt temples.

Amidst the thick of the blackness outside, he went searching for the bride in the picture. Her looks were pointed at him while her hands were extended with fingers anxiously stretched and waiting for a response.

On his face he painted a smile through which he conveyed all the longing he could muster, then held fast to her fingers which the palm of his hand was quick to fondle. After shaking hands with her, he found himself strongly attracted to her. Nothing has changed in her. Still lady-like and very pretty. Time to her was no more than a quill pen that lovingly drew a fine line under her eyes, increasing their appeal. He suddenly felt that he had been missing life for a long time, now that he came to realize that his world in the last few years was, in a sense, empty and dead without her. He felt overwhelmed by a strong urge to cry vehemently, to run to her for succour saying, "Help me, please! My mother has died. I'm now orphaned, lonely and I need you!"

A long telephone ring brought him back to his present moment's reality. It was an overseas call. His chat in English with Christina continued for a long time. Their sentences across the ocean were brim with longing, news and trivial details. He promised to call her daily at the same time. He put down the receiver smiling and recalling her strong teeth, reminiscent of a nut cracker. Ill at ease, he turned to the silent assembly and conveyed to them Christina's heartfelt condolences. He then started to look again for his cousin who, he noticed, had withdrawn into a corner. She rarely exchanged any talk with him. From afar she greeted him in silence. Her smile affected him like a hand touch. He seized an opportunity and lingered in front of her to have a few words with her. She raised to him a soft, tearful eye. She forgot everything and hung on to his lips. Sedimentary, petrified strata are now being cracked inside him by a long-dormant ghoul who suddenly emerged in a fit of frenzy.

Insomnia kept him wide awake at night. He started to jot down the names of some people who were once close to him, encompassed his existence while he still lived here: a friend whom he did not hear from since the war; the neighbour's son who became a millionaire; a woman whose bed he frequented and who now leads a life of piety; another who was married once then was eventually widowed only to return to her jaunty life style. His former boss, he came to know, died at his office of heart attack. At dawn break, he went to sleep, having already taken a decision that bordered on a whim. It was the cork's determination to float. Wishing to God that the number was still the same, he dialled the number of his old house. His heart leaped in excitement when she answered in her typical way "Yes!" Her familiar, fresh tone captivated him and made him feel as if she was laughing her way into the telephone. This voice once inhabited his heart for some time. Now there she was : his cousin and ex-wife whom he divorced in a moment of madness. She sounded as if she was happy to hear his voice. He explained to her that he only had one day left before leaving Egypt. Everything between us is over. Absolutely not. Want to see you. Why don't you drop by and meet my husband, I spoke to him a lot about you. Wouldn't it be a bit embarrassing? He's wise enough to know that the past is dead. Nothing has died, he thought to himself.In our last meeting your eyes said the secret word. The nymph is opening up the gates of an old palace that was closed down for years. She bestows a new life on the remnants of a bird that soars high after a long period of inertia. Isis gathers up the body of Osiris whose

153

fragments are scattered across the land.[1]

In the taxi, he noticed that the sun at the crossroads tended to be dilatory in parting. Tunnels, bridges and new turnings all conspired to disguise the address. He greeted the janitor who, on seeing him, stood up in respect. It all seemed like yesterday. He leaped his way up the stairs as he used to do in the past. The sound of T.V. serials still came out from the set in the second-floor apartment. He remembered to watch out for the sloping stair while turning for the next landing. Panting he stood before the door. In days gone by he used to simply turn the key but now he has to ring her bell which produces a musical tune. The light of the hall is switched on. A dark bespectacled boy with curly hair and wearing cotton pyjamas with a glittering vertical line. He knew before about the children but the surprise made him hesitate. Come in please, sir! Nothing has changed. The rosy thick curtains and the "massive" dining room with its metal statue and its plush armchairs. Only one thing has changed: his footsteps no longer made a noise. She always wanted to carpet the floor with moquette. In came the other man: her husband. Dark, bespectacled and curly-haired while his cotton pyjamas with a glittering vertical line appeared under the dressing gown's opening. He was carrying a dark bespectacled little girl with curly hair. Since the moment he arrived he remained dominant. "Welcome. Your cousin will be with you in a minute." Moments, each bound to the other, elapse in silence. The little darling managed to slip away from her father's lap and mounted his back to cuddle his neck and put it backwards in order to press a kiss. Cute and naughty like her mother! The boy came in holding a tea tray which

(1) *According to the Pharaonic myth.*

154

he put down then instantly placed himself in front of his father. A replica of his father, he thought to himself. The conversation turned round politics, political parties, bureaucracy, the weather, unemployment in the U.S., the amount of foreign aid, the information revolution and the city's outer belt which will solve your problem of transport. Deep inside, he was amazed that he did not put himself within their problems.

Finally, she arrived. She drew near him and extended her hand in welcome. My late aunt really wished to see you before she died. In his mind's eye he saw his mother and her tomb. Her husband offered him a cigarette which he did not refuse in spite of the fact that he did not smoke. She stood up to pour him out a cup of tea. I know the way you like it, only two lumps and a half of sugar. Her remark stirred up an oscillating chain of inactive memories. Itched in his imagination were the prints of his fingers and lips on her body, as if no separation has ever happened. That man who now sleeps beside her, does he see his traces on her? Why then, didn't he ask her about them? About their origin? She addressed her husband with an intimacy and endearment that their talk never enjoyed while still married. He felt exiled and defeated, a man who lingered somewhere in the backstage, far from the play and the audience. The coldness of his seclusion rolled a drop of sweat to the middle of his brow. In retaliation to what he felt of envy and mysterious regret, he found himself talking profusely of Christina as his wife, although he had been cohabitating with her for years without marriage. When he added that he used to take her sweet son Rubie to ski in the weak-end he smiled inside, remembering that this was no more than a suggestion that the brat arrogantly rejected on the pretext that he had a date with his girl friend. The husband, now ill at ease, excused himself to leave for a few moments because "the kids have school tomorrow." He then drove the children in front of him after thay had greeted the guest in a routine way. He left her with him. Now, thay were alone together. They heard a door being shut. In her sitting posture, her body stretches out in a breath-taking manner. The time is now ripe to say what should have been said from the start. The body could be tied to a chair but the heart is still free. Oh how I miss you! If she goes he will run after her. That tender, glowing and distant female! In a time bygone she used to prance up from one room to another wearing her slit satin gown.She used to stand before the stove, he following her with his fingers engaged in a vigorous exploration of her body. He would put out the fire.

She used to leave the bathroom brilliant and glowing as ever, her wine-coloured body now wrapped up in a white towel, exhaling the scent of soap and steam. When she finished drying up her black locks she used to tie them backward, thus looking like a Greek goddess standing before a master sculptor.

Another cup? Let's drink everything, let's drink merriment, sadness, and longing, all at once, for, darling you are my cup and wine. Her inquiry as to his present circumstances brings him back to his reality. Of course I care about your welfare, cousin ! When he thought of her reply while looking at the new cross- stitch picture of a belly dancer stretching on the wall, he felt as if he remembered nothing except aeroplanes, buttons and white bodies with blue eyes. He felt that he had already talked and smiled much and that now he can neither talk nor smile any more as if his tongue was dry and his throat petrified. His looks trouble her, sting her, confuse her. She turns her face away from him.He draws his face near her. He exhales the redness of her lips, fresh and natural as ever. He knows the meaning of her scowling. The message that her face conveys says to him that she may seem so near and yet, in reality, she is so far. Her husband returns to dominate the scene again. He felt that he was an intruder in that place. He was lonely there. An overpowering force was driving him away. He stood up in feigned seriousness. I'm sorry for the inconvenience. Not at all, sir you're welcome. They bid him farewell while standing close to each other at the door. His hand tore away the lining of the pocket in which it settled as he dragged himself down the stairs. His feet sank in the dust of the platform. He is now swimming in a sea of premonitions. He imagines himself drowning in a waterway. He bathes in an abandoned water wheel. He sleeps in a field of cactus in the heat of the midday sun. He vanishes amidst cotton stalks and points his gun...

Cairo is no more my home!

He went abroad. The inability to adapt to the sudden change of continents disperses the cells of one's blood veins. Travel from East to West is a chase of an illusion that attempts the impossible. The day's dark compresses the metal buildings. The skyscraper's gate is computerized. The abstract painting adds the finishing touches to his loss. Rubie is stretching before the T.V. set, sipping a glass of beer. Hi! Mom's ᴊut. Your supper's in the fridge. The bottles in the bar are empty. How was the trip? How do you bury your dead in the land of the Pharaohs? Do you put the dead bodies along with clothes and food?" He started to caress the boy's soft blond hair. The boy shuddered looking at him with suspicion. "How about going to ski next week-end." "Okay!" answered the boy in a mew, while chewing the gum in his mouth, then engrossed, went back to mechanically follow an oscillating ball that runs fast on the T.V. screen.

Translated by Hazem Azmy

*IQBAL BARAKA   was brought up in Alexandria where she obtained a degree in English Literature, moved to Cairo and graduated in Arabic Literature in Cairo University. She writes novels, short stories, and articles. She has been writing for **Sabah-al-Kheir** since 1967, attaining the positon of editor, 1980. In 1993, she was appointed editor-in-chief of **Hawa,** the weekly woman magazine, first issued by the pioneering dauntless woman writer, Amina al-Said, 1954. Baraka is a woman of many talents. She has published six novels, between 1971 and 1985, and two collections of short stories. Her first five novels went into two issues each. Several of them were produced for the cinema. She has also contributed to Islamic Studies: **A Dialogue on Islamic Studies** (1987) and to Travel Literature: **A Trip to Turkey** (1989). Her activities cover lecturing on women, literature and Islam in European and American universities, membership of literary societies and women associations, being a founding member of the Egyptian Women Writers' Association and the Egyptian Womens' Cinema Society.*

*"A Cup of Nescafe" and "Abortion" appear in her latest short-story collection **A Case of Rape,** 1992.*

160

A CUP OF NESCAFÉ

Iqbal Baraka

Salah looked at the terrace filled with plant pots. From its fence hung thick green branches of a plant whose name he knew but could not remember. The name was as difficult as all the names his ear caught or those he pronounced with difficulty in this apartment. He hid behind the old tree praying God that none of the servants nor the lady of the house would notice him. But then he unleashed his heart and pra'   God to let the lady of the house appear. She will appear. She certainly will, because everyday at the same hour she walked serenely out to the terrace, threw her slim body on a bambo seat and waited for her nescafé tray.

At twelve o'clock sharp his eyes roamed about as usual looking for her. He would know that the time had come when his hand, confused, rapped on the wall and the peeled off paint fell to the ground. He would realize that she was moving in her room when a fragrant smell spread nearer and nearer until it almost stifled him. He would then turn left or right according to his position in the room and hear her greeting him. He would answer, stammering, then sink in a quiet glittering lake which is her presence.

For six whole months, Salah did his job repainting Miss Sawsan's apartment, or as he used to pronounce it Mazmazel Sawsan as he heard it from one of the servants. For six whole months he saw her kind face, studied the dimples on her cheeks, enjoyed her captivating husky voice and watched from afar while she moved lightly like a butterfly.

It did not start like this. On the contrary, the chore of repainting the apartment seemed difficult and depressing with her glaring at him discontentedly asking him when he would finish working. She moved nervously looking at the furniture heaped up on the terrace keeping her from enoying it. Not once did she smile at him. Instead, she ignored his presence completely moving here and there as though she were all alone in the apartment, with no one persuing her with his eyes and following her footsteps while he was near the roof pretending to be busy painting. The roof needed four coats of paint not because it was old and had not been repainted for over a quarter of a century but also because Salah discovered that his position up high gave him a golden opportunity to know what was happening in the apartment. Most of the servants were on vacation or stayed in the house for a few hours then disappeared. Only she suddenly appeared at midday then hid in her room till the afternoon. When he finished his work he called one of the servants in a loud voice. Either that man appeared or she did, talked to him briefly and saw him to the door. She was not interested in the colour of the paint or whether he was doing his work well. She was interested only in his finishing this unpleasant chore as quickly as possible and that order and splendour would return to the house.

More than once she expressed her regret because she had started this foolish project.

Once she said: "I made a mistake when I decided to stay in my father's house, the house where I was born, grew up, married once then divorced."

He remembers one time after she had become used to

him and had begun to converse with him, she admitted that she was heedless and stupid. She was fed up with the monotony of her life. She cursed the day she was born to a rich father who had only her then left her when she was fifteen years old.

Exactly five years later her mother died. The family assailed the luxurious apartment pretending to be distressed but their eyes searched for their right to the inheritance. The lawyer told them that the father, while alive, had sold all his possessions to his daughter and registered the deal at the notary public. Some filed suits while others quietly withdrew but both parties did not knock at her door a second time. They were furious and sad. So in spite of a large family she was alone.

Alone within the walls of a vast apartment with the walls high and far apart, the doors outmoded and the furniture sumptuous but old, very old.

Every piece in this salon is worth a fortune and I sit here like a watchman with no worry except to guard this enormous wealth!

Imagine! I am living in a museum, about to become an old objet d'art myself!

He never answered her, just looked at her in wonder. A woman to whom fate has given everything, given generously until she was drowned in abundance - family tree, beauty, youth, culture, wealth. What then did she lack?

At first, when they exchanged displeased looks he used to begrudge her and all her class. They had it all while he, his family and his neighbours got the crumbs. He does not know why he refused to complete his education and ran away from school when he was in the third preparatory class. Was it hard luck or the curse of fate? Their neighbour's son, Mostafa, was an orphan and poorer than him but he used to spend all night until dawn intent on his books. Just one week ago he received his degree in medicine and the whole neighbourhood celebrated his graduation, while he, Salah, barely reads. All the years he spent in school did not make him like books, did not make him fond of letters. When he counts the proceeds of what he read during all those years he does not remember except a few passages of the Koran and some simple facts about plants and animals any pupil in a primary school knows.

Yet she talked to him as if he were one of the social scientists. After one month an odd relationship grew between them. He completed repainting the terrace and put the drawing-room furniture back in place to please her so she invited him to have a cup of nescafé with her. He felt no taste whatsoever in that drink and when she invited him again the next day he boldly asked for a glass of tea to improve his mood and increase his enjoyment of the moment.

Every day she sat in the drawing-room watching him paint the dining room walls, the lobby and the other small drawing-room. All the rooms led to each other without doors as if the inhabitants of the apartment kept no secrets in their hearts.

He, too, wanted to disclose his secrets to her but something tied his tongue, something stuck in his throat and prevented him from speaking. He became a listener, saying nothing.He would comment in a word or a phrase but he did not talk, did not elaborate as she did.

She offered him a cigarette and they discovered that they smoked the same brand. They became closer. She is almost his age, maybe a year or two younger but of the same generation. An unseen ray radiated from her eyes and engulfed him in a wave of warmth and security. He felt relaxed when she gazed at him, delighted at the sound of her voice when she laughed. He began to miss her.

Once she went out to see the lawyer. She was gone for just one hour but for him it was a whole long depressing day!

She came back full of cheerfulness and vitality. She insisted that they have lunch together. Having lunch together every day became a habit. She ate with relish and told him that she was gaining weight. For years nobody shared her lunch. She sat alone everyday at a full table and could not look at it. She swallowed a few morsels against her will as though something was obstructing her throat.

With him she eats with relish, laughs from the bottom of her heart at anything that crosses her mind. She would tell a joke and burst out laughing without waiting for his reaction.

One day she confessed to him that she had come to love life. Something changed her outlook. People are not what she thought they were. Some are kind and wish her well. They covet nothing.

She went out another time and stayed out for two hours then came back smiling, dreaming. She gave him an inscrutable look then disappeared in her room the rest of the day.

He felt restless. He wanted to be sure she was all right but shyness prevented his asking. Anyway, just being in the apartment filled him with a captivating brightness. The sound of her movements in her room filled him with a mysterious rapture. Suffice it that she is in the same place.

This is better than hiding where he knew not.

But she kept going out, spending most of the day out, returning only a few minutes before he finished working as if she set her watch at the time he left the apartment. She avoided his glances and spoke to him briefly but she frowned no more: the fascinating smile never left her nor did the look full of gratitude.

Her new condition saddened him. Tormented, he asked himself, "Has he done anything wrong? Has he uttered a word or made a move driving her to banish him from her paradise?"

She certainly is no more what she was. She is not even in the same state as she was when he saw her the day he started his work in her apartment.

She is now a third creature.

Thoughts clashed in his brain. When he went home and sat with his parents and his brothers he saw no one and heard none but her voice. She sat with him, among them, talking, laughing, drinking her nescafé as if she belonged. He decided to ask her, but how to begin?

He did not dare confide in his brother, the plumber, though they were close friends. His brother would laugh and make fun of him and disgrace him in front of the gang.

He will defend himself. He does not love her. It is impossible for him to fall in love with the like of her. The difference between them is vast. She does not belong in his world nor does he in hers. He understands it perfectly and the evidence is the loud music that used to emanate from her room when she took refuge in it all day. Tasteless, colourless music, nevertheless she loved it. She turned on the same record tens of times while a headache tore him apart.

No he cannot love such a woman!

She wore her fanciest clothes to go out and he used to eye her in amazement. She looked wonderful, like movie stars in foreign films but he cannot possibly walk in the streets beside a woman dressed that way: out of the question!

She also talks a great deal about books. She says that her only recreation in life is reading.

He does not read the daily newspapers and the news broadcast bores him while she listens to it attentively as if what happens in Ethiopia or Nigeria is her personal affair. What he, Salah, feels for her is something other than love.

Thus he clarified the matter to himself because he was not used to deceive himself. His feelings for Bahiga, the neighbours's daughter, move every muscle in his body, make him contemplate marriage and children.

As for Mazmazel Sawsan he does not want to touch her. She is a work of art the way she is, only she should not leave her place. He feels a dumb jealousy when she is not where he can see her.

Now that he has turned her old apartment with the depressing walls, flaky doors and dangling windows into a wide place filled with joy and light, now that he has done his duty as best he could, he wants Miss Sawsan to sit there in her comfortable bamboo seat sipping her nescafé quietly, watching the beautiful scenery viewed from the terrace and to stay put!

Distressed, he sighs as he watches her doing exactly what he had hoped to see her doing. Here, she is seated in her favoured place, but he is no more part of the scene. He is here, below the building, behind an old tree hoping no one would discover his presence!

Translated by Nadia El-Kholi

ABORTION

She touches her belly, presses her fingers on the accumulated fat, is it an illusion or a fact? Is she pregnant? After more than ten physicians assured her that she was barren? After her first and second husbands divorced her and the third too was contemplating divorce?

But she has the evidence. For the first time the evidence is real, for the first time it is not a lie or a pretence. The first time it happened she was young, twenty- five years old, when one of the aunts advised her to resort to the ruse of faking pregnancy. The aunt acted out all the symptoms before her and explained the matter in detail. The reason was that her husband was contemplating divorce and they wanted to postpone the calamity for a few months, after which God may save her and she would actually conceive. She was sure that she would conceive, deliver, feed and bring up a child like all women. Why shouldn't she be like them? What is the difference between her and her cousin Haneya who has given birth to five children since she got married: three boys and two girls, in just eight years while she had none, not one baby!

She yielded to her aunt and did what she advised her to do and pretended that she was pregnant. A month passed, then two, then four and the doubt started to seep into her husband's heart and his family's hearts. When the nine months passed her husband divorced her! He told her brothers that he was not angry because she did not deliver as he was because she deceived him and he could not live under the same roof with a woman he could not trust.

The second time Zakeya did not lie or act or pretend. The truth was apparent to everyone.

One year after she married her widower neighbour the symptoms of pregnancy were manifested. She was nauseated by food, she hated the smell of her husband and would not have him approach her for weeks, then her belly swelled and swelled and her guts moved.

She was the only one who did not believe that she was pregnant because she felt no maternal yearning deep down. At last she overcame her fears and went to a gynaecologist. After examining her thoroughly he confronted her with the sad news.

False Pregnancy!

She left the operating room with her head bent and a feeling of shame. Who is to believe in her innocence. This is her second conviction! Now is the second time she is convicted of lying. Her husband did not comment for he had sons and daughters but his treatment began to change. He pampered her no more nor did he express any feelings for her. He did not give any hope or assure her that medicine progresses and scientists invent new drugs every day, that no obstacle stands in the way of science.

Her feelings for her husband and his children changed. She started to grumble and complain and refused to continue playing the role of servant and governess. She had loved the children and felt compassion for them and imagined herself their mother who had died early while delivering the third child. She embraced the youngest son who had not seen his mother and acted as though she was his mother. But her feelings for him too changed when her belly swelled and the hope grew that she would have her

170

own son, her flesh and blood, feeding on her blood, growing inside her, sucking her milk: a son who resembles her, inherits her characteristics and clings to her. When she carried her husband's son and looked in the mirror she saw the great difference between his features and hers: he does not even resemble his father; he is a carbon copy of his mother. He reminds her of the woman her husband loved and cherished and who gave him three children. Jealousy kindled in her heart and grief squeezed her and she felt a deadly loneliness. She came to this world and will depart without leaving a trace! She felt a mortal sadness whenever the family gathered and she saw her sisters-in-law carrying their infants, their bellies full and a child or two clinging to their tails. A picture she longed for for a long time but in vain. How often she spent the night with her eyes wet with tears! How often she tossed and turned in her bed asking God humbly and submissively, "Why did you deprive me of this honour? What shall I do? What then is my role in life?"

The answer came to her in the way the women in the family acted. If they gave birthday parties for their children they ignored her, did not invite her. If labour pains suddenly attacked one of them, they gathered together and went to her behind her back as if her presence would hamper the delivery. If the subject of children was brought up and the mothers voiced their complaints, she noticed that some overdid it in expressing their annoyance and vexation with the kids while others clammed up and neither talked nor commented, just watched her reaction stealthily.

Some thoughtless phrases uttered by her husband and his eldest sister, even by her own sister, turned her life into hell but the worst hell was on Mother's Day. At first her husband used to buy gifts and give them to his children to present to her and kiss her. Gradually his enthusiasm waned and he ignored the day completely and so did his children. She too pretended that the day did not exist but the songs on the radio and the television and the advertisments for consumer's products, the shop signs and the pictures on magazine covers pointed at her a condemning finger:

"You are not a mother and you will never be!"

She withdrew within herself ruminating her pains. Her husband felt exasperated and one day, grasping the opportunity of her mother's illness and her being with her all the time, sent her her divorce papers. The intervention of her family was to no avail. She felt that he wanted her no more!

She revealed the reason. His older daughter had grown up and was capable of taking care of him and her brothers. They did not need a stepmother who never experienced motherhood and who was not willing to play the role of a servant.

Her parents submitted to the inevitable and, though tormented, said nothing. She went back home carrying a suitcase with her clothes and a few belongings. She withdrew to a corner of the house and watched her younger sister busy studying, dreaming of the day she would go to work while she, Zakeya, had no qualification whatsoever and could barely read. She envied her.

Days passed and the abyss between her and her family widened. Her father begrudged her what he spent on her and gave her the bare necessities only. Her mother wanted her to take over all the household chores because she was old and her body was fraught with countless ailments. Her sister looked down on her and snatched the magazines from her because she did not understand what was in them. She avoided sitting with her because she could not concur with her and could not stoop to her level of thinking.

At last relief came! A man double her age knocked on their door asking for her hand in marriage. She loved him at first sight and decided to dedicate herself to him. Because her family was keen on getting rid of her the marriage took place in a few days and she went to live in his home.

She felt that life was compensating her for all that past, when she found the man living in luxury. He was a merchant, still managing his shop in Al Hussein. His wife had died two years before and his children had married and gone away. He wanted nothing from her except being his companion, to alleviate by talking with her some of his worries. There were even those who took care of the household. She was only to share his happiness and his distress.

· She gave herself completely to her new life. She made use of her past experience, rectified her defects and groomed herself to avoid her mistakes. Even her sons-in-law's harassments and their provocative phrases and silly innuendos did not bother her. In her eyes the world changed and for the first time in her life she felt happy and had a goal to achieve, her new husband's comfort and happiness, sharing with him the burdens of living. She started to frequent the drapery shop he owned and to add a touch here and there. Abdel Raouf, her husband, was glad of her enthusiasm. He carried out her requests and complimented her on her good taste. Their relationship began to strengthen and her authority to widen. She found someone asking for her advice, heeding her opinions and carrying them out. Even his children felt safe with her, gathered around her and treated her like a mother. They were assured of her good intentions. They relaxed in the knowledge that she was barren and it made them happy to be certain of it as she had married twice, two men, one of whom was with children, yet she did not give birth. So she was harmless.

Suddenly happiness turned to distress and the sun was about to set in her sky forever.

She discovered that she was pregnant!

Her tears flowed hot and abundant whenever she entered the bathroom looking for an evidence to refute her fantasy and found none. Her belly swelled, so did her breasts, her stomach was upset and the dizziness never left her head. Her pallor increased while her conversation decreased. She pretended to be asleep hiding her head under the pillow and her whole body wrapped up in the blanket as though she had committed a sin.

She beseeched the sky to belie her fears, to spare her the agony of a third experiment. She cried in torment, bent and bowed tens of times every day imploring God in her prayers not to expose her, not to make a spectacle of her for the third time, not to send her back to her family's home where she was not wanted, not to deprive her of the kind man Abdel Raouf who never once hurt her.

What will Abdel Raouf say now that he is almost sixty? What will his sons say? They are already haggling about the inheritance and cannot bear to be patient until their father dies.

Doubts overwhelm her. Is it real pregnancy or a false pregnancy?

All the symptoms are different this time. Something tells her that an embryo is forming in her guts: a beautiful

174

baby who resembles her, inherits her characteristics, clings to her and feeds on her milk.

Her heartbeats quicken. She knows it is coming. Her sixth sense does not lie. The symptoms of maternity are apparent. She cries at the least provocation, her personal dreams retreat. She longs for the coming baby. In her grip she feels its smooth fragile hand, her nipples shiver at the touch of its lotus blossom lips!

She loves the world; she loves life, she wishes everybody well. She bestows her forgiveness on everyone that harmed her or called her names or hurt her feelings. She is not angry with anybody or embittered against anybody. She loves them all especially Abdel Raouf, her child's father who granted her happiness. But no! The baby's arrival will disturb her life. Maybe Abdel Raouf will have his doubts. His children will revolt, they will not surrender. They will persuade him to divorce her and plant the seeds of mistrust towards her in his heart. She has been through it all before! She swears that she has done nothing at all. never sought this pregnancy.

Abdel Raouf holds her shoulders, encircles her in his arms and asks her tenderly:

"Does a woman cry on the happiest day of her life?"

She looks at him, dazed and asks sobbing, "Do you believe that it is a real pregnancy?"

He answers boastfully, "Why not? Am I not a virile man?"

In tears she implores him :

"But... I mean... you know..."

He says with confidence and deep faith :

"It is God's will 'He says Be and it is!' "

Overwhelming joy engulfs her. She kisses his hands and face saying :

"My heart tells me it is real pregnancy."

"So be it. Whether it is a boy or a girl, it is mine and I shall protect it with all my being."

"And your sons?"

"What about my sons? I shall leave them what is more than enough and I shall make provisions for your son as well. I shall not have them tear him to pieces. In my will I shall specify everything in my will."

She could not believe her eyes. It is impossible that life can be so wonderful. Is this a man or an angel God sent her to make up for all the deprivation and humiliation? Is he really flesh and blood?

Before she drowned in a flood of her emotions she felt a coolness between her thighs. Then haemorrhage started!

After the operation the doctor says :

"The lady was actually pregnant but strong emotions like overwhelming joy or deep grief often cause a miscarriage."

Translated by Nadia El-Kholi

SEKINA FOUAD   is a journalist and a creative writer. She is ex-editor-in-chief of the **Radio and Television Maga-zine** *and author of eight short-story collections and a novella.*

A File of a Love Lawsuit *(Malaf Qadiyat Hob),* **9 Nile Street** *(9 Sharia al-Nil);* **Circuits of Love and Ter-ror**   *(Dawa'r al- Hob wa al-Ro'b) are the titles of three of her short-story collections. Fouad achieved her greatest success with the novella:* **The Night that Fatma was Arrested.** *It is the story of a young woman who almost single-handed resists corruption. The novella was adapted for the cinema and television and won the author the cinema-story prize for 1985. The short-story collection :* **Taming Man (Tarweed al-Ragol)** *brought her unprecedented notoriety and male rebuke. Fouad is a member of the Writers' Union, the Supreme Press Council and ex-member of the Shoura Council (Second House of Parliament). Some of her stories have been translated into English, French, German and Dutch.*

"She Will Come" and "The Pasha's Beard" appear in **9 Nile Street** *and* **Nisf al-Dunya** *magazine, 1992.*

178

SHE WILL COME

Sekina Fouad

Her small town was inhabited by travelling cars. The whole town consisted of the only large street through which cars drove from Port Said to Ismailiya and Cairo, or vice versa.

On either side of the road, there was everything needed for the comfort of travellers and day and night drivers. There were the beverages, tea and coffee and molasses-tobacco and al-buri[1]. At night, all colours of smoke spiralled upward. They put out the lights and left dim lanterns that did not reveal those who had come to snatch a smoke. In the day time, booths and carts of kebab and membar[2] gleamed, and the barbecue smoke filled the air. Everywhere , there were so many cafés and sandwich booths. Peddling comfort is an art, and everyone can make money. The magazines she liked and the stories she had heard from thousands of passing travellers had shown her how vast the world was and how small her town. Nevertheless she never tired of talking of its past glory when it was a main train station on the route from Cairo to Gaza and Palestine. Her town had held the two banks and embraced the Canal in between. She and her mother, father, brother and grandmother lived on the East Bank. Then the train, whose rails her mother had warned her not to cross, stopped running.

---

(1) *A kind of water pipe.*
(2) *A kind of sausage.*

When it stood parked, she lived in it with her dolls, sat in the driver's seat and blew the whistle. Then the ravens started to crow and the sea gulls flew away from the Canal. She warned her againl the bands of robbers who lived in the train, and later she heard of the bands of robbers who had robbed Gaza and reached the east part of her city. Her mother took her and fled at night, hiding her from death in the mattress cover of one of their old beds, tying it up with a rope. Through a hole in it she had put out her hand to feel what was happening around her and inspect the features of the faces that crowded the bottom of the boat.

All the travellers on the high road knew her. All sorts of things dangled inside and outside of her small booth, she cried the wares she knew and, at times, the wares she did not know. The important thing was that she cried her wares and waited.

She knew that when the right time came, she would come. There was a time for everything, and the universe had its secret and magic—and silence was meaningful. All God's creatures had a language of their own. In the Canal water, she met the talkers and the silent ones, who told her stories of time, travellers and absentees. Water over her body gurgled as she went to a distant spring, and went down and up in the water and came out like a female jinni with henna coloured skin and hair whose reflection the sunshine lit up with skeins of gold, and whose ever-blushing cheeks made the girls bet that they were coloured with pink taffeta dye. So she moistened the white handkerchief with her saliva and rubbed her cheeks till they almost peeled. She spread the handkerchief out and its whiteness fluttered without a single red spot. She then chased the girl who had slandered her to teach her, and anyone else who dared slander her, a lesson.

Her hand and tongue struck at everything. The world was small and she was intolerant of it. When she felt cramped she fled to one of two things : either she wrote a letter to her ustathah[1] or to her secret transmitter - the huge shells that she had brought with her from the other bank, her old home in Qantara East. She lifted the shells to her lips, breathed her wishes, and the wind brought back the echo, in which she heard the words that were all she wanted to hear.

When she lost her people in the war and arrived on one of those small boats which glided furtively across the Canal at night, carrying a medley of human beings, the living, the wounded and the dead, she slid her small hand in the dark looking for the features of her father or brother. In the hospital, she continued to search for a face she knew. She searched through all the wards and handed people things and gave them to drink until she became a daughter to all. Disaster, war and death coursed through her veins and became her flesh and blood and her heritage.

He laughed heartily when she swore that she had property. He raised his head from under the car whose wheels he was fixing and looked long at the owner of property, to make sure that he was not mistaken, and she hid the holes in her dress which were very neatly mended. She shook off her slipper, and removed the dust on the nail-polish on her toes. She adjusted her silk head-scarf that was made of old Indian silk embroidered with gold threads, that she had found in the remnants of her mother's old clothing and looked at him defiantly.

---

(1) A female intellectual, teacher or writer.

From his place he laughed louder, as he still lay on his back with a large iron spanner in his hand, with which he threatened her and tickled her feet that stood next to his head. He did not tell her that she had Solomon's treasures under her "cheap cotton" dress and apart from this buried treasure, she had nothing. He took a handful of sand and threw it at her face.

Unlike her usual self, she turned the joke into a tragedy, and swore that she had vast property. Her father and brother had paid their flesh, blood and bones for her share of property, so as to leave her an inheritance, and she would poke her fingers into the eyes of whoever did not believe her.

Since she had brought up the subject of her father, no one could laugh. He left everything behind him, got up, dusted his clothes and walked by her side on the bank of the Canal.

Silence reigned for only a few moments, then it was followed by the rumbling of the huge wheels on the road. Then with her acumen she started to bet, for as she had watched and watched, she had learnt the sounds, and at times, even the numbers of the cars. It was enough for her to hear the sound of a car in the middle of the night or in the crowd of the daytime to know the model and load of the car and whether it was a private car or a truck.

She waited for the car that would come and take her to her distant dream in the big city, with great people – the big world.

She nurtured a dream of something bigger than the small world here. She felt cramped by the limited areas and distances of her town which hung on the edges of a car

182

going far out in the world. She heard voices that made the world bigger and bigger – the pages of magazines, the stories of thousands of travellers.

She had been clever at school but she had dropped out a few days before the end of the intermediate stage. She had continued her education with raised expectations, and had dropped out before the end of the secondary school. Along with the land, the robbers had stolen the certificate that she had dreamt would take her to a bigger world. So what? What she knew was enough. She was qualified without a certificate.

She had tired of working day and night, embroidering head scarves decorated with coloured flowers that women would wear. She cursed the women in the world, and decided to chop off their heads rather than spend her life embroidering flowers. Needlewok tired and bored her. She changed her occupation and sold newspapers. She used to keep a copy of each paper for herself and, at the end of the day, she would read it, and through its words and pictures, she would travel to a new world.

She loved everything that the Ustatha wrote and learnt by heart her answers to problems. Her world filled her with hope, strength and confidence. She heard her on the radio and watched her on television and loved her more and more. She now understood what her grandmother had meant when she used to say: "What is lost here is compensated there." As soon as she heard the Ustatha's voice she saw her mother's open arms and her father resurrected to take her hand to cross the road. She threatened Moss'ad that with the *Ustathah* she could do without him. Whenever she was angry with him or with her mother, she would pack her belongings and take out "the Ustatha's" address, which she had cut out of the *Modern*

Woman magazine and put it with her picture in her purse, along with a faded picture of her father, her picture with her brother and her mother in the background, with only the tip showing as she was shy of the camera.

Were it not for her mother's severe illness and her love for Moss'ad, whom she loved so much that it was impossible to leave him, she would have realized the dream she nurtured during the long nights. She would have jumped onto a big truck, alongside a kind trustworthy old driver – for boldness and adventure were needed even in difficult circumstances – and asked the way to the *Ustathah* . She would have gone to her and lived with her as a daughter, pupil, secretary or maid. What mattered was that she would be sheltered by her wisdom and love, and become part of her, learning from her some of the wisdom of the world, that her words overflowed with.

In the small booth that she had set up with her life's savings and by selling her mother's only bracelet, together with the bridal money Moss'ad had paid her, she put everything that she had learnt that the traveller might need. Her teasing, her sauciness and her endless chatter about what had happened, and what hadn't and what would happen, lent a special flavour to her soft drinks and sandwiches, which at times were not so fresh.

Thanks to God who divided all wealth, she never lacked customers. She hung a blue bead and an evil eye charm on the booth and stuck on the glass a label with a sentence that a taxi driver had brought and which was like the one stuck on the back of his car: "Before you envy me, look at what has been spent on me".[1] She burnt incense when she heard the Friday call to prayer, and pricked a

(1) A specimen of slogans that taxi or truck drivers stick to the back of their vehicles

184

paper doll with holes to protect her "from the evil of the envious if he envieth." [1] She put up a big straw awning and got three chairs, which later became fifteen. When the chairs were all occupied, the cars opened their doors and their seats became café seats, while just a few yards away there were empty seats without a single customer. When ever she saw someone staring at her stand or admiring her success, she said under her breath "God is great." [2] and put her palm out spreading the five fingers. [3]

The Municipality civil servants accused her of using her booth license to open a café, and she referred to the *Ustathah* . When some people came to ask for protection money from her profits, she referred to the *Ustathah*.

Moss'ad came and told her things that she did not like: the owners of shops and booths were wondering why travellers chose to stop and park at her café, and that some travellers had made a habit of passing that way for her sake. As usual, when someone hurt her, she made scathing comments about him and all his forefathers, and as usual, she took off her engagement ring and flung it away, releasing him from his engagement since he was so easily swayed by gossip. Mentally, she cursed the day that had made her love him so much. She spoke of the big wide world, mentioned the *Ustathah* and threatened.

When her mother entered hospital and they neglected her, she referred to the *Ustathah* and threatened to report this to her.

When her mother died, she mourned and wailed her death and the world that was empty without her, but her grief was alleviated and the world seemed to still contain

---

(1) *A Koranic text.*
(2) *In Arabic : "Allaho Akbar," an invocation*
(3) *A gesture believed to keep away the evil eye.*

promise, when she remembered that the *Ustathah* was still there.

When her friend who knew her innermost thought came and whispered to her, at first she pushed her away before listening to her. She cursed her lack of understanding for that day was a feast and both ways of the road were full. The cars were standing one behind the other, hardly separated from one another by time or space and as usual all the cars stopped at her café, which was an essential part of the trip. The feast tip added to the usual tips filled her money box to the brim. She was busy answering questions, handing out drinks to some and hitting and pushing away others who claimed, as they took or passed things on, that their hands had lost their way.

Her friend in her loudest voice repeated :

"The *Ustathah* or someone who is the split image of her is in a car on the road." She pointed to a small black car that stood on the other side.

Her eyes no longer saw the crowd, nor did she near the noise. They were replaced by a vacant silence in which she only saw the black car from afar. Her eyes were glued to the car trying to make out the figures moving inside the car.

"If you are lying you will regret the day in which your mother begot you."

She did not wait for the reply. She left the booth and the crowd and leapt to cross the road, in front of a truck whose driver had pressed the accelerator at full speed and fallen asleep. She took a step back and was almost crushed by the wheels, but her childhood experience had given her a flexibility with which she avoided the crazy wheels. She paid no heed to the gasps and screams, or the eyes that were covered with hands to avoid the sight of death.

186

She once more asked her friend to take over until she returned and questioned her with her eyes and gestures. For the noise of the cars did not allow anyone to hear. She pointed to the distant black car and her friend nodded swearing by her father's soul that she had seen a face that resembled her and...

She heard nothing of what she said. Her assurances had been enough for her. She started jumping and dodging the wheels of the cars to cross to the other side, where the black car stood.

In spite of her usual impetuousity, she did not have the courage to go straight to the car. She took her time to think of a way to advance.

She took one step forward politely and in a low voice full of love and respect, advanced towards the car. She stopped, then drew back.

Inside the car was a big man. He had no head for his neck bumped into the ceiling of the car. He was swimming in perspiration, anger and the smoke of his cigarette. He was turning left and right, looking for something. What she saw did not inspire her to ask questions.

She called her friend, gesturing to complement the dialogue that was impossible because of the noise of the cars and pointing to the car, asking if this were the one. It was impossible to communicate through the lines of cars. She turned waiting for an opportunity to cross and repeated the question. As she looked round, she was thinking of the picture she loved, that had reached her from the *Ustathah*. It was signed by her and contained her best wishes for success, expressing her confidence and pride in her. Since that day she had tried to be worthy of confidence and pride. She had framed the picture and hung it at the front of the booth. Her heart beat as she thought that the picture would become flesh and blood. She thought nostalgically of her mother and the sister that she would have liked to have so that she would not be alone in the world, and she longed too for her dead father.

She would tell the *Ustathah* that she was all the family that she had left and all her loved ones.

Her joy seemed to have affected her judgement: in spite of the fact that she had the same features, the lady who stood in front of her was not so tall, was shorter, thinner and weaker and her hair too seemed thinner. What is more, she looked very tired and her eyes showed exhaustion, as if she had not slept for a month and was persistently looking for something, for which she had gone up the first few steps of the small hotel, of which only one storey had been completed.

The *Ustathah* was looking left and right and it seemed that she had found no answer to her question. She rushed towards her and called her by her name. The lady smiled and nodded. That meant that she was the *Ustathah*.

A difference in weight, hair or strength did not matter. The important thing was that it was she. The lady asked her and she hoped that she, alone in the world, would have the answer to her question.

In a tired and faltering voice, keeping an eye on the black car, the lady asked :

'Where's the toilet?"

She was astonished, and then she was surprised at herself. Was it because she was the *Ustathah* she would not need a toilet. She jumped eagerly and cried out :

"A toilet... of course there's a toilet... and a bed-room.. and the whole hotel." She called the solitary employee who did all the odd jobs at the hotel – public relations, cleaning, cooking or seeing to the request of any of the occupants of the only five rooms, which were seldom occupied, for people came there only to travel.

The hotel worker whispered: "You kno   that it's not finished and the guests use the public toilets." She asked for the key to the special room that had a private toilet. She snatched the key from his pocket before he handed it to her.

He opened his sleepy eyes to find out what had happened to her. She had never shown an interest before. Before he had gathered his wits and opened his mouth to ask, she had run to the narrow corridor that led to the poor but private suite. She opened the door and put on the light. She took a quick look at the toilet and felt ashamed but she made way for the lady.

She was sorely distressed to see the *Ustathah* leaning on the wall with one arm, while with the other hand she was mopping her brow. She was as pale as the green and yellow lemons which long ago used to grow on the trees in the gardens of her town.

In a trembling voice the *Ustathah* asked if there were any headache tablets, for she felt as though a thousand hammers were pounding at her head.

"Ah!" said the *Ustathah* as if she were uttering her last breath.

She said to her: "Tablets for headaches can be found not far off, but I shall get them for you in a wink." The *Ustathah* leaned on her to cross the threshold. She supported her and shut the door behind her. She ran to the nearest booth, the small pharmacy, brought a strip of tablets for headaches and returned to the lady.

In the corridor, she heard deep sighs from behind the door. She was scared, she rushed, banged on the door and opened it. Her *Ustathah* was leaning on the wall and vomiting. She supported her and helped her to sit down on a small bath stool.

The *Ustathah* was shivering as she stretched out her hands for the tablets. She gave them to her and filled a glass, that she found on the bathroom shelf, with water and steadied her trembling hands so that she could put the tablets in her mouth.

She helped her clean her dress in front, wet a handkerchief, wiped her face and supported her. The lady submissively stood up. She pushed the stool near the wall so that she could lean her head against it and rest. Her breathing became more regular her shivering subsided, she resigned herself and shut her eyes.

She did not know whether it was appropriate or inappropriate to tell the *Ustathah* that she had waited a long time for such a fortunate opportunity, but she said it, then felt ashamed and blamed herself because of the word "fortunate" for it was inappropriate to such a situation. She was then ashamed that she had uttered a word, for it seemed that the teacher had fallen asleep.

The *Ustathah* raised her head and asked: "What's the time now?"

She shivered as she heard the *Ustathah's* voice return to normal, just as normal as she used to hear it on radio and television. She looked closely at her watch, the hands were blurred and then faded away. Time should come to a stop, the hands of watches should stop for, at last, here was the opportunity to talk to her. She opened her mouth trying to find an appropriate way to start the conversation, but the *Ustathah* spoke before her: "It seems that it's very late, but I can't thank you enough."

190

The words surged to her lips so that she would not lose this precious opportunity that she had waited for, and she said to the *Ustathah* "I was waiting for you. I wanted to tell you..."

Suddenly, the *Ustathah* became disturbed again as the sound of footsteps could be heard approaching in the long corridor. Her hands started shivering again, she raised her hand to mop her brow and opened her bag quickly looking for something. She took a net in which she gathered her light ruffled hair, that was wet with perspiration, and then donned sun glasses which hid half her thin face, but she could not hide her swirling inner emotions.

The man who was in the car drew near, in a fit of anger and irritation. He said angrily that it was late and hot and irritating and spoke of the road, the wait, boredom, flies and the important matters that had l(r) delayed. He pointed out that a second could make a difference.

The *Ustathah* burst out saying :

"Things have become unbearable, and running after interests and opportunities even more so. Migraine used to recur once a year, then once a month, then once a day, and now every hour."

The lady's eyes met the eyes of the girl that was staring at her. She stopped speaking, smiled, pulled her elegant blouse and patted her hair.

The girl remembered the picture of her *Ustathah* on television– now she was the split image.

The clash continued without words, but as they walked to the car, their feet kicked up the dust as if they were engaged in a war with dust.

The man sat in the driver's seat and slammed the door behind him. The *Ustathah* sat on the seat next to him and countered by slamming the door even more loudly– then remembered something.

Before the engine could start, the *Ustathah* quickly opened the window and turned to look for the girl who was behind her. She found her still standing where she was. She said:

"I'm sorry. Time is always short but did you need anything?"

The girl's hand tried to touch the *Ustathah's* shoulder, but only reached the hot black iron as the car was moving. She patted it and asked the *Ustathah* :

"Do you need anything?"

Translated by Nayla Naguib

THE PASHA'S BEARD[1]

Once upon a time, a little girl was hopping by the edge of the harbour pier, talking with the birds, and hiding in the nooks of the absinthe tree. She used to go to them early in the morning on her way to school and wait for the ships passing through the harbour and emerging from the hideouts of the dawn fog. She would choose her very own ship that would leave to the end of the world and never return. The land of God is for all mankind. Until the time of departure, she plays hide and seek with the birds. Whenever they come close to one hideout of hers under a blossom of that absinthe tree– her grandfather's beard– she would run away to another blossom and hide. Her squeals of excitement would make the birds even more frisky and excited, for they would come back to chase her and she would once again hide, in the innermost palace. She wants to go closer to the warmth of her grandfather's bosom, her grandfather whom she loves so much– she loves him more than all the honeybars, the pieces of Turkish delight, or the pressed dates, she could barely get. For such things, she would save a little out of her scanty allowance. She cared about nothing in this world around her except his laugh, his compassion, and his love. Her father and mother won't stop fighting and threatening to split the house in two. Then she would flee to his bosom, his love, the gentle touch of his hand and his kind eyes, seeking shelter.

---

[1] The Arabic name of the absinthe tree – a tree of the wormwood species with white–yellowish blossoms resembling an old man's beard.

One day of the first year of school, she had decided to go to him after the last lesson and never return to the hell of her mother and father's fighting.

It was a day of her life that was never to be forgotten. In the morning, her teacher had given her a merciless beating and had humiliated her. She kept insulting her in front of her classmates, saying :

"So it has come to this – a little squirt of a girl making fun of her teacher."

The burning pain of the beating, the humiliation, and the cruelty are still carved on her palms by the sharp edges of the ruler. The fire in her hands still burns whenever she remembers the fire of her teacher's wrath because of that picture she brought her. The teacher had asked the pupils to bring over photos to fill personal data forms. When her turn came, she presented her teacher with a drawing of a 'Tom Thumb,' swearing that he was her or she was he.

The battle began with a burning slap on the face when her teacher asked her about that pigmy drawn in the picture, and she replied with what she had memorized of the tale of that tiny, tiny girl.

"My dear teacher, I may be small now, perhaps not bigger than a knuckle of the little thumb of your pretty hand, but my dreams are great indeed. With my knowledge and my work, I shall widen this needle's hole where I live and make it a beautiful home with windows that allow the sun in. I'll make the dreams wake up and walk about in this world."

Her face was plastered to the wall, for as punishment she spent the school day gazing at it, her back to the world.

194

With her mouth closed, she told her teacher all that she was never allowed to utter :

"My teacher, ever since I learned my letters and learned how to read them in lines, I have been making out of them my father and my mother and all those whom I loved but never could find - except for my grandfather. For him I save my allowance , even if it is a piece of candy we share together. And he saves for me a love that is bigger than the sea of our little town. He was the one to assure me that I was my father's and mother's daughter, the one to tell me about the police report of finding a female newborn, one month old, who had my eyes and the exact details of my face, sleeping on the threshold of the white mosque, with high walls and a tall minaret, hung by a crescent moon up in the sky.

Patting my head, grandfather laughed and said :

"It happened. It actually happened. During one of their loud fits of insane anger, they decided that each one was to take back what he or she had given to the other. They did not know what to do with you. After they agreed to split you in two halves for each one to take his share, they backed down and gave up the idea, deciding to return you to the house of God." "Oh," I screamed out of the pain in my soul. My grandfather hugged me and asked :

"What's the matter Tom Thumb?"

This has become my name, for I have chosen for myself a name and a shape other than what both have participated in shaping. I wanted to cover up as much as my puny capacity could allow – as puny as I myself was – to cover up the only thing left in common between us. So I cut up and glued in all my notebooks a drawing that I found in an old fairytale book. It was one of the books I used to sneak to under the enchanted roofs filled with hideouts and bookcases in that ancient wooden house which both have abandoned so that each one might go to a new home.

With my face to the wall, I recalled the stream of Tom Thumb's life, pushing the time on – which decided not to move – and filling the hours of this schoolday and the hours of punishment which continued until 6 o'clock. When those goat legs I stood on started to shiver, my teacher decided to end the punishment without ending her anger at the fact that she lived to see the day when her squirt of a pupil was to make fun of her.

I put my notebooks and pencils in my bag, and with a tongue stuck to my upper palate and two pursed lips so as to stop a cry from letting out I said,

"Tomorrow, my grandfather will come with me and tell you the story of 'Tom Thumb'."

I went to Grandfather. I went there where I used to find him at the small window, contemplating the sea or exchanging with the people of our district stories of those leaving or coming forth from the world's harbours. I went there where on certain occasions a nightly gathering would begin in the early evening and extend almost to dawn. My grandfather would enter into a contest with young men, women, and older men as to the ability to remember and to relate lengthy stories. Grandfather would tell more stories, remember them more vividly and more beautifully and would stay up late longer than any one else. Like him, I would not stop relating stories, learning and listening.

At my grandfather's window, I found a different scene. I did not know at the time what brought my father and my mother together in our old deserted house. I did not know why they closed the door with him inside, leaving him alone in his room, or why by his door, women whom I

196

had not seen before, were crying and wailing, all dressed in black like crows.

I spent the remaining years of my childhood angry with him because we had not agreed upon that, as had been his habit, and he had not warned me of this departure, after which we could not see our loved ones any more.

The mention of death has ever since meant to me a desolation that has the sharp edge of a knife, hot and pointed, piercing my heart.

Grandfather left to a faraway grave beyond the sea, close to a group of yellow sand dunes, and with bunches of wild flowers of a dark fiery colour spreading over them. I brought him from my window sill a small aloe and planted it there next to him. No sooner had one month passed than I found he sent it another aloe plant to keep it company in its loneliness. I used to take my books and study there, where the aloe and the bunches of flowers were and say to him and to them all the words forbidden to me. The old surviving aunt, my grandfather's elder sister, could not hear or see any more. There was no one but she in the old house now. My father and mother became scribbled lines on the back of some coloured postcards that came from afar. I made friends with the morning seagulls when they brought to the shore news of approaching ships. Among the morning birds I had certain friends with whom I woke up with the early light·to share the bread and the water which I put on the edges of my little balcony. They all shared my room. And the great, great absinthe tree at the entrance of the harbour took on the appearance of my grandfather's face and beard. Inside it I found the hideouts of his bosom and the warmth of his compassion.

Just as the aloe plant at his grave was getting taller, splitting the rocks to get a drop of water, and just as it was nourished by the sun, the night, and the moon, I also was competing with the two aloes in growing up. I used to stand next to them and ask my grandfather which was taller. I used to read my books and let him see how well I could read. I would tell him about my feats and racings with the world, about my toil and labour in order to find a place for 'Thumb' under the sun. I used to whisper to him. "Grandfather ! 'Tom Thumb' is growing and changing. New things that I don't know anything about are happening to her. I wish someone in this world would comfort me. Grandfather, out of my tree I'll bring into flourish all that I loved and wished, a beautiful life, a great love that will encompass the whole world, and..."

I hear his weeping mixed with laughter, then tears gush like white drops of pearls flowing down the trunk of the green aloe. I kiss it, trying to protect my mouth against its soft thorns, and raise my voice for him to hear me.

"And a man to love and to make of his heart the home that never was and to dissipate all the years of estrangement. With him I'll build a home made of the iron and steel of love, understanding, and communication. I'll fill its garden with flowers, its balconies and roof with bread, birdseed, and water for the birds of the same lineage of my childhood friends to eat, quench their thirst, and bathe. I'll grant my children joy, security, happiness, and compassion to heal the wounds of 'Little Thumb' hidden deep down. I'll dry my tears as well as the tears of all the children of the world, haunted by fear, hunger, and terror."

All wars will come to an end, following defeat or victory except that cosmic warfare that takes place on the fields of flesh, blood, nerves, and feelings. This will take place when two people meet and promise each other love,

Then the morning will dissipate the marriage of the night, and all words turn out to be melting butter. All the gardens, the walls, and the house will turn out to be ruins, impossible for the growth of a green branch.

In the middle of the ruins, new 'Little Thumbs' grow and are torn by the exchange of fireshots between two people who did not possess the terms or the qualifications to enable them to transfer dreams from night to day.

Palestine's 1948 war the '56, '67, '73 wars and the Gulf war – throughout all these wars, the defeats, and the victories, declaring the outcome of my war with him is still postponed. I try to manage: with patience or anger, with explosion or silence, with hope or despair. And the days never stop rising and dropping, dying out and flaring up. Nothing remains of the dream, not even the smallest part, not even its very remains.

"We will find the solution when things are more stable and the times are wiser and kinder – and we can catch our breath."

We never stop attributing everything to the times. Yet there is no time for wisdom or compassion: the days are heartless, and the events are mindless. Contradictions amount and the flood sweeps everything in its way. Madness pervades the world, and wars are breaking out north, south, east and west. And the wars taking place upon the fields of flesh, blood and nerves are more cruel and bitter.

The 'Tom Thumbs' of this world have flung away millions of frustrated happy dreams, stolen security and terror lying deep within the pupils of young eyes.

I go now to my grandfather's grave, which has disappeared together with the other features of the place:

perhaps it was the wind or the sweeping ebb and flow of the sea. Certainly he heard the bullet shots, the appeals for help everywhere, the shove of the waves, of humans skinning each other, and so he left.

Naked of every cover needed to shield the soul with security and shield the body's wounds, from afar I spied the remains of two aloes that have shrunk and gone pale. I called out to him and wondered.

"It was a dream for one 'Tom Thumb' to whom I would present the happiness and security of the world. It turned to hundreds, thousands and millions of hungry and terrorized 'Tom Thumbs.' Is misery our private heritage or the heritage of the whole world? And why while we mean to grant the sweetest of things, the best of all and the most compassionate, do we end up repeating the same cycles of inherited misery and cruelty?"

There, by the edge of the harbour pier, if you see a little girl jumping and hiding in the branches of the absinthe tree waiting for a ship to take her away to another shore, talking to seagulls, and carrying breadcrumbs and water to birds, don't believe her. For her face is to the wall, and her back is to the world.

Translated by Omayma Bakr

ETIDAL OSMAN was born in 1942. She obtained a degree in English Literature, Cairo University, 1963 and another in Arabic Literature, in the American University in Cairo, 1979. She has occupied several posts in the Ministry of Culture, mainly in the field of publishing: as member of the Department of the **Arabic Encyclopedia** *(1963-1966); the Publishing Committee (1966- 1970); editor of* **Prism : Cultural Register and Report,** *(1970 - 1975), editorial secretary of* **Fusul: Journal of Literary Criticism** *(1980- 1985) later its editorial manager (1985- 1991) and deputy supervisor of publishing in the General Egyptian Book Organization (1989- to date).*

Osman is an original short-story writer and a well - informed critic. She has published two short-story collections: **Jonah and The Sea** *(Younis Wa al-Bahr) 1987 and* **Tattoo of The Sun** *(Washam al-Shams) 1992; a critical study:* **Illuminating the Text: Readings in Modern Arabic Poetry** *(1987-1988) and edited* **Youssef Idris (1927- 1991),** *1991 in memory of our great novelist and short-story writer.*

THE SULTANA

Etidal Osman

Auntie Sultana is the strangest woman in the world; in the morning of woman born, and at night like a djinni's daughter. She lives near the fields, at the outskirts of the village. At the break of dawn she milks the cows, and cooks for the rest of the day. On festive occasions she bakes flat loaves of bread which come out of her oven like pancakes, fragrant with the smell of *helba*[1] and her fresh breath of amber.

She remedies the sick with the balsam of sweet words, native recipes, air pressure of heated glasses and medicine which she brings from the Big House down town: a drop of zink, cold or hot, cotton and bandages, a blood-like red liquid in a tightly closed bottle. She treats wounds with a touch of her hand and a special powder which, she say's is called "sulpha", it takes from the patient his pain and gives him, in return, relief.

In the afternoons Auntie Sultana, washes and perfumes herself, and adorns her eyes with antimony. For her dress she chooses the colour of green crops. Her gown drapes her neck and vests her prominent breast with tucked folds which stretch out loosely rich and undulating to the ground causing with every movement a noisy ruffle like wind-tossed tree leaves. For headdress she wears a scarf and a shawl, the scarf is so white that it would make the

---

(1) *Fenugreek: used for a drink or tonic prepared from the grains of this plant.*

newly blossoming cotton sigh of jealousy, the shawl is the colour of wheat stalks from under whose gold stretches out her night black hair, shining and curly.

Clinging to her I always followed at her heels; she would almost stumble over me as she shuttled among the oven room, the stable and the bathroom. She scolds me :

"Why don't you sit somewhere? let me do my work then we'll talk. In the evening I'll tell you as many stories as you like."

Frustrated I look at her as if my soul were pinned to her lips and the prospect of a tender promise to materialize in her affectionate eyes. I cast my head down and start crying.

"Alright, stop it now, I will."

Straight away the clouds of childish tears clear up and I would hear my own laughter, crystal clear springing from my heart.

"Shall I tell you about the king and the crow whose black colour you take for your hair or shall I tell you about the daughter of the King of Djinnis, Pomegranate Seed, and you keep her red colour for your cheeks, or the story of Solomon's ring and you acquire the language of birds or...?"

I interrupt her quickly :

"Solomon's ring."

"Alright, I will at the right time."

She forgets and gets busy doing her never-ending house chores. And I, tied to her apron strings, follow her caught by the huge butterballs of her magnificent body perspiring profusely. I kiss her cheeks and relish the salt dregs of melted butter which I love more than cream and honey.

204

My eyes are constantly engaged with her active movements; she works all day long and never seems to be exhansted as if she did not feel her body's weight. She comes and goes incessantly as if she were walking on water or air. In her motion the sea waves never stop nor is the air ever consumed.

Whenever she sits down to fix one thing or another I snatch the opportunity to throw myself into her lap. I feel I plunge into a goose and ostrich feather cushion. At times I seem to dive in a bowl of leavened dough. She takes me to her swaying bosom, I dip my head in the deep groove between her breasts; I say :

"Auntie Sultana, you have a nice smell, a woman's smell."

She holds me tight half pleased and half upset then lets me go. I see her large bosom shaking with an extended resonant laughter.

"Look at this girl, green and tiny, and look at what she says!"

Auntie Sultana never grows old, time and age do not touch her. We grew up to find that she was our aunt, and the aunt of boys and girls who came before us. She never alters or changes, never misses her habits and her evening stories never end.

When we grew up and went to the village school and the bigger school in the county town and later joined the university in Cairo we always returned for the summer vacation and found that she was the same as we had left her. Other kids came to her, she fed them and filled their evenings with her stories and warm intimations. "Those kids are my sweethearts." The same words she used to tell us. And I would leave my mother, father and brothers and go back to her sweet-smelling bosom as if I never left her lap but for moments.

I am still enthralled by her dress of the colour of fields and the tufts of her wheat-stalk shawl, my soul pinned to those serene moments when her secret words laid open the caves of talking.

Like a broken branch Auntie Sultana had no husband and no son. Nobody knew any of her relatives. There was only a picture with a shabby golden frame hanging on the drawing-room wall. It was a photograph of an old man at whose faded features we always stared and asked her questions which she never answered.

The village folk said that the man was a relative of hers who escaped his kin and brought her with him there.

Others said that he was her husband but was old enough to be her father. They said he never touched her but would only sit next to her and tell her stories of the ancestors and teach her the arts of poetry and literature. She memorizes, they said, ten thousand lines of verse, difficult and unknown, and the folk epics of Abu Zaid el Helali, Zat al Hemma, 'Antara and Hamza of the Arabs.[1]

Some people said that the man was the son of an important person who took part in the Orabi Uprising, escaped from the English authorities and the Khedive and took refuge in the countryside.

Others added that he was the son of General Mohamad Ebeid, the hero of the battle of Kasr el Nil and the commander of the Sudanese battalion, who fought valiantly and lost his life at El Tal el Kebyr. When the Orabists lost the war his mother moved to live with her family in the

_____

(1) Folk stories of chivalry and heroism.

206

county town where he was brought up. There, later, he quarelled with a maternal cousin over inherited property and left with Sultana, his actual or adopted daughter, who looked after him.

Other well-informed people argued that the man was a comrade of Saad Zaghloul[1] at the School of Law. They were intimate friends for years, then they quarelled when Zaghloul in Paris in 1919 with the Egyptian delegation, ignored Mohamad Farid[2]. The man, they said, played a substantial role to help bring Farid's remains to be buried at home.

However, some asserted that the man who came to the village to inquire about the old man was Gamal Abdel Nasser. The old man stood up and kissed him between his shoulders. That incident took place before the Revolution,[3] so nobody knew him.

We did not know the truth. On rare occasions we articulated those questions whick kept buzzing like bees let loose from their hives by boys' wantonness.

We sat next to her on one of those native sofas, munching the delicious food she cooked in the morning and spiced with her hot breath.

Intimate and cozy we huddled together enjoying the warmth which made our minds more alert. A boy or girl would suddenly say :

"Auntie Sultana tell us the story of the picture."

Taken by surprise her eyes clouded for a moment, she would say :

---

(1) Great Egyptian nationalist.
(2) Another great Egyp an nationalist leader who fought for Egypt's independence.
(3) The 1952 Revolution led by Gamal Abdel Nasser.

"He... God bless him with his mercy and light."

The words said softly were like tender hands which gently patted the old man's face and caressed his dishevelled strawy grey hair, or like amiable lips touching the wrinkled forehead. Her voice changed then restored its normal pitch as if she has just shaken off long accumulated dust on something she holds dear and would now like to leave it in peace under her skin or in the deep recesses of her heart, screened from sight.

We murmured with great curiosity excited by her incomplete answer. With a firm movement of her hand she stopped us and imposed silence.

"Let's talk of something else. I'll tell you a story, if you like it you'll sing a song and if you don't...?"

We shouted in unison :

"You'll tell us another story."

"You know, kids, everything in the world has a story." Her words had something of an electric touch which persisted with us through the evening. We asked:

"How, Auntie?"

"The dream has a story and talk has a story."

The boy says :

"We want to listen to the dream's story."

The girl says :

"No, we want to listen to talk's story."

Auntie Sultana says :

"Alright, don't quarrel, I'll tell you both.

In the old time and a very old time it was there was a city whose houses were made of marble enamelled with gold and silver. Its walls had a thousand windows with sandal wood shutters and a thousand windows of glowing red copper. The doors which were used by princes and guards only were of ebony.

The city was by the seashore, and the sea was full of fish, and the fish were coloured and winged and could fly up to the sky. The sun would burn their wings, they fell on the clouds and the clouds threw them back to the sea and there they grew new wings.

In that city lived a poor woman who had an only ewe whose milk she drank and whose wool she spinned and from whose offspring she ate. When the governor took away the woman's ewe, she went to the king's palace to claim it back. The guards did not let her in. At the palace threshold the woman sat down and wept. Her tears turned into lupine and beans. Which do you prefer lupine or beans?"

"Lupine, Auntie, it is salty like tears. What happened next?"

"The lupine seed fell into the sea and was swallowed by a fish which flew up to the sun. The wings were touched by the beams which burnt them. When the clouds threw the fish back to the sea the lupine seed, which was still inside the fish, fell out of its mouth, it had turned into a gem.

"The gem was tied to a tree, the tree was planted into a garden and the garden was bound to heaven. Gem had the power of iron and the colour of fire at times glowing like ruby and at times like pearl. It had the spirit of emerald."

"Auntie, your words are difficult."

"Listen and you'll understand. Everybody came to know the story of Gem. People said: 'Gem is a treasure with a talisman. They said: 'Gem was originally the tear of a wronged woman. She evades whoever means harm to her. They said: 'Only the fair and constant can possess her. 'They said: The one who possesses her will become a king of kings. When the news spreads, hearts filled with greed and strangers came to the country coveting the magic treasure.

One day Gem revealed herself to a native young man. She appeared to him as a beautiful girl washing herself in a garden pond. He looked at her and blushed. When she realized that he was gazing at her, she let her dark hair fall down on her luminous face; water dropped on water. He fell in love with her, he held her and would not let her go until he had brought her into the chamber of his heart."

"Allah Auntie... by God's prophet your words are beautiful but difficult like poetry."

"People rejoiced when Gem accepted to marry the young man. They celebrated the occasion, held festivities and read his fortune, he was fortunate, his star ascending to be a king of kings."

Auntie Sultana narrates her story as if she were possessed by the spirit of djinnis. Her countenance altered and changed. She stretches her hand over our heads to a recess in the wall. She disappears from the circle of light and then reappears. We see Gem, at her wedding party, strutting in a silk gown embroidered with stars and moons and a gold and silver brocaded veil. Blessed be the Creator. She stretches the other hand and brings forth the sword and the sceptre to the handsomest of all handsome young men. Praised be the Prophet and a pinch of salt in the evil eye of the enemy. We near the ululations and the songs. Auntie Sultana turns into choir and guests, boys and girls, bride and bridegroom and wedding procession. We watch her, our eyes wide open, panting, out of breath.

The king was fair, he said the one who tills, will the harvest take. He expelled the strangers, built walls round the country and lived blissfully with Gem. Nothing upset him except one thing,. something strange in which he was involved.

"Magic, Auntie?"

"Maybe djinnis?"

"Everyday he held an extended meeting which lasted from morning to evening. From everywhere people came to tell him about the dreams they had in their sleep. He listened to everyone of them and considered his dream. If he liked it he would reward the man by appointing him a personal counsellor and if he did not he would send him to Mount Kaf where dream robbers were kept. The man was punished by not being allowed to sleep for months or years after which he was sent to the executioner who cut his tongue with his sword. The inflicted punishment was a terror to all trespassers, and people...

Were afraid to talk.

Or go to the court.

Once a person dreamt of Gem.

Another dreamt of the garden.

On another night ten people had the same dream. What did the king do?

He held the regular meetings but nobody showed up. He ordered his guards to bring a huge mirror which reflected whatever was taking place in the palace and in the city. He used to sit by the mirror and talk and listen to the things he liked. But one day he failed to see his reflection. The King ordered the head merchant to get him mirrors from all countries. He looked at them and was intrigued as they all did not reflect his own image or the things which happened. The King was so angry that he issued a decree banning all mirrors.

The news spread, people were upset and the King was

aware of it. He ordered his guards to disperse all over the country and keep an eye on people's sleep and wakefulness. He became obsessed with gossip, hearsay and whatever was concealed in hearts, holes and corners. His counsellors advised him to increase surveillance and to appoint a watchman for every person. Some people volunteered to keep an eye on their own dreams and to report anything, even if it were an airy nothing, which might endanger the country's security or interest. Eventually people stopped talking and dreaming."

"Impossible, Auntie.. there should be...

People would explode.

Run away.

Kill him.

It may turn out into a disaster."

"One morning the palace residents rushed to the king to inform him that Gem had disappeared, they could not find her as if she were made of salt and had dissolved.

The King said, 'Maybe she drowned, maybe she was carried off by an eagle. He ordered the divers to fish for her from sunrise to sunset. He instructed his spies to climb the minarets and domes of all mosques to fetch the clouds and the flying birds from dawn to dusk. The King in person went out in a great procession to scrutinize the sea and the sky in order to find Gem, the pearl of his heart and the crown of his monarchy.

In the procession the king was sad and depressed, the crowd was silently watching when a little girl pointed at him and shouted at the top of her voice, this man has no shadow, he has no shadow like the rest of us.

When the crowd realized that the girl was right, there was an uproar, the guards were attacked, many were

212

injured and some people died. The King and a few of his followers managed to return to the palace to prepare themselves for the following day.

Exhausted and sad the king fell asleep. He found himself in the realm of dreams walking in crystal halls which led him to more crystal halls. The place was furnished with silk brocade carpets and chandeliers of gold, silver and pearls. The king moved on perplexed and distracted until he reached the throne hall. There he found Gem in the company of the Sultan of Dreams, his followers and countrymen. Overjoyed the King stretched his hand but his hand caught nothing but shadows. When he wanted to call the Sultan pointed at him, he was dumb struck and words died on his lips. *Touta touta*[1] and that's how the story ends."

"No Auntie you have to go on."

"I say,

'What happened to Gem?'

You say,

'I don't know,'

Someday you will know."

She says it firmly as if she were closing behind us the gates of the story and her house.

We went to sleep. I see the king wandering sadly in the crystal halls. Gem is crying. Her tears grow into lupine and beans. I am a winged fish, I fly to the sun whose unbearable heat scorches me. I fall and fall into a bottomless sea. I glimpse shadows which appear and then vanish. I recognize my mother and brothers. I feel the sharp pain of needles which sting every now and then and bitter mouthfuls of vomit which my hot stomach throws out. I hear murmurs

---

(1) *Words repeated at the end of a story told to children.*

and muffled weeping and see unknown faces which turn me on endless background of burning white flames. The flames devour me. My limbs are disconnected by strange hands. I scream with no sound. Teeth are grabbing my legs one after the other, toe after toe. My head is hanging in a tightly closed box. With my forehead I knock against a thick solid wall. It yields, becomes crystal transparent, through it I can see my mother's resigned face. The wall hardens. I faint, my sight and hearing foresake me. I plunge in a bottomless pit. From afar Auntie Sultana's voice reaches me. I don't know where it comes from but I hear her saying that it has been a long time now that the King is absent. One of the courtiers made a wax replica of Gem. The likeness was so good that whoever saw it thought it was Gem.

I hear people rejoicing and chanting *"Allahu Akbar"* as if it were the Bairam. The voices vanish.

I call: "Auntie.." the call evades me. I am carried on a stretcher in a great procession, preceded by the King, next to him Gem's statue. Fire is ablaze above and under me, the flames catch the King. I feel the melting wax covering me, its hot liquid burning my forehead and then drying. I open my eyes, I see my mother and Auntie Sultana holding a large towel drying the profuse sweat which covers my whole body.

I say :

"Auntie, I know the rest of the story."

"Say it, light of my eyes."

I hear her extended resonant laughter as she takes me to her large sweet smelling bosom.

Years later when I graduated from university and chose journalism for a career, I lived with my family in Cairo and my visits to the village were so scarce that I seldom heard about the people there.

I was sitting at my desk in my newspaper office, I was writing an article on one of the day's burning issues. The editor who was pestering me with the deadline, stood waiting to send the article to be printed. I was almost through when I stopped and tore down what I had written. Bewildered and dismayed, the editor stared at me. He had a glass of tea in his hand and there he stood not knowing whether to lift it to his open mouth and keep silent or to step to the desk and raise the dangerous question.

Outside strong winds were blowing from opposite directions. Through the open windows they swept the torn papers to the face of the editor. I filled my lungs with fresh air and felt an intimate breeze. I said to myself in an audible voice : "Auntie Sultana God bless you, a thousand times, with his mercy and light."

Translated by Radwa Ashour

THE SUN TATTOO

And for the moon have we appointed certain mansions among which a mansion overlooking a sea, an ocean and shores providing fertile and arid lands, escorting the dweller and the traveller, watched over by the Mounts of Atlas. Quarters and alleys leading to each other. Squares fragrant with the smell of spices, green tea, mint leaves, *couscous*[1] saturated perspiration, aromatic plants and the salty breeze of sea and ocean.

The courtyard of al-Fana mosque. Wrapped in white, the woman in her national dress is veiled up to her mouth, her eyes painted with the antimony of ancient lust, in her hands the playcards : "Let's see your luck."

The girls are dressed in azure blue. Their hair, plaited round their dark shining foreheads, falls down on both sides of their faces.

Twinkling and vanishing in the darkness of their braids are virgin bead stars, granules and round silver pendants whose dim rust encloses the luminous faces.

Beating are the drums of North Africa, playing are the strings of Barbary. If the questioner, with his question, knocks on the coffers in bosoms locked, they will open and the tongues of lads, beating and calling forth, will be answered by Bedouin Berber lasses :

"Beat the secret's secret of the secret, a lock of the mind."

---

(1) A spicy dish originating fiom North Africa, consisting of steamed semolina.

Enamoured and coy the youthful breasts shake. The string beads of amber, and saffron melted in enameled silver granules glazed with the colour of the sea, the fields and the sand, quiver. Intricate chains are the cycles of history: closed on their secrets which deeply mark time and the body, a tight .collar around the neck, the friction of whose links like moans resounds. The girls' bracelets tingle, their bodies shudder, advancing and retreating, drawn by the craving for release and the check of the fetter ornament. The Berber morning star glows at the very centre with a blood stone gem swaying on the proud protruding breasts, countless crescents marked body and soul and vanished in time.

The tall lad advances, his hands clasped, hiding, in the rich folds of his cloak and in the coffer of his breast, a dagger. The drum beats get louder.

"Beat the secret..."

The lass advances with a lofty proud gait, she unveils the crescents tattoo and, with no words, veils them. All discourse is a veil except the discourse of sentiment and love's ecstasy. She regards and disregards, her tattoo quivering says, take me with vigour. Bewildered and dismayed, the lad shudders.

"Unversed you are, fix your eyes on our secrets to explore."

The veiled unveiled tattoo sweats at the call. We summoned you, go tell whoever saw it and confirmed it, examined it and checked it that it is in his chest sealed, a witness of his heart. Its doors will not open and the secret will not be disclosed and none is to acquire the knowledge concealed. visible and invisible, except its heirs and lords.

The lad stretches his arms, produces the dagger whose handle is fastened with the knot of love's communion

218

deferred. He heads for the lock tattoo and the knot from which extend the two ends or the rope of seduction tied round his neck.

With his right hand which holds the pointed dagger the lad pulls the rope, its end shortens. the girl's body trembles.

"No way, no way to the whole to be sought."

With the other hand the boy catches the dagger pulling the rope which extends quivering. The girl almost retreats.

"By the name of a glance rising sublime."

The dagger between the lad's hands moves madly, closer and farther, up and down. The drum beats yet louder.

"Beat the secret's secret of the secret..."

Sharp and shining the dagger's point touches the neck. The string beads collect themselves before they break up sighing. The sharp point falls down on the breast ripping the blue azure dress, pricking the copper skin tattoo. The morning star glows with the arrows of Red Marrakech.

The congregated assembly becomes a string taut.

The dance a bow.

Whose discourse into the string flows.

In al-Fana courtyard the woman mixes the playcards : "Let's see your luck."

Kings and queens, Jacks and aces, card jokers and numerals named. She exposes them and collects them back. Her eyes fixed on me she addresses me with the art of riddle and insinuation. Through her veil I discern her golden teeth, touched with the red sun of Marrakech, glittering. She murmurs numerous words. I fail to understand. In the name *of Allah*. She gives me the virgin queen. In her hand the Jack. He strikes the flint of luck and passionate love. The King, in her other hand, lurks mischievously waiting.

Quickly she shuffles the cards, spreads them like a fan, their symbols on their downwards faces hidden. She touches my hand asking me to choose one. Her hand is adorned with tattood patterns of henna, yellowish dark red. "El henna, el henna, Quatr el Nada."[1]

When she touched me we exchanged the tattoo and the secret of the secret. My bosom filled with serene restfulness.

I say, "Perplexing is ignorance, perplexing is knowledge."

Nearby the serpent player plays the flute. From his bag appears the head of an adder. The water carrier moves around with his rattles. The adder's head, the glow of henna, the woman's eye, the eye of the sun of red Marrakech, I gaze at them. Silence breaks down, time pours out, mosaic verses joined and welded. Ra' Atum,[2] the serpent on both sides of the worshipped solar disk crowning the adored King, and the King was and still is venerated.

The water carrier goes round with his rattles appeasing the thristy with the water of Zamzam.[3] The lad whirls at the very centre, a Nubian, a Mulawi with no beard yet, his thin waist girdled with the skirts of the heavens seven. He whirls and whirls to the beats of the tambourines. He passes over the unsaid, he shakes and quakes, astounded and pale. His clear dark complexion reflects his successive mutations, wakeful and intoxicated, alert and entranced,

---

(1) *The beautiful daughter of Sultan Kumaraweh who gave his daughter an unparalled wedding celebration.*

(2) *Ancient Egyptian god.*

(3) *Holy Well in Mecca.*

enraptured effaced, the eye of sense forlorn and sense alive, a waving skirt flying spread over the head and another tightly tied to the thin waist, two circles blotting the colours of the rainbow, white upon white and in between a dark spot sparkling with passion... Beat the secret. We are in al Ghoury[1] courtyard bewildered as if birds were on our heads standing and the body became the soul's tattoo joining the two circles of heaven and earth. The bird swoops on the tattoo.

When his guardian Sheikh Abul Hassan El Gareh on a night lit by a full moon, invited him to the public bath, he was eager to go. The Sheikh put the white sheets beside him and called his followers. He helped them take off their clothes, one after the other, and gave each a sheet and then a second. He did the same to the lad and to himself. It was a generous bestowal. The lad spent the night elated as if in heaven.

"No knowledge, no eye, no sense reaches us."

The following morning the Sheikh was found murdered in the bath. it was said that he drowned in the waters of passion.

The lad had reached his point, the drum beats their climax, the dagger's blade the naked tattooed breast.

"No mind, no congregation, no dispersal, nothing."

The flower of blood was ripped open. In the soul's recesses I could hear a voice saying :

"When the light of the enlightened beams
My soul will escort Osiris
I will assume the shape of the winged hawk[2] .

---

(1) Al - Ghoury : a mosque in Cairo named after one of the Memluk sultans.

(2) The winged Hawk is Horus : son of Isis and Horus of the Pharaonic myth.

I will go out to earth

And open hell

In order to see, once more, the sun of existence."

I was in the courtyard of al Fana mosque gazing, and I could see al Ghoury next to the old bookstore, the minaret of al Hussein mosque and the dome of al Azhar. The sound's echo has resounded in my ears, it still fills them.

"Beat the secret's secret of the secret..."

Ripped open was the flower of blood, between the two mansions, the two breasts, in the domed heaven and in the eye of the sun.

Translated by Radwa Ashour

RADWA ASHOUR *was born in Cairo in 1946. She* *obtained the B.A. degree in English Literature in Cairo* *University, 1967 and the Ph. D. in Afro-American Litera-* *ture in the University of Massachusetts, U.S.A, 1975. She is* *Professor of English Literature and ex-chairperson of the* *Department of English Language and Literature, Ain* *Shams University. She is a brilliant novelist, short-story* *writer and critic. She started her writing career with two* *critical studies:* **The Way to the Other Net : A study of** **Ghassan Kanafani's Works,** *1977 and* **The Follower** **Rises: The Novel in West Africa** *1980. She then published* **The Journey: An Egyptian Woman Student's Days in** **America,** *1983. This was followed by three novels :* **A** **Warm Stone** *(Hagar Dafi')* *1985;* **Khadiga and** **Sawsan,** *1989 and* **Siraj,** *1992 and one short-story collec-* *tion. Ashour is an artist. She is passionately in love with* *people, justice, liberty, literature, the Arabic language and* *the Arab heritage. She is currently writing an epic novel on* *the Arabs in Spain.*

"The Man Seated in the Garden Waiting," and the *"Very Short Stories" are part of the story-collection* **I Saw** **the Palm Trees,***1989.*

224

THE MAN SEATED IN THE GARDEN WAITING

Radwa Ashour

At first, I did not notice his presence because I was fully involved in playing with my little boy. He would throw the ball and I would raise my head, following it as it flew up high. Then I would run with my arms open and catch it as it fell. The little one was jumping and running and kept on chattering and laughing. I, too, was running like him and laughing though my movement was heavier and the noise I made less loud.

The sun's disc was a shining orange in a clear sky. It spread its rays through the entwining branches of the many trees that filled the place. Then I saw him.

An old man sitting on a wooden bench closeby. His white marble face was almost invisible behined big black glasses. His body was shrivelled and he was wearing a dark cloak. He was leaning with both hands on a thick rough stick with many knots as if it had just been cut from its mother tree.

I raised my right hand with the ball and threw it hard. It flew up high and for an instant it disappeared in the blue sky as if it were a bird soaring until it completely escaped the laws of the earth. The ball then appeared and fell far from the little one who said:

"How can I catch it if you throw it so hard?"

He continued to grumble but I was not listening. I was thinking about the man seated on the nearby seat and

225

wondering how it was that I had not noticed his presence before. He was very close. I only needed to turn around to see him.

He was sitting without moving, his face still as if it were moulded of stone. He was peering at nothing as if he could neither hear nor see. The little one said in protest:

"Mother, concentrate on the game. You're playing without concentrating."

Then he added, waggling his finger like a teacher:

"When you play you mustn't think of anything else. What are you thinking about?"

I almost pointed out the stranger, but I stopped. I threw the ball but it did not fly high. The little one said:

"It looks as though you're tired."

"It looks as though I'm tired".

He took the ball from me and went running off with it, throwing the ball up high and running to catch it. As for me, I sat down on another wooden seat facing the man who was still motionless, his mouth pursed tight with creases surrounding it, placing his veined hands one upon the other on the thick stick. Where had this man come from? How had he come? What brought him to this place?... Was he waiting? He must be waiting... Who was he waiting for?

All of a sudden I shivered. Yes, he must be waiting. What was I to do? I wondered in terror with fear shaking me like a fierce wind that blows suddenly causing the sky to become cloudy and overcast and to close in with its blackness on the ground. "We'll return home" now, immediately and quickly. We will run back home. We will close the door with key and bolt and lock and firmly shut the windows and draw the thick curtains. Then we'll get into bed and cover ourselves from head to toe with a heavy cover so as to see nothing and nothing can reach us. "We'll return home".

I felt my heartbeats pounding and racing. I started to call my little one. I looked around searching for him among the trees. I noticed their sturdy trunks and their roots penetrating the earth, piercing it to grow above it and piercing it to grow in its bowels, twisting and entwining and spreading. I saw the trunks reaching up to the thick branches weighed down by the greenness of their leaves. Then I saw the little one holding his ball, running and throwing it hard so that it flew as if it would reach the orange disc, beyond the leafy branches. Then he would run and stretch his arms out wide to receive it and raise his head in the direction of the sun such that its rays would fall perpendicularly on him and he would look like a part of the ray.

The little one approached me, hugging the ball. His face, hair and shirt were all wet with sweat.

'Aren't you tired?"

"I'll play."

I took a rapid look at the man sitting on the nearby seat, then I turned my head, took the ball and threw it with determination. I saw it fly and once again it seemed to me that it could escape the earth law.

Translated by Amani El- Rashidi.

VERY SHORT STORIES

They were torn apart by a brutal blow. The ceiling of alienation was low, tiring to the soul. They continued to cling to each other as an old man clings to the memory of happiness and the exile to the memory of his homeland. They were united by a dream wearing a school uniform and reading books.

He gave her a house with flowers growing in between its stones. She loved the storm, the sea and the waterfall. She ran out to the open space with her arms wide open. When the rain wetted her dress, she wanted to return to the house but found the door locked.

She was like a blooming flower. He wanted her for himself, so he picked her and kept her as one keeps flowers between the leaves of an old book. Then he turned away from her, taunting her that she was dry.

She carried to him the roar of the spirit and its glittering lights. He carried to her cement for the walls of the house and found flour for bread. She came to him running and singing.

He continued his preoccupation with baking a pie for the family's supper. She said to him, weeping, "You do not see me." He was shaken and was about to feel pain. Then he patted her on the shoulder and got up to make her some tea.

She gave him possession of a garden of jasmin and Arabian jasmin. She placed a crown of vines on his head and gave him the passion of the soul and a clean shirt every morning. She found him on all four in the hen pen. He was kneeling down wanting to steal the neigbour's hens.

He was raised a stranger and an orphan. When she arrived, he opened the door wide and celebrated and gave her all the keys. She got on the pony and with her feet kicked the spurs and cracked her whip and thought him a donkey.

He was born in the country of figs and olives and a large sun. His fate led him to the cities covered with snow. He knocked on her door. She said, "Come in". So they were married. In spite of a roof and children, he spent his life leaving the lights on and the fireplace lit because he continued to shiver of loneliness and cold.

She saw his genitals and panicked. After a few months she became used to disregarding them. Then she bought a sewing machine and became adept at sewing the gaudy clothes he wore when he went out in the street.

She wove him a shirt and a life graced with boys and girls. He took it without smiling. His fist was tight and his heart was bitter. His ferocity shook the walls of the house. Then he died and the children were relieved. As for her, she wept because she found herself without a cover.

She went to someone else then returned in tears. He patted her shoulder. She left once again and returned. The third time she put his things in a closed box. Twenty years later, she became aware of the existence of the box.

230

He wanted her for himself and waited. She went to someone else, so he kept on waiting. When she finally came to him, he held her to him until she felt his fingers digging in her flesh. She screamed calling for help. Inspite of her pale face and bruises, he did not understand why she screamed and why other people ran to free her of him. For he loved her.

He taught her to walk and which political party to vote for. She saw him from her window and panicked. He was a dwarf. She wanted to run and escape. She wanted to forget what she had seen. But she stood still muttering, "So be it"... and continued with life.

She saw everything: the pale face, the motionless body over the threshold and floating in the room. She left the hospital and returned home. She prepared the children a hot meal and fed them. She said "good night". Then she went to bed and gave up the spirit.

She looked in the mirror and saw a sea and fishermen and space embroidered seagulls. She handed him the mirror. He looked and saw a low prison, a bare tree and a crow croaking.

She looked in the mirror and saw her grandmother and her mother and her daughter like a necklace with regular beads, all alike in failure and loss.

She looked in the mirror and saw the massacre: the swollen bodies, the flies and the picks that dug the common grave. She felt sorry for the mirror and held it to her breast to be stronger.

She looked in the mirror and saw the torn flag and

the boy weeping. She closed her eyes and saw the flag hoisted and the boy singing. She lived her life torn between those two pictures.

She looked in the mirror and saw the bird shivering. She said, "Tomorrow, the spring will bring him warmth." The spring came and left. She looked in the mirror and found the bird dead. She covered him and hid the mirror so she would not stumble over it while coming and going.

She felt her face and threw the mirror far away. As she picked up the fragments of glass to throw them in the garbage she muttered, "A mirror that reflects nothing but a face with creases and dull eyes... a mirror without a memory.... Stupid."

After the age of 60, she looked at her basket and found it empty. She put everything back the way it was and hung the basket on her arm and walked in the marketplaces as usual.

A woman carrying a basket and walking in the streets. Nobody knows whether the basket holds hot bread or poisoned candy.

She baked them and kneaded them and covered them with her handkerchief while they leavened, then cooked them in a slow oven. And when they became youths crowding at the elbows and had spouses living with her she was filled with bitterness. She did not undersatnd why she baked the loaves and others ate them!

She hated her belly that sprouted children harvested by the sickles of invaders. She said, "I wish I had died before them." She almost prayed to God to take her to

Him or to make her barren. But when she uncovered her hair and gazed at the sky, she wished her belly were like the fields sprouting millions of ears of corn.

Her husband did not give her the flower she had dreamt of. So she turned away from him to the child she took care of like a patient gardener. When the child grew . up, he came to her joyfully carrying a flower in his hands and cried to her, "Look mother what I'm presenting to my fiancée."

She works in a small kitchen where she passes her day, peeling onions and garlic, and pouring sweat from the heat of the oil which fills the place with its choking smoke. In spite of this she has a wide window from which she watches a flock of birds soaring in space.

She washed their underwear. She cleaned their home. She prepared their meals and raised their children. When she died, they buried her in the charity cemetery because she was only a servant.

He drew the scene with his ugly master and with his master the Christ. He drew the commando and the flower and the tattoo of the map. He drew the assassination gun and the stone gravestone and the citizen writing his will. He drew all this.... so they killed him.

He raised his weapon and died a martyr. She hung his picture on the wall. Sometimes the picture was absent like a book you once read and kept along with other books in the library. Sometimes you notice it like a mother suddenly notices her son on his way to school and sees how beautiful he is and how much she loves him.

She opened the window and saw the amazing arc surrounding the sky's dome. She distinguished the colours of the spectrum and the smell of wet grass and the crystal drops on the green trees. She whispered to herself, "Who said that the evil of the universe would prevail?"

She saw him approaching. He was covered in black, riding his horse and raising his sickle. She hurried to her loom and got busy weaving the colours of the spectrum. When he came upon her, she did not know if her racing heartbeats were fear of his heavy sickle or concern for her unfinished tissue.

Translated by Amani El-Rashidi

*SALWA BAKR was born in Cairo in 1949. She graduated in Management in Ain Shams University in 1972, then in Criticism in the Institute of Dramatic Arts, 1976. She worked for the Ministry of Provisions for six years, and as a theatre, film and literary critic in the media in Lebanon and Cyprus for five years, then devoted all her time to writing. She has published three short-story collections: **Zeinat at the President's Funeral** (Zeinat Fi Guinazat al-Ra'is) 1986, **About the Soul that was Gradually Spirited Away** (an al- Roah Allati Soriqat Tadrigiyyan), 1989 and **The Monkey Trainer** (Ageen al-Fallaha), 1992, in addition to a volume including a novella and three short stories : **Atteyya's Shrine** (Maqam Atteyyia), 1987 and one novel : **The Golden Chariot Does not Ascend to Heaven** (Al-Araba al-Thahabiyya La Tas'ad ila al-Sama'), 1991. Her novel has been adapted for the cinema. She is well received at home and abroad. She is the most translated of our women writers.*

*   "A Flower in the Swamp" appears in **The Monkey Trainer and** "The Camel" in **Al-Hilal**, 1992.*

THE CAMEL

Salwa Bakr

The traffic lights turned red and the big and small cars stopped. Everybody waited, while a little boy stamped his feet and cried out as he watched a camel cross the street :

'Look, mother. A camel."

"All right," she answered, without taking her eyes off a poster that covered the wall of a large building at the street corner, advertising a new tourist resort.

His gaze followed this large and awesome creature with his extended neck and his high hump, as he proceeded deliberately. The boy sighed contentedly and declared :

"Mother, I want a camel."

"Oh, really!"

She pronounced the words while her eyes were riveted to the blonde girl in the advertisement, lying on a beach wearing a two-piece swimming suit.

For the third time he repeated his request and pleaded with her :

"For the sake of the Prophet, mother dear, I want a camel."

She held him with one hand and carried with the other his schoolbag and another bag full of vegetables. Her handbag hung from her shoulder.

Tired of waiting for the green traffic lights, she grumbled angrily :

"A camel! What a ridiculous idea!"

His eyes were glued to the camel until it disappeared.

Then he burst out crying to affirm his determination and insist on his request :

"What's so ridiculous about a camel?"

Realizing how serious the matter was, she smiled and attempted an explanation :

"The camel is much too big, dear. It could never fit into our small flat. A camel would need a large place."

He quickly refuted her argument, saying :

"Fine. Let's buy the camel and live in a large house."

"Ha, ha, ha. Live in a large house for a camel? It takes a lot of money to live in a large house and I have very little money."

"Fine. Make a lot of money."

"Impossible, dear. I have a small salary that is barely enough for our food."

Again, he stamped his feet and cried,

"But, I want a camel. Do something and get me a camel."

The hot sun burned her head and the humid air suffocated her while the house was still a long way to go. Her patience was exhausted and she screamed :

"Stop being such an idiot! How can you cry over a camel? Shut up and hurry on. I want to get home and see to the cooking before your sister comes home from school."

Tears poured down his cheeks, fortified by his screams as he persisted in repeating a request that seemed to him both fair and simple :

"I want a camel. What's so wrong with a camel? For once, I wish you would listen to me and get what I want," he cried.

Revealing the darker side of motherhood, she bared her teeth, put out her claws and shouted at him :

238

"Shut up! Shut your mouth or I'll give you a good beating, right here, in the middle of the street and in front of everybody."

Her threats intimidated him as he was perfectly aware that they were not idle and could easily be carried out. He toned down his crying but did not stop completely. The mother softened a little and decided to follow another course of action :

"Please be quiet, son. I have a headache and my body is aching all over. I think I am going to catch the flu'. Come on, I'll buy you something sweet. Would you like chocolate or candy?"

He was fed up with her patronizing attitude. He stopped in his tracks and yelled angrily :

"I said a camel, a camel. Not some silly sweet."

She too was about to explode. Should she stop and give him a beating, or should she swallow her rage and shut up? She opted for the second solution, but he did not cease his whining. She exploded :

"Shut your mouth, you nincompoop. A six year old boy crying for a camel! Stop being childish. The camel is not a toy. What would you do with it? Play with it? How annoying!"

Her question took him by surprise as he had no preconceived idea about what he would do with the camel. Yet he still had strong overwhelming feelings for this unique and magnificent being, for whose sake, all cars, all traffic lights, everbody stopped till it crossed the street.

He rememberd the hump, the neck, the wide eyes and he sighed deeply. Confident of the validity of his demands, he silently swore at his mother.

She noticed his thoughtful silence and proceeded with her persuasive offensive :

"Also, a camel is very expensive, dear. You must be considerate and do as your mother tells you to. Don't wear me down. It's hot and I'm completely exhausted. Come on."

He, in his turn, tried to follow the same line of action and said calmly :

"All right, mother. But having a camel is really quite simple."

She quickly responded to his reasoning and said :

"All right. Do you know anyone who owns a camel? Your cousins? Your neighbours? Does anyone of them have a camel at home? Please be reasonable, dear."

He quickly knocked down her argument :

"The neighbours have a dog and my cousins have a bicycle."

She could no longer take it. She yelled so vehemently that she attracted the attention of an old man passing by. He stared at her as she said :

"Shut up. Damn your insolence."

The old man sympathized with mothers nowadays who were nervous and quick-tempered because life was difficult and food not easy to come by, because of eating useless frozen chicken and meat. He uttered a sigh, gazed at the mother pityingly and went on his way.

The boy was unaware of the external source of sympathy that was walking along beside him. He was staring at the ground, feeling wronged by this tyrannical woman, despite the obvious justness of his cause. He had a simple human request: a camel, no more, no less. She on the other hand mentioned other people. Other people may not have camels but they have many other things he does not have. Why does she bring in other people, or his cousins?

240

She decided to have a cold soft drink to quench her anger and her thirst. As soon as she laid eyes on the cold bottles covered with ice-cubes in a box in one of the shops she stopped and asked her son :

"Would you like a cold drink?"

He did not answer and continued crying and sulking, while he stared at her with hatred.

A smiling shop-assistant came to open a bottle of lemon. Noticing that the boy was crying he tried to be kind to him and offered him a choice of different kinds of sweets. Still, the boy did not respond. Having taken a long sip of her drink, the mother said :

"I've had it with this boy ! He hasn't stopped whining because he saw a camel and wants me to buy him one. How irritating!"

Once more, the assistant smiled, patted the boy on the shoulder and addressed him :

"Do you want a camel? Well, why not? I'll get you one, my boy. Don't you worry about it."

The man went into his shop and came back in a little while carrying a small camel in his hand, a red plastic camel.

The boy examined the plastic object in his hands. It actually looked like a camel. He compared it to that magnificent awesome figure that crossed the street and hesitated, amazed at the man's stupidity: how could he call this object a camel? However, he hesitated once more since he had something in his hands any way, and he kept quiet

and said nothing.

The mother had finished her soft drink. Finding that he had calmed down she remarked :

"How beautiful! It's red and quite pretty!"

The child stared at her with suspicion and contempt and remained silent.

"You know what! You can put him on the T.V. or take him to bed with you at night."

Her remark made him feel bitter, betrayed and disappointed in this liar standing in front of him. He kept quiet so long as he had this red plastic object in his hands. The man declared victoriously :

"It is so easy to please children! You just have to be patient with them."

The mother agreed as she took out money from her purse :

"I was completely fed up with his whining all the way : I want a camel, I want a camel. By God, I was about to clobber him right in the middle of the street. I barely restrained myself."

The man gazed benevolently at the boy and reasoned with him :

"All's well that ends well. Next time, my son, ask for a bicycle or an aeroplane! But a camel! You have peculiar taste. There used to be camels in the good old days. In future, they will disappear completely."

The mother smiled, happy to be out of a spot. She pulled the boy out of the shop, but, as soon as they had walked away, he calmly and persistently declared :

"Mother. I want a camel, please!"

Translated by Hoda El-Sadda

A FLOWER IN THE SWAMP

It was a wide, large, swamp, encircled with a dense growth of bushes and reeds, and interspersed with wild unruly plants. A long time ago, dark green mosses managed to spread all over the surface, so much so as to prevent a soft breeze from stirring one drop of the rotten and stagnant swamp water.

Had it not been for the creeping sound of a snake, a lizard, or some insect, the swamp would have seemed totally devoid of life. The overwhelming silence emphasized the ugliness and loneliness of the place and inspired a feeling of boredom, desolation and sheer nothingness.

Notwithstanding, there was a white flower that bloomed at the far end of the swamp. It towered brilliantly with its soft, velvet leaves, more beautiful than a narcissus, more radiant than a lotus. It was impossible to guess where it came from, or how it grew in the midst of this desolate lonely place, how it blossomed so magnificently. It rapidly diffused its fragrance, like soft music coming from afar.

The white flower perceived her beauty, breathed in her fragrance and then gazed at the ugly swamp around her and bemoaned her fate: My short life will soon end in this horrible swamp. All flowers bloom, exhale their fragrance, and reach their prime in order to make life more bright and beautiful. But here I am, in this gloomy swamp, alone, like the first star of the night. My stalk is soaked in putrid water. Beatles pass by my side indifferently. My radiant picture is distorted when reflected in this awful murky surface. Oh, I wish I were a beautiful bird in the sky so that I could go far, far away from this foul, deathlike place, never visited by honey bees or butterflies. I wish I were a flower in a luxuriant garden where I could go to sleep and wake up listening to the singing of nightingales and larks. I wish I belonged to a bunch of flowers so I could share with them the things shared by lovers when they meet, having waited for so long.

The soft flower then supplicated to heaven to have some creature, some human being, cross the swamp so that he would see her pick her softly and pin her to the hair of a bride or put her in a lovely vase so she could exhale her fragrance until she withered.

As time passed by, the sorrows of the white flower increased and she was torn with pain and regret because she neither had wings to carry her and fly away, nor a voice that would resound and be heard at a distance and attract some creature that adored flowers. In fact, she became even sadder when she realized that she could not even scream: she would have objected and expressed her annoyance with the swamp and its rotten air and unbearably putrid water.

Days passed and the lonely swamp flower, so helpless and white, waited and waited until she realized that she was bound to die, destitute and unknown, unseen, untouched by a single creature since the day of her birth to the end of her days.

One day, the flower contemplated her picture reflected on the still surface of the greenish swamp water. She shook all over, appalled by what she saw : her stalk was dried up and yellow marks of withering had creeped and

244

reached her radiant whiteness. The flower was beset by fear and awe as she realized that she had only a few days to live, that the end was near.

The flower wished it could jump, run, fly, weep, scream, not only because she was afraid of death – as she was aware that flowers were short-lived and had to die - but because other flowers died after they had given joy, beauty and magic. As for her, she had waited and waited and she was going to die in this terrible place, and her beauty will be lost to no avail, as if she had never existed, like someone who was never born, never breathed or grew or lived.

The flower was overwhelmed with sadness and torn with pain. However, sheer despair led her to the heights of hope and utter despondency pushed her to the borders of faith. She started to encourage herself, saying: As life tightens its knots, there might be a way out of darkness. She wondered with surprise: Would a butterfly or a honey bee venture to this gloomy place, would a human being or some creature come to live in this deserted and isolated swamp? Who would even consider coming for a lost flower that dives with mosses, cockroaches and the ridiculous weeds of the swamp?

But the flower was determined to live up to the image of a flower until the end and said: Never! I will not die in an unknown world nor will I leave the world without making my mark. I shall spend this night, which I feel is my last night, squeezing myself and diffusing my soft enchanting fragrance, until I overcome the stink of the swamp. Then my sweet scent will spread with the breeze and the wind to far off places and reach a lover of flowers or a lover of beauty.

The evening slowly and gradually descended at first,

but it soon quickened its pace and completely covered the swamp in darkness. Only the radiant stars shone brilliantly in the blue sky. The flower joyfully gazed at them and started to squeeze herself and exhale her strong, sweet perfume which she produced with a lot of effort and in spite of her being soaked in the stinking water of the hateful and rotten swamp.

At night, the flower did not tire of squeezing herself and diffusing her fragrance. She was encouraged by the company of the golden stars and silver moon that radiantly looked upon her. It also made her believe that there was always hope because she worked so hard. As time went by, her fragrance spread more and more, dispelling the repulsive stink of the swamp. Soon, this fragrance completely overcame all other smells and was then carried by the damp night breeze far away, into the open space.

The night was almost spent. Dawn was near and the flower did not tire of her labour as she struggled against death and annihilation. She squeezed herself dry and diffused all the fragrance in her soft body. When she could take no more, she collapsed on her stalk, lonely and pale. As she slowly faded away and was about to cross the line between life and death, she heard the chanting of a beautiful stork who was quickly crossing the sky on his last night round, before the extinction of the stars and the departure of the moon. As the stork passed over the swamp singing, he felt exhilirated, joyful and enchanted: What a magnificent fragrance! How delightful! There must be splendid flowers and mellow trees. As the flower entered the realm of death, the happy stork decided to build a little nest and bring his lovemate to live in this place.

Translated by Hoda El-Sadda

AISHA ABOUL-NOUR was born and borught up in
Cairo. She graduated in Journalism from Cairo University,
1974. She has been editing the weekly magazine **Akher-
Sa'a** (Latest News) since 1975. She edits cultural and
literary sections and is particularly concerned with women's
affairs. She has published three short-story collections:
Perhaps You Will Understand One Day (Robbama tafham
yawman), 1980; **Meeting at the Time of Lost Love** (al-
Liqa' Fi Zaman al- Hob al-Dai') 1989 and **Men too Are
Afraid** (Al-Rigal Aydan Yakhafoun), 1990 and two novels
in 1981 and 1985. She is fond of depicting conflict between
man and woman. She has won two Press-Syndicate prizes
and has had some of her short stories translated into French,
German and English.

"Meeting at a Time of Lost Love" is the title story of her
1989 collection and "The Rebel" apears in **Perhaps You Will
Understand One Day.**

THE REBEL

Aisha Aboul-Nour

She did not konw that the doors to the room were closed with tight iron locks. The only large window had curtains made of solid bars.

She had prepared herself to go out to life. She is exhibiting all her natural beauty. Her clothes are becoming and the colours are soft and matching, showing taste and good judgement. Her thick shining hair is fastened behind her small ears with one hair band.

The sound of her thin high heels is heard in the small room as she goes toward the door. The long leather strap of her bag encircles her left shoulder in a casual way. It goes all the way beyond her small waist. The bag swings with the quick rhythmic movement of her legs.

With a spontaneous movement, she pulls the door to slide through. To her surprise, it is locked. She tries anew, but to no avail. She runs towards the second door and then the third. All the doors are securely locked. She jumps on the simple furniture of the small room until she reaches the only large window in it, but she bumps against the solid steel curtains that surround it. She exclaims in terror and a big question mark lies on each iron lock and steel curtain.

What terrifying confinement?

She runs to the first door and with all her strength and fury she pushes it roughly with her shoulder. She then kicks it with her shoe and at last she bangs on it with her stubborn fists.

But the huge thick door is not even scratched. She screams with a choking voice; her screams are loud and continuous. The sound reverberates and she hears the echo in the depth of her ears, hurting her and shaking her besieged inner being.

Angrily and nervously, she spills the contents of her leather handbag all over the floor. She picks up a steel nail file from among its contents. She finds the weakest spot in the huge wooden barrier: its heart, and she forces the tip of the file with all her might that increased because of her will to be free and to escape the oppressing siege. Its heart bleeds dozens of rough wooden layers. She has managed to make a small hole that does not exceed the size of the head of a pin. She remembers the metal hair band with which she ties her thick hair behind her ears. She takes hold of it without hesitation. Her dark locks fly in all directions on her forehead and shoulders. She inserts her weapon in the weak spot of the strong barrier. She takes off her shoe and, with its thin heel she widens the opening.

She throws the shoe away when the heel breaks. Once more, she fidgets with the things on the floor to find a new weapon to help her in this fateful battle. Her fingers get hold of a pair of tweezers. She eagerly picks them up and pushes them in the heart of the cave that her will power has created.

The opening gets bigger and deeper. The weak heart of this strong body bleeds excessively. She perspires all over. She looks exhausted. She breathes with utter fatigue and feels suffocated. She refuses to give in. She rejects defeat. She has to free herself from this siege.

She takes off her tight brassiere which felt shackling. She frees herself of all the obstacles to free movement and progress in work. Many of her feminine personal belongings are scattered on the floor. She has not used many of the things yet. She picks up her expensive lipstick, her metal kohl container, her soft hair brush, her gold bracelets, the pearl necklace with a pointed lock, her diamond ring, a sharp razor blade that she uses to sharpen her brown eyebrow pencil, a big safety pin that she carries for emergencies if she suddenly loses a button and there is of course the heel of her other shoe.

She continues using her feminine weapons, with enthusiasm, speed and care. The small opening gets bigger. Hope produces festive tunes and her bright eyes are filled with the glitter of victory. The strength of her free will is about to break the siege. Life outside awaits her liberation, her truthfulness and her generosity, that slavery be abolished for ever and that she, with her own hands, ends an era of unjust rule and breaks the chains of suppression.

One unmerciful eye looks upon her through the circular opening. It observes her diligence and the likelihood of her becoming free for ever.

The mean wicked eye moves nervously with expressions of evil and anxiety. In this external world there are those who desire to keep her imprisoned. There are those who are terrified to death of her gaining her freedom and independence. The mighty eye narrows the siege around her. She has approached the end line, the safety spot. This is the undeniable truth. This wicked eye gets terrified. It forcibley imposes the siege on her. It wants her to give in, to announce her defeat in any way. But she is stubborn and patient. The eye is mad with anger as she proceeds and progresses in her work. It confines her to a small corner of the small room and devours all her primitive feminine weapons until she has nothing more to help her in the battle for victory.

Suddenly, she finds herself faced with her dear circular opening, unable to move. The siege becomes more confining and excruciating until it almost flattens her against the barrier whose heart she had almost smashed.

Like the cripple who resists in order to free himself of the burden of the handicap enforced upon him by suppression and terrorism, she inserts her ten sharp pointed nails, her last weapon, and continues widening the circumference of the circle.

Translated by Lobna A. Youssef

MEETING AT A TIME
OF ESCAPING LOVE

In a moment when the pain was excruciating and because she wanted to be a woman without a past to remember or a future to look forward to, she accepted that he becomes her companion on this painful journey; he is a man without a past that she knows about or a future that she cares for.

She thought that they were two tigers in the middle of a forest. Both were on the defensive desiring to take revenge. The next moment of anger will – no doubt - be a moment of victory over the pains of one of the sides– tempororily – at the expense of deepening the wound of the other.

Because of the sensitivity of this wound she knows that, in similar cases, it is not possible to allot victory and loss with justice to either of the two partners involved in a forest of emotions, stabbed by hundreds and hundreds of arrows and daggers.

This is why she is not surprised to hear him tell her :

"In all my previous relationships I was the one who left first."

And without desiring to provoke or challenge him, she spieaks to state facts:

"Me too. I always leave first."

She felt the tiger wandering in the deserts within him wag its tail as a sign of discomfort. He asked her, not out of sympathy but in order to devise his plan of invasion and retreat.

"Why?"

She spoke, unveiling her wound with the forgiving and capable attitude of one who gives the enemy a chance to progress :

"Because I was always the giving side, even when giving was at the expense of proving myself."

His eyes twinkled with guile and slyness and said in a voice that gave way to inner fierceness :

"Therefore you admit that the one who gives more leaves earlier?"

She said, showing the cards of her game with simple complexity :

"I admit that the one who endures greater pain leaves first."

He says with rash joy that reveals that he is arrogant and stupid :

"Then, my giving will be more."

With an unreal smile she said :

"We'll see."

He smiles proudly like one accustomed to winning at the end. He then leaves his seat in order to get physically close to her. He holds her slender palm and folds it in his own hand.

She endures - she does not show any signs of pain. With a callenging look, she looks into his eyes :

"I will not scream."

With great self-confidence that infuriates her, he said :

"Who says I am pressing?"

She remembers the old war plans during her adolescence when her older sister taught her the first lessons of life: "Attack is the best means of defence." She smiles with bitterness when she remembers the old lesson. She never makes use of it at the right time. Perháps because "the other" always comes disguised in a costume of love and innocence offering the loving rose with one hand and hiding a poisonous dagger in the other hand behind his back. She used to believe the words of innocence and with tenderness come forward to embrace the love rose. At that point, the dagger would be thrust in her chest with a betraying stab. She would falter and stumble because of the two shocks: the betrayal and the wound. But before her body hit the ground, where quick feet raced to trample on the defeated, betrayed, weak and fragile, she would stir with agitation and jump to her feet. Perspiring heavily on the forehead, and blood flowing on her body she would repeat to herself in a voice that echoed and penetrated the cells of her will power: "Be strong. Do not fall. What doesn't kill us strengthens us. This predicament will pass like others and when it does you will become stronger, you will not fall."

From the corner of his eye, he caught a glimpse of her secret thoughts. As he stirred her coffee for her, he said :

"They say women like me to pat them on the shoulder when they feel weak."

Smiling proudly, he goes closer, with his hand ready to pat her on the shoulder.

She shrivels and moves away before he touches her with his hand. It is as if she fears his fingers would touch the wound. Sitting properly and haughtily she says :

"Men too."

As he drank his coffee, he said with self-confidence:

"Men do not feel weak because they face problems

with open mindedness. They have no illusions."

Her leg shivers nervously. She speaks with exaggerated coldness, in an attempt to impart her fury :

"Strange, but your eyes say otherwise."

With a sneer that showed his fury, he said :

"And what do my eyes say?"

"That you have just overcome a big illusion."

Proudly confident, he said :

"I am not the victim of illusions. But sometimes, I wilfully open the door for them for a while."

She feels the fury of the tiger within reaching its limit. It is alert and ready to attack. At any price, her tiger wants to tear apart his false pride, to rip the flesh of his arrogance, to cause his stubbornness to bleed. But she postpones all this to a later moment. Pulling his leg, to get him to confess his real intentions, she asks :

"Am I one of these exceptional cases?"

He answers impertinently :

"Perhaps."

As she tries to control her superficial quietness, she says :

"I admire your aggressive 'frankness'."

He bends his head as a sign of gratitude and says :

"First statement of praise I've ever heard from you."

Shooting her first arrow, she says :

"This is no praise but a declaration of war."

He smiles arrogantly saying :

"Every war involves desires for gain. What do you desire to gain from me, may I ask?"

She shows her muscles as if exhibiting her strength:

"Not all wars are for the sake of plundering. There are wars fought to maintain legal borders."

He stands, walks around her seat and waves his arm as he starts to lose control over his nerves. He comes close to her ear and cries out :

"Who has expressed doubt concerning the legality of the borders? I am merely a visitor and have absolutely no colonialist plans."

She readjusts the position of her legs and yells in rebellious rage for her pride :

"What do you think I am? Abandoned land that you can trample on with your feet during your wanderings between lands and borders?"

His voice grows louder as he holds her shoulder and shakes her in anger, saying :

"You women do not know what you want. If we choose to live in your land, you accuse us of occupying it and if we pass by like travellers you describe us as pirates and invaders."

Attempting to hide a sarcastic smile, she says :

"In my special case, I have not decided yet what I want from you."

Wittily reflecting his intelligence, he says :

"I know. You want me as a prisoner of war."

She shakes her shoulder pretending not to care and trying to avenge herself for a previous insult:

"Perhaps."

His hand shakes nervously and the cup of coffee falls on the floor. He carelessly looks at the broken pieces that scatter as if the incident is beyond his scope of comprehension. Looking at her angrily, he continues talking :

"It seems to me you do not love the strong man."

She speaks adding more fuel to the fire of his anger.

"In his madness, he sets fire that destroys his pride."

As if comforted by her inference, he says :

257

"I see you love the weak man so you can be domineerng."

Quickly she refutes this accusation :

"On the contrary, the weak man bores me and reminds me of my closet filled with old clothes, one which I never open."

He objects in anger, defending the pride of his fellow men :

"Great! You love no one then?"

To correct him, she says :

"Yes, I love the strong man who knows when and how to be weak."

He said in a challenging tone :

"You are afraid, terrified in fact."

She smiles sarcastically, as if she has heard a bad joke.

"Really? Afraid of whom? Can you tell me?"

He holds on to his challenge :

"Of your awareness that you are in need."

Suddenly, he becomes silent. She too is silent. They both think while playing with their fingers. She plays with her hair locks; he lights and extinguishes his lighter. They both are startled. They turn and look toward the blank white wall, as if the lights in the room have gone out. One strong beam of light gets centered on part of the white wall as a signal that the show will be on: a special film on the love meetings that have been thwarted in the past days of each of them.

In a low voice, he said to himself, "I hate to give and not to take equally." She speaks to herself saying : "I do not like to be exploited."

At that moment, she feels she possesses the strength to confess. She looks at him and in a voice that summons strength to overcome her weakness says:

"Yes, I feel afraid. Need enforces closeness and closeness results in a wound and a wound is the seed of pain."

At the same moment, he shivers with obscure fear. He catches himself redhanded: he feels the need for closeness and to quench his thirst for a moment of security.

He draws nearer to her quietly and for the first time he caresses her hair tenderly with his fingers and says :

"Don't worry. Men too are afraid."

She reflects upon his gentleness which is perhaps a bait which he is using to trap her tiger and tear it apart. With claws ready to attack, she says :

"Yes, and they lie as well."

The fierceness of her reaction shocks him. Once more he assumes the role of the king of the jungle and says in a haughty voice :

"Men do not lie because they are free. Courage is one of the traits of freedom and courage is opposed to cowardice and lying."

She speaks sarcastically :

"Do you really live under the illusion that among you some are free?'

At that point the fierce monster breaks the bars of what they call civilized behaviour and announces open aggression. Twisting her arm he speaks to her harshly :

"You are sick - in fact, you have a psychic problem."

Her tiger emerges to be ready for the enemy. She tries to resist the harshness of his fists, she screams in anger :

"Is this because I refuse to give in?"

He speaks as he holds her arms more tightly :

"No, but because you are stupid to the extent that you don't realize how different we are in strength."

She resists with savagery until one of her arms is free. Quickly, she snatches the cup of coffee and throws the coffee àt him. She screams saying :

"You always win by using your physical strength because your arguments are weak."

This time, he does not reply. He finds it enough to pull her hair and throw her on the floor.

She is insulted and feels oppressed. She pounces on one of his legs, rips it until it bleeds. He screams and bends over his wounded leg out of pain. Terrifed of his vengeance, she gets up and runs to hide in the kitchen. In pain, he follows. She quickly attempts to close the kitchen door behind her but he is quicker. With his huge body, he manages to stop her. Trembling, she takes a few steps back, and observes the malicious look of vengeance in his eyes. She runs to hide behind the stove. He quickly surprises her with a blow on the jaw. That makes her lose balance and she falls in pain. He throws himself over her. To further humiliate her, he tears her clothes apart.

She cries because of the severity of the agony of her soul that makes her unaware of the physical pain.

She screams to announce her agony :

"You have spoiled everything. If you were not stupid and haughty, I could have given you the most ecstatic moment of your life."

She then felt that every muscle in his body weakened, relaxed and was still. His body shrank and became tame and tender. His skin became mild and expanded to form a gentle sheet that caressed the wound. From his cold sweat that wetted her skin, she felt that he was ashamed of himself.

Translated by Lobna A. Youssef.

260

IBTIHAL SALEM was born in Cairo in 1949. She graduated in Psychology in Ain Shams University, 1972. She works at the Cultural Palaces (clubs) of the Ministry of Culture. She started writing while still a secondary-school student. Her first work was published in the **Student Newspaper** of her university student union. After graduation, she spent ten years with her husband in Port-Said. This "influenced my first book, **The Seagull** (Al-Nawras), 1989," she wrote. Most of the stories in this collection were inspired by this city. Her second collection of short stories: **A Small World** (Dunya Saghira) was published in 1992. Several of her stories were published in literary magazines or newspapers, such as **Creativity** (Ibda') and **Literature and Criticism** (Adab wa Naqd). Salem is an original writer. Her vitality of spirit is strongly reflected in her stories. Some of them have been translated into English and German.

"The Seagull" is the title story of her first book; "The Bet" appeared in her second.

262

THE SEAGULL

Ibtihal Salem

"What do you know about war? For the likes of you it's over, but for us it isn't," she shouted at her dumbfounded superior. In seconds she had left his office in tears.

In the evening she met Youssef. They took the ferry to get to the other side of the harbour.

"I notice that the number of sea-gulls is decreasing from year to year," said she to Youssef with her eyes sailing in a sea of sadness.

Khaki was the predominant colour, and a stinking smell mixed with accumulated perspiration came out of the ancient building whose windows were stained with dark blue paint, and which was surrounded with barbed wires.

She made her way through clustering dead human bodies until, with great effort, she got to the lists of captives and casualties hanging on the wall.

Suddenly she realized that Youssef was talking to her :

"I saw a great number of dead seagulls on the shores while I was sailing the seas."

"What do they die of?"

"It's said, of the excessive soot and smoke in the air." Youssef answered with the sea air filling the shirt which he wore under his leather sweater whose upper buttons were left unfastened.

She took a deep breath of the air iodine and her memory swam in his eyes back to the days when they went round the light-house counting the seagulls and dreaming, while the migrating birds were caught in a playful little wave stirred by a soft afternoon breeze.

Youssef grew up and rode big waves over the sea, whether it was calm or rough, and she was preoccupied with everyday concerns. She recovered from her trance when she felt Youssef's fingers caressing her hair.

"Let's come down to what is more important. Is there any news about you?" he said while getting out a packet of foreign cigarettes from the pocket of his jeans.

"I had a row with my boss. I requested a day off to transfer my son to a school nearer to our house, but he turned down my request."

"Doesn't he know?" said Youssef taking a deep breath.

Youssef was a sailor, and she was, and still is, his friend, his haven whenever he yearns for one.

She drew closer to him while watching his shadow that fell under the faint lantern of the ferry.

Days were figures in a black line waiting every month for a barred window to open; and nights meant cold walls and fixed eyes waiting for a knocker who never turned up.

The ferry struck the harbour quay and the bump threw her into his arms. A slight shudder went through her body.

She answered while she was setting foot on land, "He knows."

They turned into a side road.... Women's wailing was mixed with gun shots, and rotting bodies protruded from the rear of the 'government' van.

When the news was imparted to her, she put her languid hand on her belly, and her tears were stone dry for the fate of the forthcoming child.

Youssef waited for her prolonged silence to come to an end while her eyes went round every part of the surrounding scene.

He threw away his half-burnt cigarette and drew so close to her that his body almost touched hers.

"What was his reaction?" he asked.

She answered in a stifled voice.

"He said a lot of things. All I remember is 'What use are you to this department?'... 'I don't give extra days off unless they are unpaid.'.. 'Why should you send your son to school? Let him be taught a trade.'... I could stand no more. I exploded and told him that he had a dead heart and he knew nothing about war."

Their stroll ended up at the entrance of her house which was rather dark. Youssef held her hand and pressed it with both hands when he realized how embarrassed she was when she asked him in. She drew so close to him that she smelt the iodine in his perspiration. Her eyes measured his strong figure and dwelt on the sails reflected in his eyes. She asked him, "When will the sea-gulls be as many as they were in the harbour?"

He laughed, patted her shoulders, and said,

"Soon, very soon."

He pulled the zip fastener of his sweater up to his neck and stole away– from her– into the dark, and her sad heart followed him.

Translated by Guirguis El-Rashidi

THE BET

"Do you feel cold?" he asked her in amazement.

"Frozen," she shouted pulling together the ends of the collar of her blouse.

He pushed a button beside a small cassette player and warmth began to spread gradually into her limbs. She sat relaxed. He pushed another button and all the car windows closed.

He manipulated the steering wheel shouting:

"I love cold weather, and you?"

"I love warmth and company."

Trees and houses fleeted in the twinkling of an eye, and neon lights were reflected on the wind screen of the car.

Warmth playfully stirred up such associations that she forgot that above her knee there was a hole in her stocking which she had been trying to hide with the hem of her dress. The tip of her toe almost showed out of her worn-out shoe. She always resented the smallness of her salary which was not, and never will be, enough to buy her a coat. She thanked the good chance that made possible her meeting with that old friend in such a bitterly cold night, his catching a glimpse of her a few steps from the establishment she worked for, and inviting her to a free ride home.

She recovered when she heard his voice saying:

"Eh, where have you been?"

She took a deep breath before she answered:

"In the wide world."

He brought his face close to hers and said with a smile:

"The world, my pretty, is to make the cleverest use of your chances."

She was dumbfounded, and his features looked different as if she was seeing him for the first time.

She recollected her memories of him. They lived in the same vicinity in a small coastal town, but she had not seen him for years. She only heard that he went away to a faraway country.

She looked intently at the details of his features which were marked with rough wrinkles. The hair on the front part of his head had turned grey, though he was barely forty. In spite of his starched shirt collar, his necktie was vulgarly red, not matching his woollen check jacket.

They approached the district, one of whose streets once brought them together. When he pulled up, she wished all establishments and extra time work would be cancelled in cold winter nights so that she would not have to get out of the warm car.

"It's ice-sold outside," said she in a hoarse voice.

He turned the steering wheel shouting: "Let's have another round to carry on our chat. Life's but a lucky hour."

He drove round the market place in the square next to their street, round the depot of broken-down buses that looked like heaped junk, and then emerged into the main road.

He took out a fine cigarette box, tried to give her one but she refused pretending that she had a bad chest.

He did not pay any attention to what she said. He pressed the button of a gold lighter, and the space between their two faces was lit. She noticed that his eye lids were swollen and his eyes were dim.

He turned on a recorder which filled the place with a boisterous noise. A look of his sneaked to her legs, but she closed them instantly.

His voice came out of the smoke circles:

"What do you think?"

"The voice is reasonable, but I can't make out a word."

He shook his head to the rhythm of the tune and said:

"You know, I paid for the tape, the recorder and the Mercedes, together with an export bureau and two blocks of flats a green rabbit.[1] By God, I paid a rabbit."

He stretched his chest and resumed saying:

"By God I paid a green rabbit," and added with considerable self-confidence, "and I could buy the singer at any price he names."

She looked around in the narrow space of the car, bit her finger nails, tried to extricate herself from the embarrassment of the moment. She said in a loud voice:

"Do you remember when we used to jump the school fence and ask the boy Bessa, son of Fahima, to hold our bags and clothes for us, then ran until we got to the sea front? When my mother smelled salt in my body, she urged my father to beat me."

He knit his eyebrows and moved his head as if trying to remember. She went on:

"And when we went to the European quarter hanging behind cars and betting which of us could collect more garbage tins?"

The shriek of the brakes drowned her laughter; her head almost hit the front of the car.

---

(1) *A million pounds in large notes according to the "nouveaux riches" jargon.*

He sulked and his features became sharper. He said:

"I think that's enough. We'd better go back."

When she was aware of a stinking smell, she realized that they were near the district, one of whose streets once brought them together.

She broke the silence:

"Would you bet?"

The features of his face were reflected on the wind screen. He answered:

"On what?"

"That you couldn't stand alone for an hour at the bus stop. Didn't you say that you liked the cold?"

Amazed, he turned his face towards her.

"Is that a problem?"

"This means you agree?"

"Starting from tomorrow."

She pointed at an old house at the end of the market street.

"Let me off there."

When she got off, she strongly slammed the car door and went round to his side while he was starting the car. She shouted with her eyes fixed on him,

"If I win the bet, the car will be mine."

The frost struck its claws into her flesh, and the space between where she was standing and the cars that looked alike was covered with extending snow.

Translated by Guirguis El-Rashidi

270

MONA RAGAB was born in Cairo in 1953. She obtained a degree in Economics and Political Science from Cairo University. She is cultural assistant editor of **Al-Ahram.** *She started writing while still at school and has published various short stories and poems. She has published three books and a fourth - a novel - is under print. Her first work was an autobiography translated from French:* **My Life in a Thousand and One Days** *(Hayati Fi Alf Youm wa Youm), 1979 and 1983. She then published two short-story collections :* **The Masks Game** *(Lo'bat Al-Agni'ah), 1987 and* **When Women Rebel** *('indama Tathour al- Nisa), 1991. Her first short- story collection has been translated into German and some stories into English.*

Both "When Women Revolt" and "The Fervent Heart" appear in her second collection of short stories.

WHEN WOMEN REVOLT

Mona Ragab

> *Like difficult travail Revolution*
> *is of dubious avail .*

A squadron of black shiny Mercedes cars were parked solemnly by the gate of the huge building which had been lit for a number of hours. Stern-looking high-officials had been emerging from these cars, one after the other, in their rich apparel. An illustrious lady shot out from the third car to join the line of prominent figures. Another lady, who had been waiting for them at the gate for an hour, was filled with joy upon seeing them. She ran down the carpeted staircase to greet one of the high-officials warmly with a strong shake, using both hands, which almost made him stagger backwards.

They all came to discuss that grave event that had taken place three days before. Distress prevailed in their homes as that atrocious incident had shattered their placid illusions.

There was no escapee: women had to come out of their hiding places and cry out aloud everywhere :

"Stop the cancerous terrorism."

Women arrived from all directions and walks of life: left and right, north and south, the labourers, and the drudges, the non-chalants as well as the ladies of fashion.

"Women's presence needed."

That statement appeared on the invitations forwarded by the organiser of the meeting. She managed to gather all that number by making them realise the importance of their participation in that event. She received everybody cheerfully and addressed them as follows :

"Your presence tonight reflects how much you are keen on taking part in discussing those serious events."

The high-official composed himself and replied collectedly and pedantically deriving his tone from mountains of inheritad traditions.

"When great happenings take place all feelings should be bound in unison. We appreciate your partaking in this meeting and we shall readily listen to your suggestions."

Another official added :

"Your coming together tonight, clearly reveals your determination to take a stance regarding these great events."

When the gentlemen participating appeared in the hall, the ladies gave a warm applause. They stood up to confirm their appreciation of the gentlemen's co-operation.

"Finally they will listen to us," said the secretary of the conference to her colleague, as she was placing ashtrays on the platform table. But as the chairperson was introducing a distinguished guest, he whispered to her with a smile :

"I hope we will start immediately. I still have some other very important appointments."

She nodded and like a sea-captain sailing on murky seas, she started her mission. She replied buoyantly, like a free bird,

"Right away."

It was shortly after six o'clock when the large white hall became almost full. The chairperson of the conference flushed with a bright smile, as she sat among the men in the centre of the platform. She felt like a lion guarding its lair, anticipating, with a wave of enthusiasm, the penetration of the jungle of inherited traditions.

She embarked on her speech boldly :

"We are meeting tonight to voice women's stand

towards the event that had great repercussions nation-wide."

Loud cries stormed the place like luminous meteors scorching the canopy. For the first time all feminine currents were united: the oppressed. the tortured, the cultured and the vanquished. Nothing could dissipate their bitterness but hope in a future relief. These moments pregnant with aspiration, anticipated the end of that suffocating nightmare that seemed eternal.

An elegant middle-aged woman stood up and spoke impatiently:

"Let's start by condemning all sorts of terrorism."

The official on the platform interrupted:

"I hope we can formulate an accurate statement expressing the audience's view of the issue."

A stern-looking, bespectacled university professor went up to the platform and said:

"We shan't leave this place until we come to a common accord to be forwarded to all the parties concerned. But we must first reach a definite stand towards all our violated legal rights."

A tempest of clamouring applause broke out, staged by those with long hair, cropped hair, brunettes, blondes, redheads, greyheads, those with tied up hair, loose hair , hair cut short according to the latest fashion or hidden under white or blue head covers. The chairperson stared at them speechlessly. They all seemed to have uncovered old wounds allowing the gush of anger to flow.

An elderly woman stood up to speak. She looked like an old camel that had long-controlled its thirst. Her grey hairs were not totally hidden by her blonde wig. She spoke in high-flown language :

"The kitchen mentality has imprisoned women within the walls of their kitchen since the remotest times. Starting from tonight we shall not compromise the rights we are entitled to as modern women."

Another lady found her way through the crowd. She was wearing a shabby, discoloured, pinkish *galabiya*.[1] She seemed to be carrying the Himalayas on her shoulders, though her only burden was a small plastic bag containing a few coloured pieces of clothing. Distress gathered under her eyes.

They allowed her to speak. When she began, the words choked her and she broke out into a fit of tears expressing the unsaid. One of the ladies attending the meeting patted her on the shoulder and offered her a handkerchief to wipe the flowing tears. This helped her to speak. She mumbled but then broke out in a voice anguished by a heavy affliction she had endured for years.

"This evening my husband threw me out of doors after he got married to another woman. This bag holds all that I am left with after ten years of marriage."

There was a great deal of commotion and turmoil.

The great hall shook with a loud feminine outcry. The chairperson failed to stop the noise banging the brass ash-tray on the table. The women's voices sounded like seagulls, shrieks reaching the uppermost sky levels.

An embittered prominent writer gave vent to her personal grievance saying :

"Men aim their poisonous weapons at intellectual women. They describe our writing as feminist literature."

She was followed by a tall, slim-legged, attractive woman emerging from the back rows. She was wearing

---

(1) A long loose traditional garment.

jeans and a sports blouse and was holding a long cigarette. She resumed the issue :

"Men want to lock women up permanently in a dark cell. All retrogressive voices have to be stopped."

The men murmured grumbling and their lips were turned up in disagreement. They refrained from speaking and took their leave quietly. Oversatiated, they departed collectively finding excuses in other important appointments. They gave the women a formal salute and walked out with a grin. The chairperson was disappointed and tried to stop them :

"We had hoped to reach a consensus and a statement at the end of the meeting to be jointly signed by men and women!"

None of the men listened nor waited. The officials apologised for leaving, their feet propelling them towards the gates.

"Send us the official report for perusal. We promise we'll be looking into it," said the high official.

As he said that, he winked furtively at another man as they approached the gate. The assistant realized the meaning of the statement. Overwhelmed with distress she said :

"We hope you'll join us for the next meeting."

It was not very late when all the men departed. The women had decided to stay until precise recommendations to be put into effect were reached. Voices interposed, speeches alternated and views were exchanged. Like a hurricane, clashing views were put forth for discussion. A whirlwind of reproaches, complaints, and protests blasted. They burst out from the depths of an old mine. Passive tears were copiously shed but they soon gave way to fervent enthusiasm.

The hall quaked under the heat of emotion menacing a fiery outburst.

Some of the passers-by came up to find out what was going on. The chairperson clapped her hands to bring the raging alternating shots to a halt. She ordered the intruders out so as to complete the comprehensive plan in complete privacy.

"I beseech you for some order so as not to lose sight of the main issue."

After the evacuation of all the intruders, she spoke in a voice that she wanted to reach the whole room :

"We declare the establishment of the Women's Defence Association, here and now."

She was gratified by the warm response she received from the agitated faces flushing with fury.But was that the flush of fervour or was it the effect of the make-up on their faces? She did not ponder much on that nor was she discouraged. What counted was that these women had responded to her appeal with glowing hope and fervent remonstrance.

At eight, in the heat of the discussion, a black cat came purring. A frightened young lady sprang up amidst the crowd of women and quit the hall. One of the panel members caught sight of the clock marking a quarter past eight, so she left her seat apologetically. They asked her :

"Are you leaving when we're still laying the foundation stone?"

She apologised to all of them on account of its being time for her baby's evening feed. Another young lady, in her twenties, withdrew silently. She had whispered to her companion that her boy friend was waiting for her outside. She had not seen him for a number of days.

A fourth lady departed hurriedly upon remembering that her daughter would be back from her maths private lesson at eight. She was followed by the tenth and twentieth who claimed other urgent excuses. The chairperson's eyes reflected her annoyance. She drew out a cigarette to quell her agitation and anger, then drank a glass of water to subdue her wrath.

She yelled out calling them back,

"We haven't written out the recommendations yet."

But she was unable to stop the departing ladies nor to keep the remaining ones seated. The line trailed towards the gates and dispersed in the corridors.

"Let's then meet another time at the beginning of next month, perhaps our circumstances will be better. Perhaps we'll exert some more effort!" she added.

Three ladies approved the date of the meeting. They were the only ones remaining after the rest had vanished while she was screaming :

"Don't bury your heads in the pit of despair, ladies."

She gathered her papers and before leaving, she ended the official report with these words :

"The coming conference will be held at the beginning of next month."

She, then, picked up her handbag and walked out supporting herself against the walls of the empty hall.

Translated by Marie-Therese Abdel-Messih

THE FERVENT HEART

How often are our dreams aborted
by the cruelty of our fortune

Heavens! What a child you make of me!
The minute your features twitched, tears gushed down my
cheeks and power was subdued.At first, I would not admit
to myself that I was at your mercy. It had never occurred to
me, not for a second, that I would become a young fretful
girl in the presence of your turbulent heart that drains me
of my energies and cruelly strips me of my resistance. How
do I suddenly flutter like a blank sheet of paper with every
wince you make.

I was overwhelmed by your tears when one morning
before leaving for school you remonstrated in rage :

"No mother, you can't go away and leave me for a
whole month – that's too much; one week is enough."

I pretended not to have heard you. I did hear you, but
I acted as though your words did not hit me right in the
ears.

I had to have my papers ready, while you were set on
your studies. There was a long way for me to cover,
preparing the documents for my scholarship to study in
France. I had to drudge along a prolonged consuming
effort.

But that morning I was bewildered by your gushing
stream of tears. It was the morning when I had to complete
the last document needed. I composed myself until I
completed the bureaucratic procedures. Until then, I had
thought that my mind was firmly set on my future. It

seemed to me that my great plans were about to be accomplished. During the coming two years, I shall move freely between Cairo and Paris. I have always longed to obtain my doctorate degree abroad, signed in Parisian letters. There, it was all awaiting me, the lights of the bright future gleaming ahead. In fact, I was th˙ only one selected among scores of candidates by the administrators.

On your way back from school you inquired about the details of my voyage. I told you that I would just leave you for twenty days.

You protested very decisively: "Only twenty days no longer. Else I'll be angry with you, forever."

I could not say any more. My courage failed me and I was left to utter bewilderment and hesitation. I was unable to tell you that I should stay two months abroad, for a start, and then I'll be moving between Cairo and Paris, that going away was inevitable for me to complete my studies at the Sorbonne.

Before I boarded the plane taking me to Paris I reassured you :

"I won't be away for long. Take care of your studies sweetheart, I want to be proud of you."

Here I am finally confronting my dream. I entered my quiet Parisian room, situated in a huge white building annexed to the University. But suddenly, I was transfixed infront of the door as though I was stung by a scorpion.

I examined my primrosey, plainly furnished room, over and over. It looked cramped and gloomy, despite its ornamented furniture. How about that desk, that seemed like a dustbin out of use? My desk in Cairo, however small, embraced immense dreams. Suddenly your anguished face emerged on the walls calling me back to you.

As I was lost in thought, an Arab-looking girl barged

into my room like a rocket, welcoming me with a friendly smile. She came from Morocco, and lived in the room opposite mine, she told me. She spoke to me as one accustomed to the life in a tumultuous city :

"Unpack, change your clothes and let me take you on a sightseeing tour around this charming city, beginning with Montmartre and the Champs Elysees. There's no time here to gaze into space."

As I was brushing my hair, ready for sightseeing your face appeared on the mirror. I recalled the time you stood infront of the glass trying some bright lipstick on your little mouth. You had become thirteen then, I contemplated you as you were trying to add more years to your age. You blurted out :

"Mother, when can I wear lipstick, varnish my nails, wear high heels and drive a car?"

Without waiting for a reply, you added :

"Mother I won't get married except to the man I love."

I stood there dumfounded. I could not believe that in no time you had become a little woman, considering the ways of life, without fear or embarrassment.

I said :

"My God! when has my little one grown up?"

You roared with laughter and said :

"Mum I've become as tall as you. Let's check I'm no longer a child, mother."

And in no time, you put on the new blouse you had picked up yourself, along with the jeans that make you feel free. You let down your hair to add more charm to your face, breaking all ties with childhood bonds.

But the following days, I was involved in the administrative procedures of applying for the Sorbonne, and I was led on from one step to another in a systematic chain of procedures. Once in Paris, I got to know how to use the underground, found the nearest supermarket, and where to get the popular French bread. I was introduced to some Egyptians forming homogeneous groups within the great city.

But in the library, while I was looking up some material in some references, your face emerged within the blank pages. I turned over to the next page as if to escape your sudden invasion on the first page, but it was useless.

In the evening my Lebanese friend living in the room at the other end of the corridor, invited me to one of the discoteques with some university colleagues. My friend noticed my preoccupation and tried to console me :

"We all become homesick at the beginning of our stay. Don't worry. You will soon get over this feeling of estrangement with the quick beat of life in Paris. You won't find a minute to spare once your regular classes get started."

She went on :

"Pluck up some courage. It will only take you a month to get accustomed to live on your own here."

There, in a small Parisian café, I found myself amidst a number of French and Arab artists. This opened up to me vast possibilities of freedom of expression. They spoke about setting up an exhibition entitled: 'The Inner Self'. Its conditions were to paint what goes on within one's inner self without any controlling factor.

That night I couldn't go to sleep. I caught myself drawing a featureless woman gazing at nothing, walking on a tight rope. I decided to participate with that drawing. When they asked me for its title, I could not give it any. I had put it all down, the way it flowed out from my inner depths, and I was unable to explain it. Unexpectedly, I was awarded first prize.

The next morning, my Moroccan friend, living in the room opposite mine, came along with me to join the rest of the company who were celebrating my unexpected award. We all met at the small cate. But suddenly I left the café without giving any reasons.

My Moroccan friend who had been living for years in Paris was astounded to see me at noon the same day, my passport ready. She kept saying :

"You must be mad. You've got the opportunity to study in Paris and you withdraw your papers before one month is over. Anybody would just crave for such a chance."

She went on, heedless of my preoccupation :

"You must be mad."

When I asked my French Professor for a leave, he was exceedingly provoked and addressed me with an air of superiority :

"What has happened?"

I replied :

"Some urgent matters."

The over-confident, smart Frenchman said :

"Easterners are quite emotional."

I said :

"I'll be back next year, don't worry. I've just come to tell you I'll be back. I'm sorry. It's some urgent matter. I'm not sure whether I belong here or there. Once I decide I'll be back."

At midday sharp, I was waiting for you in the school playground. I stood there motionless gazing at your class room. When the bell rang I reached out for you vehemently.

Before cuddling in my arms you asked me :

"Why have you been away from me for so long mummy? I haven't seen you for twenty-five days."

Amidst the torrent of your protests and my anxiety, I gave you my unsteady hand on our way back home.

Translated by Marie-Therese Abdel-Messih

NEAMAT EL-BIHEIRI was born in Cairo in 1953. She is a 1976 graduate of the Faculty of Commerce, Ain Shams University. She belongs to the youngest generation of women writers represented in this volume. She has published two short-story collections : **Half A Woman** (Nisf Imra'a,) 1984 and **The Infatuated** (Al' ashiqoun), 1989, in addition to a collection of children's stories: **The Good Fire** , 1988. Not unlike some of the other writers in this collection, El-Biheiri often focusses on women characters involved in a love relationship in which they play a positive role. However, her forthcoming collection carries the non-committal title : **Stories of a Lonely Woman** (Qissas Imra'a Wahida).

Al-Biheiri has already had two of her stories translated into English.

"The Infatuated" and "The Sand Dream" appear in her second collection of short stories.

THE SAND DREAM

Neamat El-Biheiri

Two days ago I received the news of his forthcoming marriage. It had been quite a long time since I saw him last. All the members of the family, even those who knew the old story, agreed to go to the wedding.

At night, the house was empty, so I opened the window revealing the moonless sky. A bee buzzed near my ear then flew through the window. Following it with my eyes I envisaged the family house in which we lived, he and I, and the honey plate.

We used to lick the honey like two kittens, and following each lick, he made me promise not to hurry, for the plate was large and the honey was like the days we lived in the "family house".

Each one of our mothers and our uncle's wife had her private bedroom.

The three bedrooms were next to each other, while that of grandfather and grandmother were at the other end of the house, near the entrance.

At night when the doors are ajar and "El Sitt's"[1] voice is heard singing "good company prolongs the night," mingled with the scent of incense and the night, we slip like beams of light, sit on the window sill revising our lessons, filled with fear of the stout small-poxed teacher's cane. The smell of incense flows, he runs to the kitchen to bring the honey plate, the night merges with the smell of honey and

---

(1) *"The lady" or Umm Kalthoum, a prominant Egyptian singer.*

the fragrance of incense and our breaths. Suddenly, his slim weak-sighted mother comes out of her room, breaking the silence, she looks at him reproachfully, he grabs my hand and leads me away.

At the old school, our comrades' eyes chase us to the end of the playground. We eat our sandwiches and we draw our dream on the sand with a pencil. When they approach, we erase our "sand dream" with our fingers. They always ask him "Why do you keep her company even during the recess?" He answers gallantly, "We are cousins." I laugh and they laugh whispering that he has many female cousins in school, who sit withdrawn at the back of the class. Our comrades move away and we start anew.... We pile the sand to one side and we draw our dreams of a job and a home in which we are no longer children. I hide from him another dream of a home in which his slim weak-sighted mother does not live. When the recess bell rings, the sand particles slip slowly and tenderly from our fingers, but the dream lingers on between our embracing hands like a wheat grain in a bird's beak.

The teacher with the concave eye-glasses chooses me to read the morning news. I stand facing the students. I hold up the newspaper and read the headlines about the aid coming from the West. I only fear his bright eyes looking at me. I can see the scars on his legs showing from beneath his shorts.... I miss the line I'm reading in the newspaper and the Weastern aid gets lost too.

The school bell rings and we walk "two by two", as decreed by the slim teacher. He refuses to walk with his partner and waits for me by the narrow cement stairs whose smell I've never forgotten.

In the classroom, he hammers down the protruding

nail in our seat, and orders me to be careful when standing and sitting. I nod approvingly. Before the exams he reviews the lessons with me and refuses to let anybody cheat from us. He opens the desk's drawer putting his head in and whispers to me "Your shoes are torn." I laugh and turning right and left, I whisper back, "Your trousers are torn." We close our notebooks and leave when the recess bell rings.

Sitting on the wooden seats fastened to the ground, the supervisor chooses us to help her distribute the pastry and yellow cheese – types of food we do not see or eat outside school.

We sat eating in silence. I found a rusty half razor in my pastry. I showed it to him, he threw his pastry in the sand, and went round to all our school fellows throwing their pastry and yellow cheese from their hands. He ran and the students followed him. Through the dust aroused by his feet I saw them like little ghosts. We decided not to take this meal from the supervisor any more.

The stout supervisor used to look at us angrily. Once, while I was looking at her buttocks, I fancied jumping onto them with him and sitting on them driving her as if she were "Father Ali's"[1] donkey.

When we grew up, we used to chase each other to the corn field. We used to hide behind the tall yellow corn ears and pick up fresh flowers which had a strange taste to our lips, and a shuddering feeling to our bodies. Suddenly, we would hear his mother's voice telling us it was time to leave.

He helps me onto "Father Ali's" donkey on my way to

---

[1] In rural areas father, in this context, does not refer to the actual father, but to on elderly man, generally a near relative.

the train station. His mother hits the donkey's backside. It runs on the dust. I hold tight to its neck so that it won't overturn me on one of the manure heaps piled by the pond's edge. His mother laughs and I remember that it is the first time I see her laughing till her teeth show. I hear the sound of his feet as, scared, he runs until he reaches the donkey's backside, he pulls it, gets me down and I slide over his body. I feel the same warmth and the same shudder I used to feel there... among the tall corn ears.

My fear disappears. Nothing wakes us up except his mother's shrill voice telling us it is time to go.

In the wide city streets we walk hand in hand to the river's edge. Remembering the honey plate he tightens his grip, "Would you like something to eat?"

We laugh together and the river echoes our laughter, waltzing, the plants gathered over it forming a green island. I used to like this view. It reminds me of the "sand dream" we used to draw in the school playground: the home, the job, the heavy-leafed tree and the ever-full plate of honey. A humid sprinkling from the river reached us.

One day nobody was at home. He insisted on unbraiding my hair. I was afraid of that moment. The smell of the honey we liked merged with that of the incense and our breaths, and we merged together in tender silence.

On the next day he went to his mother and told her of that desire which had dwelled in us since we were kids. He told her of the "sand dream" we used to draw at the far end of the school playground.

His mother struck her slim breasts and told us that we were both breast fed[1] by her, and if we get married and

---

(1) If 2 babies are breastfed by the same woman 3 times, they will be considered sister and brother and thus cannot marry.

have a child, it will cry in the house like the crow of illfate.

In our room, my thick braided mother swore that that weaksighted women never breastfed me, and that she reme-mbered our day of birth as if it were yester night.

By the door of our other uncle, his daughters with their gloating eyes... sat.

Translated by Nihal El-Ganzoury

THE INFATUATED

The old dilapidated buses entered the bus terminal as apprehensively as they themselves did. There stood the wooden booth of the terminal supervisor immersed in the smell of bus exhaust and the drivers and conductors urine.

They stood stealthily in their khaki clothes, with slim statures under the sneaking light coming from the windows of rows of blocks of flats on each side of the road. They were looking towards the camp, dreading that the trick of each night would be discovered... for night in the camp is oppressive and tyrannical while night in the city tickles their imagination. They sneak out one after the other like night creatures, they pass through the large iron gate, promising the night guard a packet of super cigarettes or of tea on their return. They quickly slip towards the dream that flutters with them like the wings of little pigeons, looking for love and freedom. They were eager for the moment when the supervisor would announce which bus would be leaving first... and it was the one they have always feared with its crazy driver and weak- sighted conductor.

They occupied all the seats. Through the front door mounted the bus driver drawing a last whiff from his cigarette then throwing it on the ground without putting it out. From the back door lazily mounted the conductor. He adjusted the concave glasses on his eyes cursing the department, its supervisor, passengers and the black day on which he took that job.. he did not calm down until he spat out of the window. He struck the back of the wooden ticket holder with the tail of his indelible pencil while looking intently into the soldiers' faces. He charged them reduced fare,[1] while he continued muttering his curses, swallowing the late night resentment. He went to his seat at the back of the bus behind the wooden table, emptied his pockets and started counting the money in the dim trembling light of the bus. It was difficult to count that large amount of money in 5 and 10 piaster bills. The soldiers were looking out of the broken windows and the camp's darkness was following their eyes but they were sure that it would not reach the city. For there they will find the cafés which are open till morning, shops selling juice and food and the voice of "El Sitt"[2] filling the night with fragrance, and the lights hanging over the windows of the cafés like amber beads hanging on women's chests in their villages. As for the women with their plump bodies wrapped in colourful clothes, they are the city's fragrant plants and blossoms.

One of the soldiers, pushing his cap to the back of his head, says: "Women are the musk and ambergris of the city." They laugh swayig from one side to the other swearing that walking through the city from end to end is less tiring than sleeping on the camp's beds with their rough covers. These pale grey coloured bed covers heaped on the beds look like wild animals with spiky hair staring at them defiantly. They very quickly fold them in a sly attempt to harmonize with them, and not in accordance with discipline as the sargeant thinks.

---

(1) *Soldiers usually pay reduced fare in public means of transportation.*
(2) *"The lady" or Umm Kalthoum, a prominant Egyptian singer.*

All their visions of the city, its nights and women appeared through scattered lights on both sides of the road but passed quickly as the bus hurried on. The camp darkness still kept following them from the broken windows although the bus had left the station.

From the windows they continued to see the dark quiet streets. During the day, while bringing the food supplies from the city, they tried to count the numerous electricity posts which were lined at regular distances on both sides of the road. At night these posts were not seen, as if they were uprooted at night to be implanted in the morning. The soldiers rested their heads on the backs of the seats infront of them in an attempt to sleep. They closed their eyes but they knew each feature of the road by the sound of it. So when the bus passed over that road bumper it meant that they were near the university with its beautiful college girls holding their books and notes. The soldiers sighed saying in the same breath "education is good". At the next turn the driver slowed down giving a chance to the cars heading left to ascend to the private hospital situated on a high hill like an elegant villa surrounded by trees on all sides. That rattling sound meant that the bus had reached the "Seven-Up" factory. The soldiers' heads were leaning over the backs of the front seats when a young woman in a blue dress got onto the bus, probably she was one of the factory workers. The conductor gave her a ticket. She stared into his face and leaned on the seat handle. It seemed that she knew him for she smiled at him more than once on her way to the seat. The sound of her shoes on the bus floor littered with cigarette butts and squashed tickets woke one of the soldiers up. Not waiting until she sat, he whistled an intermittent tune to his mates. They woke up like scared mice, and a state of disorder swept through the bus. The young woman did not take any notice of it. All her tender moves and eager looks were for the conductor. From her pursuit of him, it seemed that she took that bus just for his sake. A few moments passed and the young rural soldiers felt that the young woman's presence had given the night on the bus a different flavour. Those sitting at the back of the bus saw her long and flowing hair showing from under her simple scarf, those in the front turned their heads to look at her face with its beautiful features and at the two ends of the purple scarf knotted under her chin and pointing like two arrows towards her breasts. Those sitting near her in the middle of the bus saw her face, her scarf and her relaxed but tired buttocks. A few more minutes elapsed, another soldier whistled an intermittent tune. They were repeating the tune as if it were a special language they understood. They used it to exchange messages and dreams. They then started exchanging seats so that everyone would get a chance to see the young woman from all sides. They all saw her face, hair, back and breasts. Her features being fixed in their minds, they exchanged the same tune but this time it was uninterrupted, a sign of their content with what they had seen.

This went on for a period of time which could not be exactly determined, for all their awareness of time was that spent in their exchange of dreams, looks and longing during the night ride from the camp to the city. In a moment which seemed like a recession of the dream, the young woman rose from her seat, walked some steps calculated according to the speed of the bus, held to the iron bar on the ceiling of the bus and stood by the front door. For a moment it did not seem that she saw all these faces looking at her, she went past the eyes, heads and caps, and looked straight at the weak-sighted conductor. He was busy counting the large amount of threadbare small bills. It looked as though he wanted to get rid of them, so he started asking if anybody wanted a change of ten pounds. He didn't know that the hands that went into the pockets, were only feeling their emptiness and that they would only come out with khaki handkerchiefs to wipe away the sweat on their foreheads. The young woman's face looked sad in the trembling light of the bus, it was not affected by the happiness in their eager eyes. The purple scarf surrounding her face was light but taut, the blue dress with the straight vertical red stripes rounded out near her breasts and buttocks, then it tightened at the waist. Wanting to look at the road to determine how near her station was getting, she leaned over the window; the soldiers saw a larger part of her buttocks this time. They looked at her as if they were hypnotized. The conductor's rough voice was heard asking if any one wanted a change of five pounds, he continued staring at the heads and napes until he saw the hands going into the pockets, but to his disappointment they only came out with khaki handkerchiefs to wipe away the sweat. One of the soldiers lighted a cigarette, had one whiff then passed it to the second one who did the same thing then passed it to a third. It passed round to all the others. Smoke came out of their mouths, and through it the young woman in her blue dress with its vertical red stripes and her purple scarf seemed like a jinnee. One of them, who was near her when all the strings of smoke disappeared into vacuum, stared into her face which seemed to him like the permit given to him by the sargeant, her features were like minute words: his name, the date, and the dimple in her chin was like the signature he got giving him leave of absence to visit his village, family and his cousin.[1] The young woman took a quick look at the conductor who was again asking if any one wanted the change of one or two pounds, but no one answered.

The young woman bent once more out of the window so as to determine how much of the distance was left, the soldiers' breaths heaved longingly for a touch of her face. Suddenly the brakes were pulled... the young woman fell on the floor.

When she looked up she saw a trap of soldiers' faces and hands being laid for her. Everyone desired to touch the dream and to hold it. Their hands were stretched out to hold her lest the bus door should open suddenly and she might fall under the wheels. She held onto their hands and stood up. The trap disentangled and she got off the bus.

Each one of the soldiers went back to his seat staring, in the trembling light, at his hands which had touched the maiden's face, body or the hem of her dress. On the other hand, she was getting far like the few strips of light which passed quickly as the bus hurried away.

Translated by Nihal El-Ganzoury

---

(1) In rural areas marriage with a cousin, until recently, was very common. A young man's cousin being often his first love.

ACKNOWLEDGMENTS

I would like to express my deepest gratitude to Mrs. Enaam Selim, Mrs. Mahasen Shaaban and Mrs. Nagia Koheil of the Foreign Cultural Information Department for all their valuable help during the various stages of preparing this book.

To all the friends, colleagues translators and particularly to the authors of the short stories in this collection, I owe a debt of gratitude, for their kindly bearing with me, giving or lending me books and copies of reviews and responding to many telephone calls.

General Egyptian Book Organization - Press